Never to Die II: Armenia and Her Reawakening

George Mouradian

ISBN-978-1-68506-037-4 (sc)
ISBN-978-1-68506-038-1 (eBook)

InfusedMedia Co. LLC
www.infusedmedia.co
1-888-251-6088

Dedication

This book is dedicated to the Armenian soldiers who fought against Azerbaijan from 1991 to 2020 and especially to those who died in their attempt to free Nagorno Karabakh from ruthless and intolerable rule of the Azeris.

Also by George Mouradian

Armenian InfoText, a mini-encyclopedia
Handbook of QS-9000 Tooling and Equipment Certification
The Quality Revolution: A History of the Quality Movement
NEVER TO DIE: A Historic Novel about Armenia
and the Quest for Noah's Ark

Your Journey Into Armenia
Notable Armenian Sayings and Family Relations
Guideline to Your Magical Marriage
Evils of the World
The First Crusade
One Hundred Years of Denial
The New Religion: What's Going on in the Sports World?
Detent: Will the World Ever Have Peace/
The Executioners

Table of Contents

Preface

Vartouhi Zerouni, widow of Azad Zerouni, made the decision in 1968 to leave Turkey after the tragic death of her husband and move to Armenia. Her uncle also had just died of a rapid form of lung cancer, making her decision all the more sound. There was no reason for her to stay in Turkey, especially with discrimination that was so rampant. When Azad went to Yerevan several weeks ago he talked about conditions in Armenia were a lot more improved over the years since the country was dominated by Joseph Vissarionovitch Stalin (1879-1953). Now that the tyrannical dictator was dead, succeeding leaders of the Union of Soviet Socialist Republics (USSR) were much more tolerant and helpful to Armenia. Yes, the Soviet Union was still a dictatorship, but a bit more forgiving.

Later in Armenia among her escapades, she delivers a son, Azad Jr., attends Yerevan State University (YSU), becomes a journalist, and ventures into "what's going on in Armenia." Some of the occurrences are extremely exciting, some challenging and dangerous, and some very natural. Vartouhi was in a position where she was able see what was occurring and report on the impact to the nation and to the Armenian citizens.

When I originally started writing Never To Die II in 2017, I had visions of Armenia becoming a grand nation again. After the "Velvet Revolution" in early 2018, my mind-set was reinforced. At the time this vision appeared to be on its way. However, in fall of 2020, analysis of what was occurring sent me different messages. But first, let's go back to 2018 where seventy percent of the voters backed Nikol Pashinyan (b.

1975) looking for the government to stop the corruption, improve the economy, and generate opportunities for employment. They wanted the unscrupulous oligarchs and politicians to be accountable. At first President Serzh Sargsyan (b. 1954) acknowledged the will of the people but later his supporters objected to the measures that Pashinyan was taking along with other maneuvers that were strongly questioned and debated. This created problems for the new prime minister and the country.

The 44-Day War in 2020 was a rude reawakening for Armenia. The victory and peace signing in 1994 engulfed Armenia in a euphoric state. Not only had we won a victory in Artsakh, Armenia held 20 to 25% of the surrounding Azeri territory. At the time of defeat, Azerbaijan was afraid Armenia would march all the way to Baku, thus agreeing to a peace treaty. In 2020 everything was the opposite and has literally turned into a calamity. Armenia lost the second war, no one seems to be sure of the peace terms, and there was a cry for the prime minister to resign.

The vision for the future is nebulous. Armenia has existed for 6000 years and prayerfully on to eternity. She has been a strong Christian nation in the later centuries of her life and will continue to do so. There is no question that she has to regain a healthy status by building up her strength both militarily and economically and has to learn to work tougher. One can predict the future, but no one can predict its accuracy. We have to wait to see what happens.

Vartouhi left Turkey in early 1969, became an Armenian citizen, and a loyal supporter of the country. The book starts a factual time line beginning in 1969 and moves steadily to the Nagorno Karabakh - Azerbaijani War that came as surprise initially, but analysis of the events showed Armenia should not have been surprised. [Significant events before 1969 are mentioned where appropriate to the overall story.] As a journalist and a college professor after graduation, Vartouhi has discussions with significant individuals not only in Armenia but other countries in the world. The interviews provide some analyses of the particular episodes. Many of these other countries have an interest in Armenia and vice versa. Events in Turkey are covered with a watchful eye as most people in the know are aware that the ancestors of the Ottoman Empire would love to rid all Armenians in the world. Vartouhi, in time, develops into a star reporter who covers, or gets involved in the noteworthy events that occur in Armenia, Artsakh, and Diaspora. If events in other countries have any effect on Armenia, in one way or another, these occasions are also embraced. The analyses and comments should aid readers in their own personal interpretation of what's going on.

One the things I tried to do was to show birth and death dates of the real characters who make-up the history of the book. Unfortunately, Google and Yahoo were not able to supply me with all the dates I wanted but I was able to obtain quite a few. In what I was able to obtain at least enables readers to know when these people are a part of the overall make up of the story.

Acknowledgements

Never to Die II has 'many people to be thankful for. Experts in warfare, political, scholarly journalist, newspapers editors and magazines all contributed to the book. Sometimes there would be question the validity of what was written, but then it was my job to find the truth of what is being told.

Edmond Azadian, Steven Piligian, Philippe, Kalfayan, Harout Sassounian, *Armenian Mirror-Spectator, The Armenian Weekly,* and even *The Walll Street Journal* all contributed to *Never to Die II.* I thank these experts and more for the help they gave me in writing this historic book.

Chapter 1

Leaving Turkey

Vartouhi Zerouni had no idea about the tragic deaths of Azad, her husband, and Jean Claude Charboneau, the leader of the Mt. Ararat expedition that was looking for Noah's Ark. After her marriage to Azad, she was content to be a happy house wife living with her uncle and seeing her husband occasionally when he came to Dogubayazit for supplies. When Major Vehib, the Turkish explorer on the Ararat Team, and Michelle, Jean Claude's wife, came to her home after they had taken the bodies to the funeral house, Vartouhi senses something wrong because Azad was not with them. When she saw their faces she knew something terrible had happened. They had the look of some great tragedy. Michelle had no idea of how she was going to tell the young bride what happened. She looked at Vartouhi, and started sobbing, hugging her and saying, "Vartouhi, I'm so sorry. There's been a terrible accident," she said in weeping tones.

"What, what are you saying?"

Finally it came out, "Vartouhi, Azad is dead."

Again she said, "What are you saying? What do mean he's dead? What happened? Where is Azad?"

Michelle slowly went through the events of what happened and that her husband, Azad, and Abdul were at the director's funeral home and they were victims of a local avalanche on the mountain.

Vartouhi broke out in sobbing tears. "I don't believe it," she said as the tears poured down her cheeks.

As the news of Azad's death sunk in, the trio and Vartouhi sat down discussing the events of the tragedy while the tears were flowing. Even the major, a warrior who has seen many catastrophes and deaths and did not any fondness for Azad, had a bit of moist eyes. Vartouhi knew there was no love between her husband and the Turk, but sometimes deaths of people who work together or know each other can develop strong emotions.

Vartouhi was in dilemma as what to do. A minor local earthquake can be fatal if one happened to be in its deadly path. Unfortunately, the team got caught in nature's wrath. The grieving pregnant widow had no relatives or close friends except her uncle who was recently diagnosed with a rapid form of cancer. She originally planned to stay in Dogubazit to take care of him but she now had no desire to stay in Turkey.

A week later Vartouhi got more bad news. Her uncle who she had been living with succumbed to the lung cancer he was carrying. The doctor told him previously that he would have to operate to cut it out, but he did not have much hope. The cancer was at fatal stage. Khoren Margar had been smoking for years, had a persistent cough, but continued his cigarette chaining while not giving it much thought. Finally the cancer caught up to him. The doctor did not give Khoren much of a chance even if he would have operated. A week later, Khoren passed away leaving Vartouhi alone.

Two weeks later, Vartouhi started making calls to the government offices to obtain the necessary documents to make the move to Armenia. Surprisingly, Major Vehib helped her in attaining the required papers and told her he would drive her to Markara where she she could enter Armenia.

Chapter 2

Arriving Yerevan

In January of 1969, after Vartouhi completed all the details of selling her uncle's house, she decided now was time to make her move to Armenia. She had already received all the documents she was ready to go and was now all a matter of making the change. Major Vehib who had been very helpful, told her he would drive her to Markara but she would be on her own after that.

When she arrived at the border, it was a basic routine to pass through as she had all the necessary papers. She ordered a taxi and went straight to Ararat Electronics where she asked the receptionist to see Aram Pilibosian. She asked for her name and said, "Fine, I'll let him know you're here."

When she found Aram, she said, "There's a gorgeous looking woman who would like to see you. She's in the lobby waiting for you."

The chief engineer was surprised and curious, "Did she give you her name?'

"Yes, it was Vartouhi and what sounded like some Italian name."

Aram knew a couple of Vartouhis, but why would they want to see him? He did not make the connection with Azad. When he saw Vartouhi he introduced himself, "I'm sorry but Shoshig did not get your name straight."

"It's Vartouhi Zerouni, I'm Azad's wife."

The engineer looked shocked, "Wow, where's Azad? How come he's not with you?"

She hesitated a second or two as tears came to her eyes. Then sobbing she said, "Aram, Azad is dead."

"What? What do you mean? What happened? How could he be dead?" asking while not believing what he was hearing.

Vartouhi regained some of her composure, but still crying said, "He was caught in an avalanche with their team leader and one of their helpers. They all were bombarded with huge rocks. All three of them were killed."

"Oh Vartouhi, I'm sorry. I really liked Azad, He was like a younger brother to me. We really hit it off even though we worked together for only a few days. My family is also going to feel remorseful when they hear the bad news. You have to see my parents tonight."

"Oh that would be nice. I really appreciate the invitation," she said not knowing anyone in Yerevan.

After they talked a bit more about what happened and briefly discussed Vartouhi's plans, Aram told her he would drop her off at the hotel and then pick her up around 5:30 so he could take her to the house.

At the Hotel Armenia, it was almost in the same situation and condition that Azad had described to her when he returned from repairing the sonar. She recalled how he described the room, the lobby, the country side, the beautiful tree lining boulevards, the spacious Lenin Plaza, and the people scurrying around. At Aram's house she met the family, Tavit the father, Hera the mother, Lilit 16, Nina 12, and Karnig 8. The family members all said they were real sorry about Azad's passing. The father and mother said he was like a nephew, especially because the grandfathers were both born in Govdoun, Historic Armenia. The children were all well-mannered, asking a lot of questions. Lilit appeared especially more mature for her age, a characteristic that Vartouhi noted and admired.

When the question came up as to what Vartouhi's plans were, she told them she was planning to go to college and study journalism at Yerevan State University (YSU).

Aram responded, "I think you'll like that. Yerevan State is well known for being a good school for journalism. You haven't enrolled or anything like that yet have you?"

"No I haven't. I really have not done anything. I want to get an apartment near the school, then find a baby sitter."

They all looked at her and said, almost unanimously, "You're not pregnant are you? You don't even look pregnant." Litit looked especially more interested.

She caught her mother's eye, "Mother do you think?" It was like Hera could read her daughter's mind, "No I don't think so and besides, you know you still have a lot of school work to do Lilit."

"Mother you know I have no problems in school. All of my grades have been top honors."

"Well, we'll have to see. We still have some time to think about it and you haven't talked to Vartouhi yet."

Vartouhi who was all ears to this mother/daughter conversation interrupted when there was a lull, "It sounds like it might be a good idea, let's give it a little time."

Vartouhi enrolled in YSU and found a nice apartment midway between the school and Aram's father's house. It did not take her long to find an accommodating apartment. It was located in a six-story building with a good sized living room, a kitchen and one bedroom. The rooms were all neat and clean, but the stairways leading to the apartments were run down, littered with trash, and in need of repairs and paint. When she asked why the entrances to the apartment were so messy, she was told all the apartments in Yerevan were that way. Later, when she visited other students and new friends, she found the statement to be generally true. For the time being it appeared to be what she wanted.

The book now "fast backs" to 1918 and continues from there in a forward manner. Then the text eventually returns to 1969 when Vartouhi arrived in Yerevan. In effect the narration is in a time line from 1918 to the present with Vartouhi returning back into the story. Later her son Azad also enters the account. Much of what the two are evolved with coincides with some of the major events in developing stages of Amenia. Vartouhi in time, earns a PhD in Journalism, becomes a professor at the Yerevan State University (YSU), and also becomes an outstanding reporter

Chapter 3

1918-1933

On May 28, 1918, Armenia declared herself an independent republic. The country could only make such a proclamation after the combined battlefield victories of Sardarabad, Karakilisseh, and Bash Abaran. Ottoman Turkey had lost much of her empire due to battlefield defeats in World War I and was now trying to win back some of her lost territory. Turkish troops started advancing toward Armenia, murdering on the way. They were stopped and defeated at the three Armenian cities noted above. The Armenians realized there would be another Genocide if they did not stop the Turks. Every able-bodied Armenian grabbed any weapon he/she could find and contributed to the defeat of the Turks. The "Little Ally" defeated the Turkish Army on its own. This was a last ditch effort by the Ottomans in attempting to subdue Armenia and complete their maniacal desire to massacre them all. However, the Armenians defeated the Turks in the Balttle of Sardarabad on May 22-28, 1918. The three major defeats in Armenia sent the Turks back into Anatolia. [See May 25, 1968 for the inaugural dedication of the Sardarabad Monument].

After the Allies' (mainly the French, British, and Italians) victory, the Versailles Treaty was signed on June 28, 1919. Among its many requirements were the restrictions on the Central Powers and basically wrenching the Ottoman Empire apart. Mustafa Kemal (1881-1938), the heroic general of the Gallipoli Defense, was able to muster a Turkish National Army after the British asked him to squelch a rebellion of remnant Turkish troops in Anatolia. Kemal rather than subduing the rebels, joined the insurgents in mobilizing a new Turkish Army. The Allies had required the Ottoman army to disburse, but the Turkish general was able to start a new one.

Back in the Caucasus, the victory in Armenia was not a long-lasting euphoria. Independence is a tremendous responsibility and living conditions have to accompany the situation. The Genocide and Turkish murders had caused hundreds of thousands of impoverished, hungry, war weary, diseased victims into the tiny sanctuary republic that could hardly contain herself. Half dead refugees were pouring into the country. The government had to establish some order. But it was hardly enough. Relief and sanitary facilities were imperative. The refugees had to be fed and clothed and there had to be some sense of normalcy. The other problem was that Armenian leadership had not seen independence for over 500 years and therefore had no experience in the operation of a nation. But the nation did form a governmental republic electing a premier and all the other necessary officers to run the country. In fact, Armenia was the first nation in the region to have democratic elections and the first to offer women suffrage. The task of independence was extremely difficult. The nation's infrastructure had to be confirmed; vital water, power, health installations, and all the other concerns had to be established from the ground up.

In addition to the immediate problems that had been established, the June 4, 1918 Treaty of Batum granted Armenia her independence but had many restrictions and impositions. However, even with the existing problems, Armenia did establish a government. For little over two and half years, she struggled to solve the difficulties that she was perpetually encountering. Slowly and surely the reins of government had become more manageable. But there was another danger from the west. Kemal's National Army was causing havoc and murder as in the past. Mustafa Kemal and Vladimir Ilich Lenin (1870-1924) had made previous agreements to divide the two and half year old Armenian Republic in half. The Turks halted their advancement at the Armenia border and Bolsheviks took over what was left, thus becoming one of the Soviet Republics. The Bolsheviks ruled 70 years, with an absence of a two month rebellion of independence from February to March 1921.

After the armistice was signed, Greece invaded Turkey making measurable inroads into western Anatolia. The intent was to regain the Greek territories that had been in her possession for centuries. Kemal's newly formed troops stopped the advance that had penetrated well into Anatolia and started forcing the Greeks back to the Mediterranean. In fact, there were still an estimated two million Greek Turkish citizens living in Turkey at the time. Their ancient families go back thousands of years. In three years the Turkish advance forced the Greeks all the way back to Smyrna. Kemal had turned the tide. The Allies were now out of Anatolia.

Outside of Armenia, other related activities were occurring. The Armenian Revolution Federation (ARF) established Operation Nemesis in July 8, 1920 (debates were held as early as September to October 1919), with the aim of assassinating the perpetrators of the Armenian Genocide. The operation had nothing to do with the Armenian government and was secret for all intents and purposes.

The ARF's main target was Mehmet Talaat Pasha (1874-1921), the major instigator and culprit of the Genocide. He was executed by Soghomon Tehlirian (1896-1960) on March 15, 1921, in Berlin.

Seven other Ottoman Turkish leaders were assassinated by the Operation Nemesis. Turks including Djemal Pasha (1872-1922), one of the Unholy Three, military commander and ruthless provincial governor, was assassinated on April 17, 1922, by Stepan Dzaghian (1886-?), in Tiflis (now Tbilisi).

Enver Pasha (1881-1922), another of the Unholy Three and perpetrator of the Genocide, was killed, by Hagop Melkumian (1885-1962), on August 4, 1922 in Tajikistan.

In addition to the three main perpetrators, Arshavir Shiragian (1900-1973) assassinated Said Halim Pasha (1863-1921), one of the main organizers of the Genocide on December 5, 1921, in Rome, and Cemal Azmi (1868-1922), the "butcher of Traprzone," on April 17, 1922, in Berlin.

Aram Yerganian (1900-1934) killed Fatali Khoyski (1875-1920), one of the central figures of the Special Organization (*Teskitat-i Mansus*) that sent hundreds of thousand non-Muslims on their Death Marches, on June 19, 1920, and Dr. Behaeddin Shakir (1874-1922), Ottoman doctor and also a central figure of the *Teskitat-i Mansus*, on April 17, 1922 in Berlin.

Missak Torlakian (1889-1968) executed Behbud Khan Jivansshir (1874-1921), another executor of the *Teskitat-i Mansus* deportation and massacres, on July 18, 1921, in Constantinople.

At the end of the war, all of these Ottoman Turks, and more, were originally condemned to death by both the Allies and the Ottoman Turkish Courts-Martial. Some were sent to Malta to await their executions. A few minor officials were put to death and some were freed in the exchange of prisoners. However, the majority of the top perpetrators were able to escape from Constantinople to Odessa in a German torpedo boat. It took the Nemesis assassins to find where the Turks were hiding and to execute each of them as planned.

For 70 years Armenia lived under the dictatorship of the Soviet government. It was mostly a government of tyranny, but it did have a few measures of economic progress. The first dictator was Lenin, then after his death, Joseph Stalin. Humanitarian conditions were not only brutal and cold-blooded for Armenians, but also for the whole of the Union of Soviet Socialist Republics (USSR). Once Stalin controlled the reins of power, intellectuals, writers, Soviet military commanders and politicians, church leaders, potential rivals, politicians, and even the peasantry were targets of the intolerable dictator.

The first year of the 1920s saw a lot of killings to rid the population of dissenters. After the death of Lenin, Stalin did everything he could to become the leader of USSR. By 1929, he had rid his challengers to declare himself the dictator of the Union. Stalin incorporated purges in 1936-38 that devastated the population of the Soviet Union. Incarcerations were so frequent that suspected victims slept with their shoes on because they had no idea when Soviet agents would come to arrest them. Most detainees were murdered or sent to the Silatvian gulags with no trials. All told, the result of Stalin's purges amounted to 25,000 Armenian deaths. Even with all her problems, Soviet Armenia was able to sustain herself.

After the Sovietization of the Caucasus Region in 1920-1921, Armenia became under Soviet rule in December 2, 1920. Nagorno Karabakh and Nakhichevan became a part of Soviet Armenia and remained that way until 1923. Stalin for some reason decided to cede the Karabakh enclave and Nakhichevan to Azerbaijan even though the populations of Armenians were 94 and 75 percent, respectively in the two regions. There was considerable debate in the move but Stalin's final proposal was not challenged. After the dictator's order, Azeris moved into the enclaves flooding the area with Muslims causing much discrimination and restrictions against the Armenians. Many scholars believe Lenin had previously made an agreement with Kemal Pasha that he would make the move; Stalin was only carrying out the arrangement. By 1960, hostilities generated between the two groups and only worsened as time went on thinking Turkey would become a Communist state. [see 1988 and beyond to see what developed 65 years later].

While Soviet Armenia was going through the developmental stages of a governing state, Armenians in southern Anatolia were trying to attain some measure of autonomy. Mustafa Kemal had taken over the reins of the government and was making inroads into Cilicia and also defeating the Greek forces that invaded western Turkey in 1918. The Greeks advanced well into Anatolia but were stopped and forced back to the Mediterranean arriving in Smyrna in 1922. The Turkish advance was as typical as in the past where Turks had massacred Christians en route even though they were told not to by Kemal. When the Turks got to Smyrna, the Christians were massed on the shores and docks hoping for some form of rescue as Allied ship waited in the harbor. The Severs Treaty was written in 1920 but Kemal had ignored its ramifications and was advancing his National Army against the Greeks in eastern Turkey and against the French and Armenians in Cilicia.

The situation in Smyrna was deplorable. Thousands of Greeks and Armenians had fled from the advancing Turks and crowded into the city. There was no other place to flee except into the Mediterranean. The wave of Turkish forces entered the sea port in an orderly fashion where the leaders greeted the Turks. There was no fighting, as the Greek troops had abandoned the city days before. The Metropolitan and the religious leaders of the city came to welcome the Turks who accepted the group graciously, but after the formalities, the group was arrested. The metropolitan was clubbed, stabbed, and beaten. They had his eyes gorged out and had his nose and ears cut off. After that horrifying and deadly act, it was all bedlam in the port. It did not take long for the Turkish soldiers and riffraff to start their massacres, rapes, looting, destroying, and setting the Christian sections of the city on fire. The estimate of the death toll in the city went as high as 100,000.

In another part of Anatolia, the Armenians of Cilicia were having problems with the French protection. In 1918, after being told to return to their homes in Cilicia after the massacres and death marches, the French relented on their promise for an independent Armenian Cilicia. Worse yet, they permitted Kemal's forces to continue their massacres and rapes. In the turmoil that pursed during the 1918-1920 period, the Armenians had one day of independence. On August 5, 1920, Miran Damadian (1863-1943) proclaimed Cilicia to be an independent country under a French mandate. The proclamation was nullified the next day. The net result of the two year period was no Armenians were left in Cilicia, primarily due to the secret deals among the French, British, and Turks. Five days after the proclamation, the Allies and the Ottoman Turks signed the Sevres Treaty (August 10, 1920). In effect, the treaty outlined the borders set by President Woodrow Wilson (1856-1924). The treaty was not accepted by Mustafa Kemal who was at odds with the Ottoman Government and was in the process of setting up a separate regime.

Armenia After World War I and Woodrow Wilson's Mandate for Armenia

The above map shows Wilson's Mandate for Armenia that included cities such as Erzurum, Bitlis, and Van, and other towns listed in the Sevres Treaty of August 10, 1920, and the land acquired by the "Little Ally" during the war. The treaty was accepted by the Turkish Government, but rejected by Kemal Ataturk and the US Senate that did not want anything to do with the European Powers any more. Kemal invaded Armenia in the Spring of 1918 where his troops were defeated at Sardarabat, Bash-Ardahan, and Karakilissa thus establishing the First Republic of Armenia. The Treaty of Batum was signed between Armenia and Turkey in June 4, 1918.

In the Fall of 1920 Turkey again invaded Armenia while the Russians seized territory from the north. The two sided occupation was too much for Armenia where she relinquished to both countries. The Republic of Armenia gave up 50% of her western territories and the northeastern section became a Soviet Republic. In Soviet Armenia, private property of the church was confiscated and the priests were harassed. After Stalin proclaimed himself dictator in 1929, it got worse. Assaults against the church accelerated but later eased momentarily to improve relations with Diaspora Armenians. In 1932, he allowed the leadership of Khoren I to be Catholicos of All Armenians. Yet in 1938, he had him murdered along with others in the 1936-1938 Purges. The Catholicate of Etchmiatsin was also closed in 1938, but continued underground and in diaspora.

General Antranik Ozanian (1885-1927), outstanding fedayee leader and Commander of the Armenian Army, died in California on August 31, 1927, and then later, was buried in Paris. In 2000 his remains were honored and interred in Yerablur Cemetery, Yerevan. Gen. Antranik had a long career in fighting the Ottoman Turks first as a young fedayee, and then he aided Bulgaria in her War of Independence in 1912. After the war he returned to Anatolia defended Armenia as fedayee leader, fighting the Turks before and during World War I. Countries all over the world have erected his statue in his honor. He is regarded a National Hero in Armenia.

1930

The Catholate of the Great House of Cilicia was established in Antelias, Lebanon.

The Chapel and Cathedral of the Holy See of Cilicia

The above photograph shows the Cathedral of Saint Gregory the Illuminator in Antelas, Lebanon that became the location of the See of The Great House of Cilicia in 1930. The See's movement reflects the long journey over eight and half centuries from Armenia to Cilicia (Hromkla, Sis and other cities), then Antilias. The first move was in 1058 after the Seljuk Turks invaded Armenia and created havac with the country. The catholicos had to move to different cities in Cilicia due the Armenian princes relocating there. In 1441, The Cathlolicos of All Armenians moved back to Etchmiadzin where the country had regained some of her freedom. The catholicos presiding in Cilicia wanted to stay there because hundreds of thousands of Armenians still lived there [this was true even though the Armenian Kingdom of Cilicia had fallen to the Mamluks in 1375]. After the Armenian Genocide, The Great House of Cilicia was forced to leave Sis and move to different locations until it found an abanded Near East orphanage in Antelias were it established its new home.

Christmas Eve of 1933 was a black day in New York for the Armenians. During the Holy Cross Armenian Apostolic Church service, Armenian Nationalists stabbed Archbishop Ghevond Tourian (1879-1933) to death. The reason for the assault was the archbishop's disrespect for the Republic of Armenia's flag at the 1932 Chicago World's Fair. The archbishop had demanded that the 1919-1920 Republic's flag not be flown together with the other national banners. The murder caused a serious rift between the Etchmiadzin and Cilician Holy Sees of the Armenian Apostolic Churches and Armenian Diaspora world wide.

One event that happened in early 1933 was the opening of the Yerevan Opera Theatre (also known as the Armenian National Academis Theatre of Opera and Ballet named after Alexander Spendiaryan). The opening of the theatre promoted the creation of new national operas and ballets, which under Soviet rule opened the door to gain international recognition. There were upgrades and enlargement in the following years with performances in major cities throughout the world. The opening of the opera house together with other innovations introduced Armenia to other nations as a cultural country.

Chapter 4

1936-1938, Stalin's Great Purge

From 1924 to 1936 Armenia withstood the varying degrees of Soviet dominance. Armenia had become a Soviet Republic under the stern leadership of Communism. They had a revolution in February 1921, but were put down in a manner of a couple of months. The Communist did a lot of house cleaning, killed a few thousand Armenian patriots, and sent thousands of others to Siberia. The wide scale Soviet terror included the repression of the peasantry, ethnic cleansing, purges of government officials, Red Army military personnel, intellectuals, widespread police surveillance, suspicion of saboteurs and counterrevolutionaries, and arbitrary exhaustions, and just about anyone who looked suspicious. There was no end to who was arrested and executed or sent to Siberia. Historians estimate the total number of deaths due to the Stalinist repression in 1937 to 1938 was between 950,000 and 1.2 million. Bolshevik governed the tiny republic under the watchful eyes of Moscow making sure they carried the party line. Yet even those who did, often fell to the party's supremacy. The Great Purge was also referred to as the Great Terror.

The period from 1936 to 1938 was one of the most savage reins in the Union of Soviet Socialist Republics (USSR). Stalin had been in power since the death of Lenin and served as an abrasive and murderous ruler, where the rule of terror seemed more to his character than one of any tolerance. Stalin was fanatical to both foe and comrades and would have them killed or sent to the Siberian Gulags if they demonstrated harm or challenge to his rule. Leaders high in communist positions were also in danger if they showed an ounce of ambition to his position. In 1936, Lavrentiy Beria (1899-1953), Stalin's secrete police chief, killed Aghasi Khanjian (1909-1936), the First Secretary of the Communist Party in Armenia, for "being the enemy of the people." Official Soviet reports indicated he committed suicide. Khanjian was among the thousands of other Communist leaders who died one way or another. The first secretary who died mysteriously was extremely popular with the Armenian people and was one of first advocates to promote the return of Karabakh back to Soviet Armenia. Another leader who was killed during 1937 was Yeghishe Charerits (1897-1937, Yeghishe Soghomonyan) while he was in a Yerevan prison. He was recognized as "the poet of the 20th century." At first, he supported the Soviet reign but later saw its maliciousness but was still revered as a writer and public activist.

When Stalin first became leader of USSR, Armenia was basically an agricultural country and slowly developed into an industrial production center. Soviet rule was extremely brutal at first lasting almost a decade. When Stalin came to power he was especially harsh with the Armenian Church, but later softened due to the communist desire to have a better relationship with Diaspora Armenians. However, in the middle 30s he reversed his policy and renewed his attacks on the church eventually resultied in the murder of Catholicos Khoren I in 1938. The killing and brutal treatment of the church eventually caused the church to go underground and continue in diaspora. It was not until 1941 that Armenia was permitted to elect a Catholicos of All Armenians.

In the early fall of 1937 Stalin dispatched Anastas Mikoyan (1895-1978), Lavrentiy Beria (1899-1953), and Georgy Malenkov (1901-1988) to Erevan to oversee their liquidation with a list of 300 Old Bolsovicks. The list of 300 grew to 4,530 who were all executed by firing squad. The list was made up by mostly communist members, who were accused of being anti-Soviet (Moscow did like communist being nationalistic), having counter- revolutionary activities, or being members of the Dashnak party, or Trotskyism. Mikoyan tried to save some Armenians during their mock trials, but was powerless in overcoming urges of the Soviet dictator.

The killing of leaders was not the only method of getting rid of people. "The Great Purge" ended up in the death of 20,000,000 Soviet citizens, much of it through starvation, oppression, and Soviet policies. Tens of thousands of Armenians were executed and deported under Stalin. Intellectuals such as writers, religious leaders, military commanders, communists, and even the peasantry were victims. Anyone or any group Stalin thought was a threat or competitor to his rule was a target. One of the big surprises for Armenians is the lasting life of Anastas Mikoyan who was one of the first to become a top Communist leader and keep the position for a long time. Mikoyan by some means or shrewdness outlived many of the other Communist leaders and was one of first to make an outspoken speech against Statin after the tyrant's death.

As with other Soviet Republics, Stalin was responsible for the death of 1000s in each of the republics, and maybe more. Tens of thousands of Armenians were executed or deported to Siberia. One of the unknown reasons to many scholars was Stalin and Beria aim to reduce the population of Armenia to under 700,000 by deporting or killing some of the population. This was in order to justify an annexation of Armenia into Georgia. The plan did not work because Soviet Armenia's population grew from 880,000 in 1926 to an eventual plus three million. Stalin may have had this in mind when he annexed Nakhichevan and Nagorno Karabahk to Azerbaijan even though many Communist leaders thought the two enclaves should be a part of Armenia. Another fact about Armenia is that she had the highest fertility rate of all the Soviet republics for a long time.

Barat Borian (1882-1938) a staunch Soviet statesman and historian, wrote about how the Revolutionary Committee (oganization set up to manage a conquered country) dictated the conditions in Armenia under the Soviet system.

"The Revolutionary Committee started a series of indiscriminate seizures and confiscations, without regard to class, and without taking into account the general economic and psychological state of the peasantry. Devoid of revolutionary planning, and executed with needless brutality, these confiscations were unorganized and promiscuous. Unattended by disciplinary machinery, without preliminary propaganda or enlightenment, and with utter disregard of the country's unusually distressing condition, the Revolution Committee issued its orders nationalizing food supply of the cities and peasantry. With amazing recklessness and unconcern, they seized and nationalized everything – military uniforms, artisan tools, rice mills, water mills, barber's implement, beehives, linen, household furniture, and livestock."

Borian was loyal party member and a person who had several responsible positions during his lengthy communist career. He was an example to what happens to comrades who do not tow the line or to prefer to tell the truth. Borian was one of the victims of the purges in 1938.

October 22, 1936, unrelated to the purges but an extremely significant event for Armenians was the death of Gomidas Vartabed (Soghomon Soghomonian, 1886-1936) who died with a broken heart as a result of what he witnessed during the Armenian Genocide. He was a global revered musicologist who introduced outstanding church and ethnic music to the world.

Chapter 5

World War II 1939-1945

September 1, 1939, was the start of all hell breaking horror, and bedlam on Earth as Germany invaded Poland. The Nazi blitzkrieg of heavy shelling and bombing of Poland forced the surrender of the country in 27 days. France and Great Britain declared war on Germany on September 3, 1939. The Soviet Union invaded Eastern Poland on September 17, 1939. Little did the world realize that this was the beginning of a six year nightmare that would involve all the major nations in the world and result in 45 to 60 million deaths including six million Jews.

June 22, 1941, Germany invaded USSR. An estimated 300,000 to 500,000 Soviet Armenians who served in the war, almost half of them did not return to their homes. The estimate is a considerably high number because the population of Soviet Armenia was two and half million. Germany advanced well into the Soviet Union at the beginning of the war, but ran into a stalemate at the industrial city of Stalingrad. On August 23, 1941, the Battle of Stalingrad began while Turkish troops gathered on the Caucasian border waiting for the Soviet industrial city to be conquered so they could advance into Armenia and Russian interior. Fortunately for the Armenians, the Soviet Army in Stalingrad surrounded and captured 400,000 German troops. The siege of battle reversed where the Soviets started their offense to the west. Turkey that had amassed a large contingent of troops at the Armenian border ready to attack USSR changed her mind about invading Armenia. Later in the war when victory was on the horizon for the Allies, Turkey entered the war on the side of the Allies. Due to her late entrance to the hostilities, she contributed nothing during the war.

The war in Europe officially ended in an "Unconditional Surrender" by Germany on May 8, 1945. German units stated surrendering earlier on May 2, and continued on in different locations until the May 8th date. However, even after that date, isolated pockets kept fighting until all of them eventually surrendered. In some respect, Soviet Armenia was fortunate in that Germany wanted to destroy Stalingrad before she entered the sub-Caucasus region. If she had conquered the industrial city plans were made to invade Soviet Armenia and Soviet Azerbaijan. The Azeri oil fields were tempting targets and Armenia probably would have seen another Genocide. Turkey was waiting for the appropriate moment. Armenia still paid a dear price of missing soldiers and high fatalities during the war.

War in the Pacific ended a little different in that two atomic bombs were dropped on Hiroshima and Nagasaki causing Japan to surrender. On September 2, 1945, Japan officially "Unconditionally Surrendered" to the Allies on the USS Battleship Missouri ending the World War II.

April 4, Vahan Tekeyan (1878-1945), the "Armenian Prince of Poetry," died in Cairo. He was one of the most poetic persons in diaspora and editor of several Armenian newspapers.

On May 8, Germany "Unconditionally Surrendered" to the Allies. Italy fell earlier and Japan followed in September 2, 1945.

October 24, the United Nations (UN) was founded in San Francisco in an attempt to unify all the countries in the world, maintain international peace and security, develop friendly relations among nations, achieve cooperation, and be the center for harmonizing the action of nations. The organization had initiated with 50 countries that established its charter. It headquartered in New York City in 1952 and has grown since.

Chapter 6

The Cold War 1947 -1991

After the end of World War II all nations rejoiced that we finally had peace on the planet. But the rejoicing did not last long as the USSR started on its determined program of expanding her influence and dominance again even though Stalin claimed during the war that the USSR would remain the same. European countries especially were concerned resulting in the establishment of North Atlantic Treaty Organization (NATO). On April 4, 1949, NATO was founded by 12 countries. By 2010 the number of members had grown to 30. By 2020 the number remained at 30.

1947-1948

By 1948 the Soviet Union had gotten footholds in seven Eastern Bloc countries from Albania to the Baltic States. All had Communist leaderships. Stalin was looking for more countries to put under the red banner. Winston Churchill (1874-1965) presented a speech in 1946 stating that "An Iron Curtain" had descended on the communist border The Western European countries saw the danger in this expansion and were alert to the fact Statin had reneged on his promise that he would not expand communism. But he did. The US troops remained in western Germany and also kept a presence in other Western European countries. The United Nations (UN) was established with US encouragement in October 24, 1945. These acts helped to stop the expansion. However the competition initiated an arms buildup between America and the Soviet Union that had developed the atomic bomb in August 29, 1947, after several years of research and development. Soviet Armenia was not involved directly in the Cold War, yet managed to keep a relative sound economy going during this time period, but still had to exist under the dictatorship of Joseph Stalin.

1953

March 5, Joseph Stalin died. The Armenians and most of the other Soviet citizens celebrated mental cheers. However, the Communist government still prevailed in Soviet Armenia.

September 14, Nikita Khrushchev (1894-1971) became First Secretary of the Communist Party of the Soviet Union. In his inaugural speech, he starts the De-Stalination program of the deceased dictator. He loved to bang his shoe on his UN desk.

1955

On September 6-7, riots were occurring in Istanbul as a result of Turkish pogroms. There was not much information except the Turks were going frenetic destroying and ravishing homes, businesses, churches, and beating Armenian, Greeks, and Jews in the streets. The next day, reports came that organized Turkish thugs were brought into the city by the truck loads to start the riots. The death toll was an estimated 25 people with hundreds injured. The police did nothing except to watch the wildness and hostilities. The hateful aggressiveness did not stop until the military was brought in.

December 21, reports were received that Karekin Nejdeh (1886-1955) was killed in Siberia. Gen. Nejdeh, who was a national military hero, served Armenia in several capacities. He was a prolific writer and organized the Armenian Youth Federation (AYF) in 1933.

1956

February 20, Zareh I Payashian (b. 1915) was elected Catholicos of The Great House of Cilicia after which the See broke away from the Mother See of Holy Etchmiadzin.

1957

October 17, Avetik Isahakyan (1875-1957) prolific writer and poet died in Yerevan,

December 3, the statue of David of Sassoun (Sasuntsi Davit) was recreated and inaugurated in Yerevan reflecting the epic battles of the "Daredevils of Sassoun" in Armenia in the 10th Century. An original statue was constructed in 1939 but was destroyed. In 1997, Yerevan decided to restore the statues with significant changes from the original. Moscow approved of the project where it was placed in front of the Yerevan Railway Station where tourist would see the statue on their arrival to the city. None of the top Communist Party officials attended the inaugural, however most of the attendees were from the Sassun area or decendents from there. [It later turned out the statue was one of most visited structures in Armenia. Winning many awards.]

The above statue of David of Sassoun is a modern classic that represent the Daredevils of Sassoun, the legendary folk heroes of

Armenia and the freedom loving people of Armenia. The legend grew mostly from the Arab and local wars in the pre-10th century. Similar structures are erected in other cities of the world, but do not quiet have the grandeur that the Yervan one has. David was brave, full of life and energy, crazy, daring and able to defeat the enemy in every battle. David and his force acquired the name Daredevils or Sasna of Tsrer. Two items that Vartouhi has never seen in the literature about the statue, but I think quite significant are 1) the sword David pointing to the rear was originally pointing to the front and in the direction of Turkey. The Turks naturally objected to the directions of the sword, so the Armenians said they would turn the statue around. The Turks said fine, so the sculpture was turned 180 degrees, but the sword was reversed to the rear of David, thus still pointing toward Turkey. The Turks never commented on the change. The second undocumented item, 2) is the person in the rear of the horse with his head buried in steed's anus. Vartouhi did not know if the Turks objected to that part of the statue or not. [However, David stands today with his sword still pointing toward Turkey and with a Turk with his head in the asshole of the horse.]

1959

March 3, the Matendaran (officially called the Mesrop Mashots Institute of Ancient Manuscrips) was established in Yervan to act as a museum, repository of manuscrips, and be research institute for Armenia. The country had a perpetually problem in storeing and protecting the books and artifacts in early historic times because she was invaded by so many othler nations. After the Matendaran was constructed the muscripts and other material were shipped from Etchmeadzin to its new home.

Matendaran

The Matendaran shown above is a unique structure that houses over 100,000 manuscripts, foreign documents, ancient poems, and relics. It would have much more, but ancient invaders of Armenia destroyed whatever books and articles they could get their hands on. It was a major task in preserving whatever Armenia could. The statue in the front of the Matendaran is Mesrob Mashdotsz with a young lad kneeling at his side. After 1930. Statues of Toros Roslin, Gregory of Tathev, Anahiah of Shirah, Movses of Khoren, Mekhitar Koshs, and Phrig were gradually added to the institution. The Matendran is located at the end of the Mashdotsz Avenue, the widest street in Yerevan with the statue of Mayr Hyastan behind it. Both structures are well seen on a high hill.

1962

In the spring, the Armenians tore down Stalin's huge statue in Yerevan and started to discuss the building of Mayr Hayastan (Mother of Armenia). Five years later on November 29, 1967, the statue of Mayr Hayastan was completed and unveiled to the people.

The statue on the left is Mayr Hayastan that replaced Stalin after he was torn down. The Soviet Union had previously vilified his death. The statue represents a mother's readiness to defend her country in the event of any problems. The giant statue stands high above Mashdotsz Avenue overlooking a widespread area of Yerevan.

Mayr Hyastan symbolizes peace but she is ready to defend her people if necessary. Architect for the statue was Rafayel Israyelian (1908-1973) and the sculptor was Ara Harutyunyan (1928-1999). The statue is located in Victory Park contains a military museum in its pedestal.

1964

October 14, Leonid Brezhnev (1906- 1982) became General Secretary of the USSR, an event that marked the beginning of the stagnation era in the Soviet Union. Fortunately, Armenia maintained a strong economy.

1965

April 24, for the first time, Yerevan generated a huge demonstration of hundreds of thousands commemorating the 50th Anniversary of the Armenian Genocide of April 24, 1915. Other Armenian citied throughout the country also protested and demanded retribution and justice for Turkey's role in the Genocide. Soviet authorities used to discourage similar demonstrations but did nothing this time.

1967

April 24, Armenia commemorated the Armenian Genocide enmass at the Genocide Memorial that is being construction. [See November 29, 1997, for official opening of the memorial.]

Summer 1967- the statue of We Are The Mountain (a.k.a. MamigBabig0 was completed by Sargis Bagdasaryan (1923-2001) and placed north of Stepanakert, the capital of Nagorno Karabakh.

Mamig and Babig
(Grandmoth and Grandfather

The stone statue on the left is a symbolism of Armenian heritage of Nagorno Karabakh. The Grand- mother (Mamig) and Grandfather (Babib) represents the Armenians of Nagorno Karabakh. The Mamig Babig Statue (also called the Tatik Papik or Grandmother Grandfather Statue) was first unveiled outside of Stepanakert in Nagorno Karabakh. The monument is noted as "We Are the Mountains." Azerbaijan created uproar when the statue was first constructed, but it remained there until Armenian independence where it was relocated on the entrance to Nagorno Karabakh on the newly constructed East-West superhigh-way into the enclave.

The Mamig Babig Statue (also called the Tatik Papik or Grandmother Grandfather Statue) was unveiled outside of Stepanakert in Nagorno Karabakh. The monument is noted as "We Are the Mountains." Azerbaijan created uproar when the statue was first constructed, but it remained there until Armenian independence where it was placed on the entrance of Nagorno Karabakh on the newly constructed East-West super highway into the enclave. .

November 29, The Armenian Genocide Memorial Tsitsernakaberd (also spelled Dzidzernagert) was officially opened in Yerevan. This was the result of the huge demonstrations that initiated on April 24, 1945, in Armenian cities demanding that Moscow recognize the Armenian Genocide. After 1945, talks were held between Armenia and Soviet Union that a monument can be constructed in Yerevan. Similar smaller memorials are recognized in other countries of the world.

Armenian Genocide
Memorial and Obelisk

The Genocide Memorial Complex (Tsitscnakaberd or Dzidzerakapert) was constructed in 1967 after the emotional outburst of the 50tlh Anniversary Genocide demonstration in Yerevan. The Memorial consists of twelve basaltic slabs that represent the twelve provinces in which the Turks massacred the Armenians. The obelisk pyramid divided tower represents the revival and divided homeland of the Armenians. Some people claim the double tower is a symbolism of the two peaks of Mount Ararat, Maidz Massis (Large Massis) and Poker Massis (Small Massis). After Armenia declared her independence in 1991, the Genocide Museum was constructed on the complex. [See '1991 continued' for the Ressurection Monuent.]

1968

May 26, Amenia celebrated the Sardarabad victory of May 22-26, 1918, at their newly constructed Sardarabad Memorial,

David of Sassoun (Սասունցի Դավիթ)

David of Sassoun represents the legendary folk heroes of the Armenians. The above statue is in Yerevan in front of the railroad station; however, other similar sculptures are built in countries throughout the world. David symbolizes the answer to the centuries-old tribulation against the invading hordes that constantly attacked Armenia, especially the Arab invasions. David was brave, full of life and energy, crazy, daring, and able to defeat the enemy in every battle. David and his forces acquired the name Daredevils of Sassoun or Sasna Tsrer.

1969

January, Vartouhi Zerouni moved to Yerevan; she introduced herself to Chief Engineer Aram Piligian of Ararat Electronics. She met Aram's family and planned to enroll in Yerevan State University (YSU) as a journalism student. (See earlier introduction on Vartouhi entering Armenia in Chapter 2.)

June 25, Azad Jr. Zerouni was born. Vartouhi made arrangements with Aram's daughter, Lilit, and wife, Hena, to take care of the baby in a few months as she planed to enroll in YSU. She had previously talked to the family about the planning system where the 16 year old Lilit would be watching Azad when she was not in school and the mother would be in attendance during the day. Vartouhi would take the baby home every evening.

September 5, Vartouhi enrolled in Yerevan State University as a journalism student.

1971

June 17, Paruyr Sevak (1924-1971, born Paruyr Ghazaryan) died with his wife in a car accident while driving from his home to Yerevan. He was known as one of the best poets of Armenia and a member of the Communist Party, but was critical of its corruption and some policies. In Vartouhi's journalism class several students mentioned that he was murdered by Soviet agents due to his criticism of the party actions. Sevak was buried in Yerevan.

September 6, Azad started his kindergarten class in Yerevan. He had previously enrolled in the pre-education classes that were helpful for Vartouhi in her studies. She thought the Soviets had done a good job in setting up the education system. To her knowledge, Armenia had become one of the leading nations in having a high literacy rate, one of the highest in the Soviet Union.

1972

May 5, Matiros Saryan (1880-1972) died in Yerevan. He was a famous painter known as "The Master."

September 7, George (b. 1927) and Rose (b. 1932) Mouradian visited Armenia. They were enjoying visiting all tourist sites and occasionally went to a restaurant. In one eatery, George was enamored by a little boy speaking such fluid Armenian with his mother adjacent to his table. He commented to the mother how well he speaks. He and Rose started a conversation with Vartouhi where they talked about life in Armenia and America. "Were you born in Armenia? Your son speaks such beautiful Armenian," Rose asked.

"No, I was born in Lebanon and Azad, who is three now, and I have been living here for a little over three years. I moved here from Turkey three years ago after my husband died."

"Oh, I'm sorry about that. How did your husband die? You look so young to be a widow. But how do you like living in Armenia?" Rose asked.

"My husband was in a research team looking for Noah's Ark three and a half years ago and was killed in an avalanche with the leader of the expedition. I was living with my uncle in Dougubazid at the time, but after he died of cancer, I decided to move to Yerevan."

"Oh, we're sorry about that as well, but do you like living in Armenia?" The two Armenian Americans asked.

"It's been okay so far, but quite different than what I've been used to."

"And how is that, if we're not getting too noisy?"

"No, you're not getting noisy, but when I was younger I lived in a beautiful house in Beirut. The city was called the "Paris of the Middle East." My father was a doctor and was doing quite well. Unfortunately, he and my mother died in an automobile accident, so I came to live with my uncle who had a simple small house in Dogubayazid, Turkey. He had a garden in the back of his house with several fruit trees. After he died, I left that frontier town of Dogubayazid and came to Yerevan, which is different than any other place I ever lived. I'm in a nice, neat apartment in town but it has external hallway entrances that need a lot of maintenance and cleaning."

"You sound content. You're not working anywhere are you?" Rose asked.

"No, I'm my third year at Yerevan State as a journalism student. And yes, things are going fine. I have a nice family taking care of Azad while I'm in school, so it's working out okay for now. That's where he's learning his beautiful Armenian."

"That sounds good too, but what about the rest of the people you have to deal?"

"As far as what I've observed, they're fine. Living conditions were really tough during Stalin's totalitarianism, but the quality of life is much better now. The country is still a dictatorship and has economic problems on occasion. You know everything is owned by the government, the houses, apartments, the banks, the factories, the news media, restaurants, schools, hospitals, farms, stores, and on and on. Everyone has a job if they need work. You probably saw the old ladies sweeping the streets. The government still has a secret police that watches you closely, but most of the people do as they wish with some restrictions.

Our conversation ended soon after Azad was getting a little restless. Vartouhi said she would like to meet George and Rose again to learn more about America and for them to learn about Armenia.

1973

January 27, Kourken Yanigian (1895-1985) assassinated Los Angeles Turkish consul general and vice consul in Santa Barbara, California. Yanigian lost 26 members of his immediate family during the Armenian Genocide and has been carrying the grief all these years. He viewed Turks not to be human beings but as symbols of decadence. Yaninian called the police who arrested him, was convicted of murder, and was sentenced to life imprisonment. His plea for Turkey's denial of the Armenian Genocide and that of the prosecutors were representatives of denial fell on deaf ears during the trial.

1975

June 20, the Armenian Secret Army for the Liberation of Armenia (ASALA) was founded in Beirut, Lebanon. The organization was followed by other similar groups that wished to show the world what Ottoman Turkey had committed during the Armenian Genocide. The first Turk to be assassinated by the ASALA was Ambassador Danix Tunailigil (1915-1975) in Vienna on October 27. Another Turkish ambassador and his driver were killed soon after in Paris. Other attacks and assassinations soon followed.

August 1, the Organization for Security and Co-operation in Europe (OSCE) to secure peace and harmony in the European countries was founded in Helsinki, Finland. Armenia is one of the 57 nations that are associated the OSCE.

1978

May 2, Vartouhi heard that Aram Khachaturian (1903-1978) had passed away in Moscow. She noted that he was a world-renowned composer who wrote cheerful, rhythmic, and sensuous music. Interviews with local citizens indicated that they were extremely proud of him and that they loved him as person.

May 25, the Battle of Sardarabad Monument was inaugurated. [See photo on following page.]

Sardarabat (Սարդարապատ) Monument

The above photograph shows the monument dedicated to the Armenian heroes who fought against the Turks on May 26, 1918. Two other two major victories were Bash-Ardaran, and Karakilisseh. The battles were the last-ditch effort to save the nation from obliteration. It was defended by soldiers old and young, including wormen and children. Armenia declared her independence two days after the victory. The monument is represented by two idolized Urartian winged bulls at the entrance and the bell tower (shown in the shadow). A pathway of eagle statues leads to a large arched wall depicting ancient warrior scenes and a museum in the multiplex. Once a year on the anniversary of battle

Armenian and Artsakh leaders, accompanied veterans, relatives, friends, and interested parties, lay a wreath at the memorial. A special area is layed out who have died in battles defending Armenia. .

June 2, the ASALA attacked the Turkish consulate in Madrid. The Turkish ambassador, his wife, and the chauffeur of his car were also killed.

1980

September 12, a Turkish military coup erupted in Turkey due to the mass killings of rival factors. Hrant Dink (b. 1954) and several other prominent Armenians who had nothing to do with coup were arrested and tortured together with the Turks who were fighting each other. The Armenians had nothing to do with mass killings, but the Turks used the fighting as an excuse to harass and victimize them. The Turkish assaults on the non-Muslims were not forceful as the 1955 attacks but they still did a lot of harm and damage.

1982

January 28, Hampig (Harry Sassounian, b. 1963) assassinated the Turkish Consul General at a Los Angeles street intersection while in his car. The news made the American headlines. At the trial, the prosecutors indicated that the young assailant was motivated by to the events of the Armenian Genocide to shoot the consul general for vengeance of the Genocide. He claimed the shooting was not just a crime but was a justification for the killing. Sassounian was sentenced to life imprisonment. Unfortunately, the killing was not considered a justification for the murder.

August 7, ASALA attacked the ticket-counter at the Ankara International Esenboga Airport. The two hour machine gun assault killed nine people and injured 76.

1983

February 9, Catholicos of the Great House of Cilicia Khoren Paroian I (1914-1983) died in Antelias, Lebanon. Karekin Sarkesian (b. 1932) was elected as Catholicos Karekin II.

June 16, Karekin II Catholicos of the Greater House of Cilicia visited President Reagan in the White House. The president was awarded the Grand Cross of Cilicia. Reagan thanked the catholicos and added that he "was greatly honored"

July 15, the ASALA attacked the Orly Airport check-in counter in Paris. Eight people were killed, 55 were injured (four deaths were Frenchmen, two were Turks, one was a Swede, and one American). The bombing caused a schism within the ASALA as to why the gunmen in the attack had to be so violent and had to kill non-Turks. French investigators claimed the killings could have been worse, as they thought the bomb had exploded prematurely and was originally planned to detonate while in flight.

July 27, the Armenian Revolutionary Army (ARA) attacked the Turkish embassy in Lisbon, Portugal. The assailants called the "Lisbon Five" attacked the Turkish embassy where a Lisbon policeman and the wife of the charge of affairs were killed. One of the assaulters was also killed during the initial attack. After unsuccessful negotiations four of the assaulters committed suicide. A statement from the ARA headquarters was sent to the Associated Press, "This is not a suicide, but rather, our sacrifice to the altar of freedom."

1984

March 24, Hovhaness Shiraz (1914-1984) died in Yerevan. Vartouhi remembered the greatly- loved poet from her school days in Beirut. She knew he grew up in poverty as an orphan but gained an outstanding reputation as a poet. His poems have been translated into 50 languages. In her article, she made sure she noted that he was married to Silva Kaputikyan (1919-2006), another well-known writer.

May 3, a Turkish nationalist bombed the Alfortville Armenian Genocide Memorial in France, injuring thirteen persons. The bombings followed other attacks in France.

1985

March 11, Mikhail Gorbachev (b. 1931) became General Secretary of the Communist Party of the Soviet Union. He introduces the policies of *perestroika (*reconstructing*)* and *glasnost* (openness and transparency). These ideas rekindled the thought that Nagorma Karabakh should be a part of Soviet Armenia like it was in the centuries past. The policies created disturbance in Moscow, and also stirred all *kinds* of ideas in Armenia.

March 21, the Arpa-Sevan tunnel started its operation of bringing water from the higher-elevation rivers of Armenia to Lake Sevan. The tunnel was essential to restore the draining waters of the lake due to irrigation and hydroelectric power generation.

March 28, a commentary from Beirut reported on an armed robbery massacre in the Bourj Hammoud quarter where five people were shot. The victims were killed in cold blood followed by looting the value of 20 million Lebanese pounds of jewelry. When Vartouhi heard about the robbery and killings, she thought how sad that Armenians were stealing from Armenians, and then topping it off, by killing them. The "Middle East Diamond Company" store was managed by Hrant Kurdjian (1925-1985) who was first killed followed by the murder of four Armenian workers. The murders were considered one of "the bloodiest most serious crimes in Lebanese criminal history."

April 12, fifteen days later the police arrested two brothers, Raffi (1960) and Panos (1958) Nahabedian who were found with the spoils in Raffi's apartment. Five days later, a third brother was arrested. Hratch Nahabedian was apprehended at the Larnaca Airport in Cyprus. All three brothers used to work with the shop owner, Hrant Kurkjian and had an easy walk-in to the shop before the killings. The three brothers were sentenced to deaths, but escaped from prison and vanished without trace for three decades. [In 2015 they were identified by families of the victims to be in Vienna, Austria under assumed names. Raffi had died in 2012, but the other two brothers were still at large.]

July 2, the United Nations Sub-Commission on Prevention of Discrimination and Protection of Minorities adopted a report acknowledging the Armenian Genocide as a case of genocide. However, since that date, there has been very little activity since that time on the subject [See March 25, 1919, to note a letter that was sent to Sadik Arslan, Turkey's Permanent Representative to the UN.]

1986

April 26, the destructive breakdown of the Chernobyl Nuclear Power Plant in northern Ukraine resulted in an immediate death of 54 people and possibly more. The accident prompted Armenia to debate the shut down the Metsamore Nuclear Power Plant due to the similarity of the two plant designs.

Chapter 7

Nagorno Karabakh/Azerbaijani Confrontation, 1987-1994

1987

June 18, the European Parliament recognized the Armenian Genocide condemning the Turkish denial. Turkey as usual counters with diplomatic protests but the parliament held its grounds.

October 18, a minor rally occurs in Yerevan's Freedom Square for the unification of Karabakh and Armenia. Other demonstrations and petitions followed within Soviet Armenia and Nagorno Karabakh for the unification.

October 27, Vasken I, Catholicos of All Armenians, met with President Reagan in the White House. The catholicos wished good health on the first lady who was recuperating from a sickness and expressed in English, "God bless America the beautiful." He also referred to 1700 year history of Armenia "where our people struggled for the Christian faith and liberty." The catholicos gifted the president with a souvenir plate of Etchmiazin and discussed ways America could provide additional help to victims of the 1988 Earthquake.

October 29, the last recorded armed assault of the ASALA was in Beirut where the bombings and assassinations first started. In this diplomatic attack, two French security guards were killed and one was wounded. An ASALA spokesman claimed 84 incidents were conducted in the 12 year period where 96 people were killed and 299 were injured. Vartouhi did not think it was a record to be proud.

December 1-2, the Azeri police beat and arrested several Armenians, including women and senior citizens of Chardahly, Nagorno Karabakh for protesting against the firing of their village leader. Complaints were sent to the office of the Attorney General and the Minister of Interior of the USSR. There was no response from the office. Vartouhi commented to her editor, "What did you expect from an Azeri police department and a rebuttal from the Soviets?"

1988

February 12, the first major protest occurred in Stepanakert with the local Armenians demanding the referendum for the unification of Nagorno Karabakh with the Soviet Armenia to be accepted by the USSR. To date there was no encouragement from Moscow.

February 13, a mass of Armenians in Stepanakert, the center of the Nagorno Karabakh Autonomous Oblast (NKAO), demanded the re-unification of NKAO with Soviet Armenia. It did not take long for Azerbaijani Muslims to start massacring and destroying their Armenian citizens of NKAO or forcing their deportations. [The NKAO was initiated by the Armenian Communists back in 1923, purportedly making Nagorno Karabakh an autonomous region, but it never really got to that stage due to the Azeris moving into the area and taking an aggressive role in mistreating the Armenians who originally made up 95% of the population. A similar situation occurred in Nakhichevan, which eventually became 100% Azeris due to the forced depopulation and abuse of Armenians. The population of Nakhichevan was 75% Armenian before the Azeris initiated their programs of intolerance, abuse, and depopulation.

February 18, Vartouhi and Azad, who is now nineteen years old and a student at YSU, participated in a gigantic demonstration in Yerevan to petition Moscow to reunite Nagorno Karabakh to Armenia. The demo originated as a result of Gorbachev's policy statement on *perestroika* and *glasnost* that he originally invoked last year. The Armenian population was tempted by the restoration of Karabakh back to Armenia. Vartouhi pointed out that Gorbachev's announcement ignited a strong flame in the Armenians to correct a wrong that Stalin perpetuated back in 1923.

February 19, anti-Armenian riots started in Sumgait with massacres and beatings. The Azeris expanded these slaughters and killings to other towns.

February 20, a petition was signed by 80,000 Armenians reluesting that Nagorno Karabakh be returned to Soviet Armenia. A surprising occurrence happened where the session of the NKNO Soviet of People's Deputies passed a resolution "On Petitioning the Supreme Soviets of the Azerbaijan SSR and Armenian SSR for NKAO Transmission from the Azerbaijan SSR Structure to the one of the Armenian SSR. In other words, NKAO would now become a part of Armenia SSR. Great news for the Armenians, but how did the rest of the Caucasus region react to it?

Two days later, February 22, a furious crowd of Azeris from Aghdam advancing toward Stepanakert was spotted by the police and Armenians. Two Azeris were shot dead.

February 26, six days after the signing of the NKAO resolution 500,000 to one million Armenians rallied in Yerevan in support of NKAO's re-unification with Armenia SSR.

The next three days, February 27-29, Azeri government pogroms intensified against the Armenians. Armenian Azeri citizens were killed in Sumgait and Baku. Armenian homes and businesses were ravaged, people were attacked in the streets, and terror reined. Protests, disorder, and killings continued through the year.

March 8, Gorbachev met with leaders of Armenia and Azerbaijan to discuss the public demands of unification of Karabakh with Armenia. Nothing concrete came out of the meeting except the leaders were told to stop the fighting, but the killings continued.

March 23, the Supreme Soviet in Moscow rejected the demands of the Armenians and nullified the dictates of the local Armenian Communists offices. Vartouhi saw the disappointment in the Armenians, but was not sure what the next step would be. The Azeri massacres and killings continued. Two days later Gorbachev himself rejected the Armenian claims of reunification and forbade further demonstrations.

However, the Armenians ignored Gorbachev's orders. On March 26, tens of thousands of determined citizens demonstrated again in Yerevan.

June 15, the NKAO Soviet Supreme Council again voted for the unification of Karabakh and the Republic of Armenia. Two days later, June 17, the Soviet Azerbaijan Supreme Council opposed the transfer.

July 5, protesters at Zvarots Airport confronted Soviet troops, where one man was shot dead, and dozens were injured. Vartouhi could see that the Armenians were determined to keep the unification issue on-going.

The issue of unification went back and forth between Moscow and Yerevan. Nothing was resolved but the murders continue.

September 21, following the numerous hostilities between the Armenians and Azeris, Moscow declared martial law in the region. However, that did not stop the destruction and massacres.

In the fall, 150,000 Armenians in Azerbaijan decided to exit Azerbaijan in large numbers. In Vartouhi's class, several of the students said they thought the Armenians in Azerbaijan had enough of the killings and terror to make the exit decision a necessity, but it was a matter of safety for themselves and their families. Their ancestors had been living in Azerbaijan for centuries and had contributed much to the culture structure of the country, but that did not make any difference to wild and frenzied Azeris.

On September 22, wholesale clashes occurred between the Armenians and Azeris living in Stepanakert. Vartouhi discovered it was the first time guns were used in the riots. One Armenian was shot dead and 24 people were injured. Moscow brought in Soviet troops to stop the conflict, but these soldiers and the police were largely ignored. Other clashes occurred in the surrounding towns but were not as serious. The disputes created refugee problems on both sides of the border as people sleeked safer areas to live in.

November 22, the Soviet Armenian Supreme Council recognized the Armenian Genocide.

November 24, the Soviet Armenian parliament was forced to dissolve and a state of emergency was declared. Thousands of Azeris were expelled from Yerevan. Armenians also exited Azerbaijan by the thousands. Clashes brought about hundreds of deaths on both sides.

On December 7, at 11:41 AM, a horrible earthquake struck the city of Gyumri (formerly Leninakan and Alexandropol), Spitak, and the surrounding areas. The 6.8 cricketer quake devastated Gyumri, destroyed Spitak completely, and did considerable damage to the outlying towns. The death toll over was 25,000, with over 100,000 injuries. Destruction of property left tens of thousands homeless. President Gorbachev who was in Washington, DC, dropped his international duties and returned to Armenia to assist in whatever the Soviet Union could do to help the victims and restore damaged property. Aid from foreign countries all over the world (even Turkey) was offered in any way they could. Food, clothing, medicine, construction equipment, and any other available supplies were sent to the devastated region. Foreign doctors, nurses, and construction workers volunteered their help. Hospitals provided medical equipment and supplies. The quake was a huge disaster for tiny Armenia and the undertaking to help the victims required tremendous assistance. In order to assist in finding homes for the homeless, railroad boxcars (*domeeks*) were brought into the area to provide temporary housing, but it was not nearly enough to take care of all the homeless.

In summing up the year of 1988, Vartouhi had a discussion in her class. All of the students agreed that the year has been in extreme chaos and that the turmoil was still going on. Demonstrations in Yerevan, Baku, and other cities had been chaotic and often deadly. The Azeri pogroms contributed much to the deaths. Other problems included the strikes, railroad and street stoppages, exchange of refugees, and the occupation of Soviet military in both Armenia and Azerbaijan. The oscillating declarations of unity of Karabakh with Armenia on and in acceptance, then off again, had been extremely difficult for almost everyone.

1989

1989 started with the same potential deadliness and confusion as the previous year. On January 12, the Soviet Government decided to put Nagorno Karabakh under direct control from Moscow.

The Azeri massacres and deportations of Armenians out of Azerbaijan continued at the start of 1989.

March 16, the Metsamor Nuclear Power Plant was shut down.

December 1, the Soviet Armenian Supreme Council and NKAO Supreme Council declared the unification of Armenia and Karabakh. The Azeris have mass protests and intensify their harassment and massacres of Armenians..

Further verification in a joint resolution on the re-unification of NKAO to Armenia SSR was supported by the united session of the Supreme Soviet of the Armenian SSR and the National Soviet of NKAO

In August, Azerbaijan started the economic blockage of Armenia and NKAO. .

1990

On January 13-20, pogroms against the Armenians restarted in Baku.

Chapter 8

Armenian Independence

1991

January 10, Vartouhi was assigned an interview with Khatchik Stamboltsyan (b. c. 1950), Chairman of the Parliamentary Commission Disaster Areas and Refugees. Her first question to the the chairman, "It's been a little over two years since the disastrous earthquake in Leninakan (now Gyumry) and Spitak, are we making any progress in the area?"

"I'm sorry to say, not really. We have made some progress, but there is so much more we could have done or are doing now. Great plans were made on paper concerning what we were going to do, but there were all kinds of excuses and thus no real progress."

"Exactly what has happened?" Vartouhi asked.

"Oh, we've had a lot of difficulties. Only 10% of the buildings have been replaced. In the three major cities that were hit, only 25% of the structures have been rebuilt. Sadly, in some places, houses have been constructed, but have no water, sewage, or electricity services. In other areas, projects were left half empty as workers went home because when the blockage went into effect building supplies were cut off."

"What seems to be the problem? I heard when Gorbachev left New York abruptly to care of the people who have been injured and start reconstruction right away. But from what I'm hearing, it didn't happen.

You would think someone as high a rank as the leader of the Soviet Union would have enough clout to get things started, but you say we have made very little progress."

"You're right Vartouhi, but like I said, 'It didn't happen.' All kinds of excuses have popped up. Meanwhile, thousands of people continue to live in huts, tin shacks, train boxcars, or whatever makeshift shelter. At first there were all kinds of help, dozens of foreign countries sent money, workers, supplies, and anything to help out, but as time went on, rescue operations and help slackened due to the sense of overwhelming needs."

"Everything sounds so extremely sad. Is there any hope that situation will improve?"

"Again I'm sorry to say, over 350,000 people remain without homes, schools are only for 5,500 children, no Soviet hospital has been built anywhere in the earthquake zone, and the list goes on and on. There's a lot of wishful thinking, but it doesn't look good."

"What can we do to help out?"

"Oh there are hundreds of things. We always need funds. Donations would be extremely helpful. Getting more foreign companies to send supplies, especially concrete and building materials and get Turkey free passage into Armenia. Getting Russia to help more. Gorbachev initially promised $10 million, but we never saw it. Also to get an Armenian on the Recovery Commission that is made up of Communist Russians who do not care much about what goes on in Armenia. They are more concerned about poverty conditions in Moscow than here and also to have an Armenian reporter serve an Armenian newspaper in Leninakan to let them know what is going on in the city and vicinity."

The interview continued on with additional discussion on what can be done to the earthquake victims who have really have been suffering for over four years. Vartouhi told Stamboltsyan she hoped the article would help to provide more funding and additional attention from the Armenian and Soviet legislators.

1991 continued on with Armenian Independence and the construction of the Resurrection Monument.

The Resurrection Monument

The Resurrection Monument and Genocide Museum were construrcted soon after Armenia gained her indepenendence in 1991. The monument and the Genocide Museum are a part of Tsitsernakaberd complex. Also seen at the monument is the Phoenix bird that symbolically will rise from the ashes to regain its former spendor. The modern Khatch kar represents Armenian's dedication to Christianity.

September 23, after turmoil and coups in the Soviet Union, Armenia officially claimed her independence. Three weeks earlier, September 2, Nagorno Karabakh Republic proclaimed her independence in Stepanakert. This was the beginning of long conflict between Karabakh and Azerbaijan and a struggle for the Republic of Armenia to establish a sound government.

Vartouhi has been teaching at Yerevan State University (YSU) for a number of years now and had a number of interesting students. She also served as a reporter for an Armenian newspaper. In 1991, a young man of 16 had entered YSU as a journalism student. He was like any other student except the professor noticed he had something in his character that was outgoing and dynamic. The student was in his second year journalism class. He was an exceptional energetic student who was in perpetual conversations with other students on what is going on in the Soviet Union and how these actions affected Armenia. His name was Nikol Pashinyan

(b. 1975). In a typical conversation after one of her classes, he asked the professor, "What do you think is going on with the Russians?"

"Oh, I have my ideas, but I'd like to hear what you have to say."

In a way Nikol thought this was a copout but it was the professor's way of getting the students to think. Nikol thought for a few seconds, then said, "Whatever it is, I think it's quite dynamic and maybe even a little upheaval. I personally never thought the Union would breakup, but I think the people have had it where some of the leadership has recognized it and are more or less stirring the pot. There has been so much corruption in the system, lying of industrial leaders, farmers stating they made their quotas but not even close to their assigned shares, and I could go on and on."

"How can you say all that Nikol?"

"Just look at the records. The Soviet hierarchy has been setting up Five Year Plans for decades and a lot looks like they were working. Managers would tell their leaders the quotas were being met, but in actuality they were not. In addition to the incorrect reporting, the distribution processes were not the greatest in the world. Meanwhile we had shortages of goods and the economy going downward. I think some of the people just felt they were being scalped."

"You know we had some pretty good times when Nikita Khrushev (1894-1971) became first secretary of the Communist Party. The economy grew, but later when Leonid Brezhnev (1906-1982) and his successors became Soviet leaders, the economy failed to improve. In fact, in some cases went down," the professor commented.

"I don't know what happened that far back in 50s because I was born yet, but everything I have read tells me Armenia was a hell hole during Stalin's rein. No one was safe, not even his friends or cohorts. Stalin made sure no one would be taking his place. I don't know how Mikoyan (Anastas 1895-1978) was able to stay in the butcher's good graces, but as far as I know he was still a respectable citizen of the government when he died."

"Yes, we all know pretty much what a tyrant Stalin was, but in the long term, even with dictator's inhumanities and brutalities, Armenia did make some progress."

"Okay, I'll grant that, but some of our later leaders, namely Boris Yeltsin (1931-2007) [first president of the Independent Russian Republic from 1991 to 1999] took measures that I personally I think brought about the downfall of the USSR. If he wasn't such a drunk, I think he could have done a better job," the student commented

"Nikol, I think you pretty much answered your own question. Yeltsin was the man who suppressed eight hardline communists who attempted a coup to restore the Union. But I also think if it wasn't for Mikhail Gorbachev's *peritsroika* and *glassnost* policies, the breakup would not have happened [Gorbachevwas general secretary of the Communist Party from 1985 to 1991 and as president of the USSR when he made his revisionist speech]. His openness and restructuring was the introductory idea that kindled the nationalism and restoration of Nagorno Karabakh's demonstrations. We weren't rebelling we just wanted Karabakh back to her original owners. Unfortunate;ly the Soviets did not support the idea." In fact, the huge demonstrations in 1988 got Azerbaijan so riled up she started her pogroms of massacres and deportations of her Armenian citizens. It was the Genocide all over again."

From April 30 to May 15, Soviet and Azeri forces deported thousands of Armenians from Shahumyan, Azerbaijan/Karabakh region, to prevent their massacre by the Azeri madhouse.

July 5, Mikhail Gorbachev lectured on the Nobel Peace Prize that he was awarded last year. He talked about the reduction of military forces, peace and cooperation among nations. He elaborated on his proposal and policy of *perestroika* and importance of self-determination of nations. He declared the Cold War over and a threat of a nuclear war being practically gone. He said the Iron Curtain is no longer in existence. Many other aspects of peace and harmony were discussed. Vartouhi read the speech, thought it was really great, but prayed to herself that what Gorbachev said would become a real entity in the future.

From August 19 to 21, a Soviet coup d'état was made in Moscow. The end result was a topple of the Soviet Government and the establishment of the Russian State lead by President Boris Yelsen.

The Republic of Armenia and the Republic of Karabakh

The above map shows the Republics of Armenia and Karabakh after their declarations for freedom im 1991. Nakhichevan still remained a territory of Azerbaijan.

September 2, Nagorno Karabakh officially proclaimed herself as independent republic in Stepanakert.

The proclamation ignited the flame that initiated a conflict between Azerbaijan and Nagorno Karabakh.

September 23, Armenia officially voted her independence from the Soviet Union.

On October 17, Levon Ter Petrosyan (b. 1945) was elected first President of Armenia. Nikol Pashinyan (b. 1975), one Varouhi's young students, was one of his ardent supporters.

December 8, the Commonwealth of Independent States (CIS) was organized to bring the former Soviet states together to facilitate and strengthen the cooperation among member states in the political, economic, ecological humanitarian, cultural, and other fields. The 12 member states included Russia, Armenia, Kazakhstan, Kyrgyzstan, Tajikistan, Moldova, Turkmenistan, Ukraine, Uzbekistan, Azerbaijan, Georgia, and Belarus.

December 10, Nagorno Karabakh reaffirmed her independence in a referendum.

December 26, the Soviet Union officially dissolved.

By year's end, even with independence, everything was still in a tumultuous state in Armenia and Karabakh. Both countries had declared independence, but Armenia's economic structure and government requirements were in their infancy. Nagorno Karabakh was foreseeing a probable war with Azerbaijan.

1992

1992 was the start of a rough year for Armenia. The country was independent and the reins of government were in place, but you have to admit not very efficient. The water and electric power systems were being operated intermittently, food shortages were apparent and there was no fuel to keep the homes warm. In fact, the populous started chopping the beautiful boulevard and park trees in Yerevan in order to warm their homes. Some city leaders wanted to stop the carnage of cutting trees, but President Ter Petrosyan said, "Let them do it. The people have to stay warm." Some citizens claimed they were better off under Communism than with our freedom here today. All kinds of problems were developing not only with Azerbaijan, but also with local utility systems.

As the war with Azerbaijan had gotten more aggressive, it prompted Azad to join a team of doctors to serve near the front lines. The make-shift field hospitals enabled doctors to perform critical operation to save the lives of soldiers, and sometimes civilians, as soon as possible. Many times it was a matter of life or death how fast as operations could be performed. Azad earned his medical degree a few years ago and was one of the medical personnel to volunteer near the front lines. Doctors and nurses often worked steadily for more than 24 hours depending on the number of wounded who had to be cared for. It was an endless job when critical conditions mandated 24 hours a day to perform the procedures to heal the wounded. Medical personnel had to take an occasional rest in order to keep working.

In one of Vartouhi Zerouni's journalism classes in 1992, the question arose that Armenia was beset with numerous treaties that have been detrimental to the country. The professor asked if any student would be interested in writing an essay on the subject? Nikol was the only student who raised his hand. The professor was not surprised.

"Nikol, it looks like you got the assignment. I don't think it would be necessary for you to go back any further than the World War I, if that is acceptable for you?"

"Fine with me. I'll give it a shot, "the young 17 year old replied.

"Is two weeks enough time to finish the assignment?

"I think that would be enough time. that is, if you don't require a lot of detail."

'That'll be fine."

Two weeks later, Nikol Pashinyan (b. 1975) turned in the following report.

Treaties Concerning Armenia Since World War I

The following treaties reflect the outcomes of various conflicts that relate to Armenia after the battles had subsided. The chart show the Name of the Treaty, the Date of the Treaty, and Comments on the Treaty.

Name of Treaty	Date	Comments
Brest-Litovski	3/3/1918	Treaty between the new Bolshevik Russia and the Central Powers. The treaty took Kars-Ardahan away from the Armenians giving the regions to Turkey and was extremely harsh on Russia.
Treaty of Batum	6/4/1918	Recognized the new Republic of Armenia, but imposed many restrictions on the new republic.
Treaty of Mudros	10/30/1918	Armistice between Allies and Ottoman Turkey ending the war and establishing the Turkish border to prewar Russian territories.

1918 Armistice	11/11/1918	This was the agreement between the Allies and Germans to stop the fighting. Separate Armistices were signed earlier with Ottoman Turkey and Bulgaria.
Treaty of Versailles	6/25/ 1919	Stopped the war in Europe
Severes Treaty	10/10/1920	Established Armenian borders in Anatolia outlining close to what President Wilson proposed in his Fourteen Points. Ottoman Turkey accepted the treaty but was rejected by Kemal Pasha.
Treaty of	12/6/1920	Established basic terms of Soviet Armenia after Turkey's undeclared Alexandropole war against Armenia
Treaty of Moscow	3/16/21	Also called the Treaty of Alexandropole Brotherhood. The treaty confirmed the boundaries of Russia and Turkey where Armenia had no input. Armenia was accepted as a Soviet Republic.
Treaty of Kars	10/19/21	This was mainly a treaty between Kemal and Lenin. The treaty finalized the boundaries between Soviet Armenia and the other two Soviet Repblics. Kars, Ardahan, the medieval capital of Ani, and sadly the region of Surmalu where Mt. Ararat is located were ceded to Turkey
Treaty of Lausanne	7/21/23	Finalized World War I boundaries, but left the "Little Ally" completely out of the picture. There was no mention of Armenia in the treaty.

The professor thanked Nikol for the report then discussed it with the rest of the class. The general agreement was whenever Armenia was in the picture she was usually on the losing end being overpowered by the larger nations. It was not what you would call a good feeling.

1992 continued

January 6, the Nagorno Karabakh Parliament declares the country's independence.

January 26, the Nagorno Karabakh Republic (NKR) forces initiated a serious defeat to the regular Azeri army near the Armenian village of Karin-Tak in the Shoushi region. The victory became a moral booster for further Artsakh successes.

January 30, the Organization for Security and Co-Operation in Europe (OSCE) now renamed to Conference for Security and Co-Operation in Europe (CSCE) created the Minsk Group to encourage a peaceful, negotiated resolution between Armenia and Azerbaijan in the settlement of the Nagorno Karabakh-Azeri conflict. Even with the group in place, there still was no peace in the region as the Azeris continued to refuse to practice any peaceful measures. Deaths were very common as Armenians were killed from Azeri rifle shootings continuously.

February 25, by February, the conflict had turned into a full scale war. On this day, the Karabakh and Commonwealth of Independent States (CIS) [that was organizes as early 1920s to bring peace to the region] forces had surrounded Khojaly and broadcasted to the town through loudspeakers and informants that the Karabakh forces were going to take over the city. The Azeri civilians were being offered a safety corridor to Aghdam and they would be allowed to move freely with no harm. On the next day the departing became a disaster when a few men in the crowd started firing at an Armenian outpost and the Armenians returned fire that turned into a shooting melee. The end result was 663 dead Azeris. Later reports indicated the barrage was caused by an Azeris who wanted to disown one of their generals. The incident became known as the Khojaly Massacre, but the Armenians claim they were not responsible for it. The deadly incident turned into an international argument as to what organization was really responsible for the massacre. Today the dispute is still being argued and will probably go on well into the future. [Go to March 3, 2021, to see what happened 27 years later].

Also in another area of Karabakh, an attack occurred on the village of Maragha but was repulsed by the local villagers. Most of the young male members of the community had left to fight the Azeri forces in more crucial areas. Fortunately the town was able to defend itself and no locals were killed.

March 1, Vartouhi decided to get married to an Armenian member of parliament, Simon Cashigyan who has been an extreme activist in the Armenian liberation movement and annexation of Nagorno Karabakh to Armenia. The journalist had many pursuers but never paid much attention to any future relationship. She had matured into a super-reporter and was just too busy teaching and doing her journalist job. She also carried on the memory of her first husband, although she would not admit it. She had a small wedding with Nikol Pashinyan as best man and Hera Pilibosian as maid of honor. The whole Pilibosian family was invited to the wedding. Vartouhi asked Simon to have Pashinyan for his best man because she had built up quite a student/instructor resonance with him through several of the courses he took. He was also a friend of her new husband even though there was a difference in age.

March 2, Armenia became a member of United Nations (UN) and initiated many programs involving the organization.

March 24, the Minsk Group of nine "neutral" countries: Russia, the US, France, Italy, Czech Republic, Belarus, Germany, and Turkey, plus Armenia, Azerbaijan, and sometimes Mountainous Karabakh was set up by the CSCE Council of Ministers by a mandate. The group's function was to conduct preliminary negotiations to determine the final status of Mountainous Karabakh. When Vartouhi saw that Turkey and Azerbaijan were was also members of the group, how would Nagorno Karabakh ever have a fair and equal outcome?

April 10, the horrible war of ethnic cleansing continued in Karabakh. There were literally no Armenians left in Baku, Sumgate, Kirovahad, and other Azeri settlements. A stronger Azeri force attacked the village of Maragha where 45-100 people were beheaded on the spot;

49 (including 9 children and 29 women) were taken hostage of which 19 were never heard from again. The incident turned out to be a real massacre.

April 14, the Armenians tore-down Lenin's statue in Yerevan.

The Armenians returned to Maragha on April 22-23 to bury their comrades where the Azeris again attacked resulting in additional deaths.

May 8-9, NKR forces captured Shushi in a significant victory and also secured the Goris Land Corridor to Armenia. The Armenian commanders call the victory a "Wedding in the Mountains."

June 10, Vartouhi's editor asked her to conduct an interview with the Artsakh commander who is now stationed in northern Karabakh. "There's a lot of activity going on there and I would like you to interview him as he has been doing a terrific job."

Vartouhi had talked to other soldiers in the past and written articles about them. She was expected to meet them close to the battle line. She told her boss she would go, but wanted to talk to her husband first. That evening she told Simon and Azad who was home on leave, that she would be leaving for Shahumanian.

"Vartouhi, are you crazy? There's a hell of lot of hot activity there and you have no idea what can happen to you," Simon told his wife.

"Oh, I don't plan to be directly on the front line, but I will be close enough to see what is happening. I'm pretty sure nothing dramatic will occur when I'm there."

Azad who was also present, said, "Mom the war zone is no place for an unarmed woman. You don't have to go'" Azad had been spending most of time in the field hospitals near the line of contract and had a good knowledge on how dangerous his mother would be in if she fulfilled her assignment. He managed to come home about every two-three weeks to catchup on sleep, otherwise it would be easy to screw-up when doing operations.

"Azad, there are a lot of women on the front line. The editor asked me to go and I feel it's my job. And beside the fact, I want to go."

"Well I can't stop you if you really want to go, but don't expect me or Simon to come rescue you if you get into any kind of trouble."

June 12, a large Azeri offensive captured the town of Shahumanian. Vartouhi was now on the job assignment with the Karabakh troops during the defense of the city and had a chance to interview the commander of the Karabakh forces after they had set up their security camp outside the combat area.

The reporter asked the commander, "Do you think you will be recapturing Shahumanian again?"

"We were undermanned and maybe a little over confident that they would not be attacking us. We thought with our recent victories the Azeris would not go on any offense. However, we were wrong. It was something like the Germans attacking the Americans during the end of World War II."

"Commander that was a long time ago. What happened there? America and the Allies won the war didn't they?" It was obvious that Vartouhi did not know the details of the "Battle of the Bulge" even thought she read a lot.

"It happened in the winter of 1944-1945 when the American troops were making victories all over the war front. Germans were retreating in mass. Then in a last ditch effort, German forces attacked the American troops in the Ardennes region of Belgium, surrounding them. Hitler's troops were ready to annihilate the Americans. Fortunately it did not happen. American reinforcements were brought in and the Germans went back to their retreating. As to your question, 'Will we be recapturing Shahumanian again?' Yes, we certainly plan to do so."

That night Vartouhi was staying at an occupied house well behind the "line of contact" with four soldiers. She wanted to be near the action so that she could accurately report on what was going on at the front. The commander wanted her to go back farther, but she insisted on being near there if action would occur. As it was, the Azeris knew she was at the front and their intelligence found out where she was staying. They also knew she was one of the top reporters in Armenia and that she would bring in a large ransom if they captured her. At around 2:00 AM in the night, Azeri commandos infiltrated the Karabakh lines and raided the house. Two Armenian soldiers were killed and two were captured along with Vartouhi. It was done with utmost silence where no one knew what happened until breakfast in the morning. The commander of course was devastated thinking the journalist was his responsibility and he had allowed her to be captured. They could not do anything until they heard from the enemy, but they set up an intelligence group to determine where was being held.

In Azerbaijani territory, Vartouhi was treated with respect but was asked numerous questions by Azeri intelligence officers. She was surprised they did not torture her, but maybe they were more interested a huge ransom fee. They wanted to know what she knew about any of the Armenian Karabakh plans. She of course told them she knew nothing, "I'm only a journalist. I only report on what I see and hear and have absolutely no idea what kind of plans the military is thinking. And beside the point, I think it's against international law you people are holding me as a civilian." she wasn't sure that was correct but she thought she would try it anyway.

The Azeris ignored the remark continuing to ask questions. They told her she is being held for ransom and if they don't receive what they want she may be executed as a spy.

"I think your charge is ridiculous," Vartouhi said with a smirk on her face. The reporter was concerned, but you could not see it in way she responded.

June 13 -14, Nagorno Karabakh forces took over Lachin. Azerbaijan makes a ludicrous claim that Armenia attacked China (China in the Armenian language is pronounced 'lachin'). Armenia finally has an open corridor to Nagorno Karabakh.

The Conference for the Security and Co-Operation in Europe (CSCE) was created. The Minsk Group continues to look for a solution to Karabakh, but the group was unable to keep Azersi border shootings down.

June 20, it was a little over a week that Vartouhi had been captured. She was told that the Azeris have been negotiating with Armenia for her release, but were told they were asking too much. She told her captors that she did not think she herself was worthy of a million dollars, so why did the Azeris think she had that kind of value? As she discussed this and other concerns, she was always thinking in the back of her mind about a plan of escape, continuing to observe where her guards were, how they behaved routinely, and which ones seemed to be more alert that others. The Azeri intelligence officers would meet with her at least twice a day trying to pry some measure of useful information. So far, they had learned nothing except a few personal items about her.

One day the question came up about Azerbaijan's claim to Armenia. "You know Armenia has historically been a part of Azerbaijan and should return back to us."

Vartouhi grinning with sneering look toward the officer's face, "What are you talking about? There wasn't even a country named Azerbaijan until 1918. You were a nothing. And you would not have seen the likes of Nagorno Karabakh in 1923 if it wasn't for Joseph Stalin. Armenia has been around for over millenniums, Azerbaijan has been a figment of your imagination. Armenia has been in existence for a long time and will still be around for another few millenniums. We will never die. Your claim of an occupation of Armenia in the past is a pipe dream you have fabricated. It was the Seljuk Turks who occupied Armenia back in the 11th century not the Azeris. You were only tribal enclaves in Iran at the time." Of course the argument went nowhere because the officer ignored what Vartouhi said.

He was well aware of Azerbaijan's past, however, refused to believe what his captive was saying. He did have a look of curiosity asking, "What is this pipe dream you're talking about?"

Vartoouhi could hardly hold back a smirk, "It's the fantasy Azerbaijan has injected into her people. No time has your country dominated Armenia and it's something that she never will. Go ahead with your propaganda and dream of your fictitious vision, because you will still be dreaming even after you wake up."

While all this was going on Vartouhi continued her astute observations as to what was going on around her. She had a good idea where she was located as related to the "line of action." She kept thinking how she could get out of this entrapment, but she did not show any signs of her thoughts. The Azeris had no idea that she was continually thinking of some escape plan.

On June 27, she was awakened at 2:00 AM by someone gently shaking her. "I'm an Armenian commando, please do not be alarmed. Please do not say anything," said the Armenian soldier.

"How did you know where I was? How did you get here?" She was ready to ask more questions, but the soldier put his finger on her lips.

He again said, "Please do not say anything. We'll tell you all about it later. Get dressed and we'll be leaving here. Rub this paste on your face and wear these black gloves." Again he said, "Please do not say anything. We have to be absolutely quiet."

Vartouhi got dressed in the dark and was slowly guided out of the house she was being held in. The leader of the group of four commandos held her hand as they made their way in the darkness toward the line of contact. The leader gave a pair of night goggle after which she noticed her four rescuers were wearing them also. After about two hours stumbling on the rugged terrain while the soldier was holding her hand, the leader finally said, "It's okay to talk, but please hold your questions until we we get to the command post."

At the command post she learned that Armenian intelligence was investigating her whereabouts and finally found out she was about a mile behind the line of contact in a small house guarded by four Azeri soldiers. Azeri intelligence officers made daily trips to the house to question her and assure that she was being treated properly. They were well aware that she was a famous journalist and thought she would be worth a high ransom. The four Armenian commandos knew exactly where she was being held and how many men were guarding her. They had to kill the four guards to get to her. The journalist learned all the above as she talked to the command post and Armenian intelligence officers. Overall, she was grateful and happy with the rescue and glad to be back in Armenian hands.

December 2, Vartouhi was now safe and sound back in Yerevan for the last few months and heard about a Michael Stone (b. 1980), retired professor of Armenian Studies at the Hebrew University in Jerusalem, discovering a "Bird Mosaic" north of the Damascus Gate of the Holy city. The mosaic was considered one of the most beautiful of the hundreds of floor mosaics in the churches and other structures in the city and surrounding regions. The mosaic had Armenian writing on the tiles. When the reporter heard about the discovery, she called the professor to find out more about the big news. She asked him if he could tell her the significance of the finding. He told her, "This is not the first time a bird mosaic has been found in the area. There are hundreds of similar once throughout the city in religious and official places. This one had Armenian writing on it and is one of the four that we know about from the Byzantine period."

"If they are from the Byzantine period, wouldn't that indicated the Armenians were in Jerusalem during early time?" Vartouhi asked.

"Oh, yes of course. I'm sure you know Armenians conducted pilgrimages to the Holy city in the 4th century after she became a Christian state in 301. Armenian monks established sanctuaries that eventually developed into a Patriate in the 7th century (Patruate Abrahan 637-665). There are current quite a few Armenians living in the city, but their numbers have really come down."

"I've heard that from several journalists, but what about the bird mosaic that you discovered?"

"As I said, this is not the first time a bird mosaic has been found in Jerusalem."

"The article did not say anything about when. It was worded like you were really excited about the discovery."

"I guess I was excited because this one was really beautiful. The first bird mosaic was discovered in 1894 in the process of building the foundation for a house. The one I found was at another structure. In fact, I've been finding these bird mosaics for years. The article made it sound like this was the first one."

Now that Vartouhi got most of the information on the bird mosaic, she asked about how he got interested in the Armenians. She found out he was born in Leeds, England in 1938. Three years later his family moved to Sydney, Australia where he studied the classic languages and earned a degree in Semitic Studies and the Classics at the University of Melbourne. He migrated to Israel in 1960 where learned a wealth of knowledge about the Armenians and how active they were in the early Christian period. He said he was fascinated by their history and culture.

After his tenure at the Hebrew University (1960-1961), he transferred to Harvard University where he earned his doctorate in the concept of eschatology (a branch of theology that is concerned with the ultimate, or last things such a death, judgement, heaven, and hell). This was all followed by being a lecturer at the University of California. He returned to Israel in 1966 at the Hebrew University where in 1980 he became a full professor of Armenian Studies. He retired in 2007, but continued his research and lecturing as a professor emeritus.

Stone had a long history of lectures and research studies all over the world. These included, but are not limited to; Harvard University, University of Melbourne, Leiden University, University of Pennsylvania, Yale, University of North Carolina, Armenia, and several colleges within the Hebrew University. He is a member of the editorial board of the *Revue des Etudes Armeiennes Journal* (Paris), served as a member of the scientific board *of Patmabanasirakan Handes* (Yerevan) and a member of editorial board of the Dead Sea Discoveries. He is the founder of the Biblical Literature Pseudepigrapha Group (USA). That's all Vartouhi could say was, "Amazing." [see November 17, 2003, Prof. Stone lectures at the Armenian St. Nersess Seminary.]

Chapter 9

Armenia/Azerbaijan Fracas then War, 1994-2020

1993

February, A rare three day summit was held between Catholicos of All Armenians Vazgen I (b. 1908) and Sheikl-ul-Islam Alahshurkur Pasha-zade (b. 1949), Chief Sayyid of the Muslims of Azerbaijan in Montreux, Switzerland. The summit was organized by the World Council of Churches (WCC) and European Churches. The primary reason for the summit was to bring peace to the region that the religious leaders thought was crucial to people involved in the conflict. A joint communique from the heads of the major fathes read "… this is not a religious conflict. Armenian Christians and Azerbaijani Muslims have lived and will live in peace." Vartouhi thought this was a misnomer but did not make an issue of it. She thought to herself that Armenians have been living in Azerbaijani region for centuries and have contributed immensely to the culture and welfare of the country, but have always been discriminated against. But now it was even worse.

April 3, Nagorno Karabakh Republic (NKR) forces take over Kelbajar

April, Turkey closes her border with Armenia.

June 4, Azeri Colonel Surat Huseinov (b. 1959) who was dismissed of his rank by Azeri President Abulfez Elcibey (1938-2000) because of his defeats in Karabakh, began an insurrection causing the president to flee. Haydar Aliyev (1923-2003) took over the presidency. It did not take long for Aliyev to impose an iron grip on the media and opposition protestors essentially establishing a police state. As far as Armenia was concerned, he also was a no-good Azeri.

June – August, in the Nagorno Karabakh War Armenian forces take over Agdam, Fizuli, Jebrayil, and Zangela

June 17, Russian mediation achieved a bilateral cessation or artillery bombardments of Agdam and Stepanakert.

July-December 16, Russia manages to instigate ceasefires in the Azeri=Karabakh War, but Azerbaijan keeps breaking the agreements.

November 22, Armenian dram monetary system is put into circulation.

November 30, the Councilors of Mininisters of the Conference on Security and Cooperatkopn in Europe (CSCE) met in Rome to seek as impass to the Azeri Nagorno Karabakh conflict in search for peace. Much talk resulted with a lot of ideas. Since any CSCE resolution must be based on the consensus of 53 member states there was some question that any measure any measure would pass.

1994

Armenian Tree Project (ATP) was established by Carolyn Mugar in Wobum, MA and Yerevan. The organization mission is to emphasize the use of trees to promote economic self-sufficiency, improve the standard of living while promoting the environment and many more causes. The ATP works with cities, farms, school grounds, parks and any place else where improvements can be made.

February 8 to 11, President Levon Ter Petrosian visited the United Kingdom with a large delegation of Armenian officials. It was the first time in 600 years that a head of Armenian state visited Great Britain. [King Levon V visited the country in 1385]. Talks took place, trade agreements were made, meetings and lectures with international and scientific organizations were conducted, musical interludes directed, and even discussions on the possibility of having English mercenaries help out in Karabakh. Nothing developed from that idea. The Armenian president and his delegation were treated royally, but there was not much military assistance on the way. In fact three weeks later, Prime Minister John Major (b. 1943) visited Azeri President Heydar Aliyev (b. 1923). Varouhi had no idea what they talked about except it was probably on the shipment of oil to the UK.

March 17, Armenian forces shot down an Iranian C-31 over Stepanakert by mistake. The plane was flying from Moscow to Tehran and was carrying the families of Iranian diplomats. All 32 persons on the plane were killed.

April, Armenian Fund U.S.A. (AFUSA, also called Hayastan All Armenian Fund and other similar names), is a nonprofit corporation that was formed to raise funds for the Republic of Armenia and the Mountainous Republic of Karabagh infrastructures and the rebuilding of the two countries. The corporation was established by an unprecedented coalition of all major Armenian organizations to mobilize the resources of the entire Armenian American community. It has 19 subsidiaries throughout the world. The collected funds are to be utilized for roads and highways, electric and water pipe lines, sewers, health care, communication systems, housing, and support for scientific and cultural institutions. The corporation should not be confused with the United Armenian Fund (UAF) that is another worthwhile fund for assisting the two republics in their survival and to ensure their strong futures.

May 5, a ceasefire and protocol was agreed between Armenia and Azerbaijan ending the Nagorno Karabakh War. Armenian won much of the territory surrounding the enclave.

Republic of Armenia and Nagorno Karabakh 1994

The map above shows Armenia, Nagorno Karabagh Republic (NKR, name changed in 2017, and to Artsakh Republic in 2019), and the occupied territory of Azerbaijan after the 1992-1994 war. The Peace talks were initiated soon after the war. The map was copied from the April 6, 2019 issue of the Armenian Weekly. The map does not show the east/west super highway going from Goris to Stepanakert, the north/south road from Hadrut (Stepanakert) to Martakert, nor the east/west highway from Vardenis to Martakert. The roads will contribute to binding the republic together and with Armenia and improving the Karabagh economy.

Armenians have been living in Karabagh for over thousands of years, but Statin decided wrongly in 1923 to cede the mountainous territory and Nakhichevan to Soviet Republic of Azerbaijan.. Their respective Armenian populations were 95% and 75%, respectively. In 1985 Mikhael Gorbachev's speech on perestroika and glasnost opened the door for Soviet Armenia to regain Karabagh and correct Stalin's unfair doing. Unexpectedly, the movement caused the conflict.

Peace talks are continuing between Armenia and Azerbaijan and the Organization for Security and Cooperation in Europe (OSCE), but to date they are still discussing cease-fires and tranquility. Representatives from France, Russia, Armenia, and United States meet periodically to devise a peaceful settlement between the conflicting nations

December 28, President Levon Ter Petrossian ordered the temporary suspension of the Armenian Revolutionary Federation (ARF) due to its secret organization called DRO that was charged with drug trafficking, espionage, and corruption. The Supreme Court suspended the whole ARF organization for six months.

1995

January 12-13, the Supreme Court holds administrative hearing and holds the ban on the ARF for six months.

June 14, Azad completed his internship from the Heratsisa Yerevan State Medical University and was hired as a junior surgan at the Nork Marsh Hospital in Yerevan. Vartouhi had a small reception for him with a few of his and her close friends. While he was studing and experiencing his internship he had an opportunity to assist the doctors in the field hospitals in Artsakh. After Armemia won the war in 1994Azad completed his medical training..

July 1, Aram I Kesheshian (b. 1947) was consecrated as Catholico of the Great House of Cilicia. Nikol Pashinyan was expelled from YSU for writing too many articles on politics. He also met Anna Hakopyan (b.1978), a freshman at YSU, where they soon got married. Vartouhi thought the ousting charge was uncalled for as Pashinyan had an outstanding academic record, was a highly esteemed student, and was a person who continually seemed exceptional from a political point of view.

Karekin II of the Great House of Cilicia was voted to become Karekin I Catholicos of All Armenians.

July 5, Armenian Genocide Museum Institute opened in Yerevan.

November 5, Metsamor Nuclear Power Plant reopened restoring available power to Armenia.

1996

September 15 – October 2, 32nd Chess Olympad held in Yerevan. Team Armenia won three Gold Medals and three Bronze. Vartouhi wrote that she expected Armenia to do as well as she did because the small nation she demonstrates superiority in chess tournaments.

September 22, Levon Ter Petrosyan was elected to second term.

September 23 -26, election results were contested. Protestors occupied the National Assembly building.

1997

Work started on the Goris Stepanakert highway. George Mouradian had the fortune to ride on eastern section of the highway in September reminding me of traveling through the mountains of Pennsylvania, only much higher in Karabakh.

March 20, Robert Kocharyan (b. 1954) became Prime Minister or Armenia.

September – November, George taught at American University of Armenia (AUA). He lectured at YSU, SARM-Armenian Institute of Standards, and visits Karabakh. He found the students energetic, generally intelligent, and eager to learn.

1998

February 3, Levon Ter Petrosyan resigned mainly due to his proposal to negotiate with Azerbaijan to return the territory conquered by the Armenian in return to have Nagorno Karabakh become independent. There were too many Armenians who objected to the idea.

March 16, Robert Kocharyan elected president; the results were contested by the opposition.

May 6, President Kocharyan lifted the ban on the ARF.

August 17, Russian financial crisis caused trade problems with Armenia and other former Soviet Republics.

1999

May 30, Unity bloc wins plurality to Armenian parliament. Vazgen Sargsyan (b. 1959) becomes Prime Minister.

June 11, Karen Demirchyan (b. 1932) was elected National Assembly Speaker. Demirchyan was assassinated four months later together with seven other parliamentarians (see October 27, 1999)

August 28 -September 5, the first Pan Armenian Games were held in Yerevan. The games included 65 cities and 23 countries and were originally set up to play every two years, but was later revised to play every four years.

September, Nikol Pashinyan founded and became editor of the *Haykagan Zhamanak* (Armenian Times). The newspaper eventually became the largest newspaper in Armenia. Vartouhi thought it was great to be hired by one of her former astute students. Pashinyan's wife, Anna Hakobyan (b.1978) who also was one of her students, became editor-in-chief a few years after and was given the unofficial title as "The First Lady of Armenia" after Pashinyan became PM even though the tile is usually given to the president's wife.

September 22-23, first Armenian Diaspora Conference held in Yerevan. Vartouhi was hoping that this would initiate a strong working relationship between the Armenian Republic and the diaspora. Other unification assemblies have been held in the past, but there is expectation that this one will result in some positive progress.

October 27, deadly shootings occurred in Armenian parliament. PM Vazgen Sargsyan, National Assembly Speaker, Karen Demirchyan, and six other were assassinated by an armed group led by Nairi Hunanyan (b. 1965) in the Yerevan Armennian parliament building. Hunanyan was sentenced to life in prison.

2000

March 22, former NKR Defense Minister Gen. Samvel Babayan (b. 1965) leads an unsuccessful assassination attempt against NKR President Arkadi Ghukasyan (1957) in Stepanakert.

2001

Jamuary 25, Armenia become a member of the Council of Europe

September 25, Pope John Paul II visited Armenia to participate in the 1,700[th] anniversary of the adoption of Christianity as a national religion in Armenia. Vartouhi had an opportunity to interview the Pope and found him quite amiable and friendly. "Thank you for your visit to Armenia Your Holiness. We are always glad to see you visit our country especially on days like today."

"Thank you for the honor and welcome. I appreciate you inviting me to your Armenia on your 1,700[th] anniversary of your adoption of Christianity. The occasion is something to be very proud of and the fact that you have had the strong faith for such a long time. My visits to Etchmiadzin, Dzidernagapert, Khor Virab, your people, and all the wonderful religious sites have been gratifying and enlightening. You know I've been to Armenian several times and I do enjoy coming every time."

"It's wonderful you feel that way Your Holiness. Did you get a chance to descend down the pit at Khor Virab."

"Yes I did and somehow you feel a tinge of additional faith when you realize that your Saint Gregory was imprisoned there for 13 years and then bring Christianity into your nation. You have a wonderful story to tell your children and us to tell the world. You might find it interesting that we plan to erect a large statue of your venerable Blessed Saint Gregory in a couple years in the Vatican."

The discussion wandered into other topics such as the Armenian Genocide that the pope is strong recognition advocate and of any other similar occurrence ever happening again even though the Rwanda Genocide did occur a few years earlier.

September 25, Poghos Poghosyan (1958-2001) a Georgian citizen of Armenian origin was killed at a Jazz concert in central Yerevan by President Kocharyan's bodyguard. When Vartouhi found out about the murder she wanted to learn more as she suspected a matter of injustice. Her investigation revealed the Poghosyan was murdered by the president's bodyguard, Aghamal Haroutiuian (b. c. 1966), also known as Kuku, by a brutal beating in the lavatory of the Poplavok Cafe in the capital. Poghosyan who was a little intoxicated gave a witty "Hello Rob" to the president who supposedly was insulted. Charles Asnavour

(1924-2018) just happened to be with the president said nothing. Stephen Newton (b. 1945), a British national and journalist working for the European Union in Armenia, happened to see the beating and stopped it by shouting at Kuku who walked out of the toilet. Poghosyan looked like he was still alive, but he thought just barely. He told his wife to call an ambulance that arrived in a few minutes, but declared Poghosyan dead. When Newton came out of the lavatory the band was still playing. He yelled out loud to the band and crowd, "Why are you continuing to listen to the music when these bastards just killed a man here?" They stopped performing and the audience slowly exited the cafe. Newton contacted the police and told them he would like to be an eye witness when a trial comes up. Vartouhi promised herself that she would followup with the details when that happens. [See September 19, 2019, for final trial.]

2002

May 27 -28, second Armenian Diaspora Conference held in Yerevan.

2003

February 5, Armenia becomes member of the World Trade Organization (WTO).

February 19, Robert Kocharyan was reelected president. The opposition disputed the results as in almost all elections.

November 17, Professor Michael Stone lectured at the St. Nersess Armenian Seminary in Armonk, New York, astonishing the clergy and other attendees on some of his discoveries in Jerusalem and surrounding areas. He talked about the early Armenian pilgrims who came to worship in the Holy Land from the mid-4th century and who eventually ended up with 70 churches and monasteries by 7th century in and around Jerusalem. He discussed the pilgrimages to Mt. Sinai where they left Armenian inscriptions along their journey. In one particular group, 800 Armenians ventured to the mountain of Moses. Stone stated that such a trip would have been very arduous and costly. In his research he found many of the Armenian writings describing their perils and devotion to God. He showed a slide of the writing that he found on the peak of Mt. Sinai, "Der voghormyats gameghi yev khotegaosi" or 'Lord have mercy on my camel and on my guide.' Stone also pointed out many other aspects of the Armenian pilgrims in the Holy Land and about other Armenian writing in and around Jerusalem.

December 2, Nairi Hunanyan (b. 1965) and four other perpetrators of the 1999 Armenian parliamcnt shootings were sentenced to life imprisonments.

2004

February 18, a tragic event happened outside Armenia that shocked the world when the news got out. An Azerbaijani soldier, Rami Safarov (b. 1977), hacked to death an Armenian soldier, Gurgen Margaryan (1978-2004), in a hotel room in Budapest, Hungary. The two soldiers were in a NATO English Language Training program with army personnel from other countries. The Azeri planned to kill another sleeping Armenian, but fortunately the door to his room was locked. Safarov was convicted of murder and sentenced to life in prison. Eight years later he was freed from the Hungarian prison with the understanding with Azerbaijan that he would finish out his years of penalty in an Azeri prison. But the agreement did not work out that way. Safarov was welcomed back to Azerbaijan as a hero and even received a promotion later. Vartouhi found the incident very upsetting as countries all over the world protested what a rotten deal it was. Nations demanded that Azerbaijan should complete his punishment. When Vartouhi analyzed the situation it was learned that Azerbaijan gave a huge loan to Hungary and that this was her way of paying the Azeris back. The reporter wrote in her article that sometimes countries play in corrupt and stinking political ways.

2006

August 26, Silva Kaputikyan (1920-2006), the well known writer and activist died in Yerevan. She was the leading "Poetess of Armenia" and the "Grand Lady of 20th Century Poetry." She was a member of the Communist Party but strong advocate of Armenian national causes. Vartouhi also noted she was the wife of Hovhannes Shirak (1914-1984).

2007

January 19, Hrant Dink (1954-2007), well known editor of the Turkish Armenian *Agos* newspaper and avid humanitarian, was assassinated in Istanbul by Osgun Sanast (b.1990), a minor-aged Turkish reactionary. Following his murder tens of thousands of Turks filled the streets of Istanbul chanting, "We are all Hrant, we are all Armenians." Sanast was arrested and held for trial [See July 2, 2007 for trial results].

July 2, Ogun Samast (b. 1990) was convicted of murder of Hrant Dink and sentenced to 22 years and 10 months in prison. Others were initially arrested and released, but Samast was caught on video committing the crime. Yasin Hayal (b. 1981) received a life sentence for organizing the crime.

2008

February 8, Serzh Sargsyan (b. 1954) was elected president of Armenia. Runner-up and past president Levon Ter Petrosyan disputed the results. He was inaugurated on April 9, 2008.

February 20, Ter Petrosyan led several large protest demonstrations contesting the results of the presidential election. The protests continued for days after which President Kocharyan declares a state emergency. Nikol Pashinyan was also put under arrest, but went into hiding.

March 1, another large protest was organized to continue the demonstrations against the presidential election. This group had over 10,000 protestors where the police backed off, but later came with army units. The protestors were beaten with truncheons and electric shock devices ending in the death 10 people and dozens arrested. Vartouhi thought it was a sad day for Armenia.

September 6, Turkish President Allahabad Gul (b. 1950) visited Yerevan for the Turkish-Armenian national football game. Vartouhi noted it was the first time a Turkish leader had visited the country. During interviews with him and Armenian President Serzh Sarksyan she observed a cordial relationship, but not from the populate. Boos were chanted at the stadium when the Turkish National Anthem was played, and when placards were shown. Turkish responsibility and denial of the Genocide lined the streets and arena wherever Gul appeared. Very few people thought this would be a friendly start between the two countries. Some hoped that it would. Vartouhi's interviews with the presidents indicated they thought relationships could be improved, however the reporter did not think so. When she talked to Gul she reminded him of the eleven month prison sentence a Turkish journalist received for reporting that he was of Armenian descent. The president told her he was 100% Turkish.

2009

October 10, Turkish and Armenian foreign ministers signed two Protocols in Zurich that were intended to develop and normalize relations between the two countries. Initially there was great optimism about the historic agreement, but political bickering between the two countries resulted in a suspension of the Protocols six months later.

When Azerbaijan heard about the Protocols she was furious that one of the provisions included the opening of borders. President Aliyev responded by calling Prime Minister Erdogan a liar and ignoring the interest of Azerbaijan in the Protocols. Aliyev was full of outrage that Turkey would even think of such a measure especially with what is going on in Nagorno Karabakh. Aliyev went so far as stating, "They (Turks) will be on black list always."

2010

September 19, Mass was held at Holy Cross Cathedral on Aktamar Island, Lake Van for the first time since 1915. Partiarch Sahak Mashalian (b. 1962) led the liturgy but the service was not attended by higher clergy from the Armenian Apostolic Church in other countries beside Turkey.

October 16, Wings of Tatev, the longest reversible aerial tramway in the world was opened in southern Armenia. Vartouhi and Azad decided to take ride on the cableway that extends from the village of Halidzor to the famous Tatev Monastery. Both mother and son really enjoyed the trip of 5.7 km. (3.5 miles) with 28 other passengers.

2011

January 10, Areni 1Winery, that was discovered in Armenia's Vayots Dzor Providence in 2007 was confirmed to be the oldest winery in the world.

April, when US Ambassador to Azerbaijan wanted to visit Nakhichevan he was blocked by Azeri officials who told him that reports of destruction was fake news. However, the fake news was Azeris who were expressing a notorious lie. Individual and NGAs reported massive destruction of almost anything Armenian have been totally whiped out. tThere are no Armenians left in the once Soviet enclave that contained 75% Armenians. [Other sections of this book describe how Nakhichevan has been decimated to the point that there are no Armenians there or there are any cultural edifices remain that reflect Armenian presence for thousands of years].

December 21, at the French National Assembly approved the Armenian Genocide denial law. Turkey as usual recalls her diplomats and threatens trade sanctions.

2012

January 2, the French Senate approved the Armenian Genocide denial law.

February 28, the Constitutional Council of France overturned the Armenian Genocide denial law much to the displeasure of the Republic of Armenia and the Diaspora Armenians.

On August 31, Ramil Safarov, the ax murdered of Gurgen Margaryan was extracted to Azerbaijan. Armenia cut her diplomatic relations with Hungary. International countries cried out their disdain to the deal Hungary conducted with Azerbaijan. Safarov got a promotion to Lt. Colonel in Azerbaijan making the ax murder's action even more sickening for the Armenians.

2013

February 18, Serzh Sargsyan was reelected president again. There were still disputes concerning the results.

February 19 to April 9, mass protests occur against the presidential election. This time runer-up Raffi Hovannesian (b. 1959), son of Richard Hovannesian (b. 1932), led the demonstrations. Hovannesian was appointed foreign minister in 1991 when Armenia declared her independence. He was asked to resign in November 1992. Vartouhi found out it was due primarily to a speech on the Genocide he presented in Ankara.

July 20-25, mass protests in Yerevan resulted in the cancellation of a transportation fare increase. Vartouhi wrote an article where the voice of the citizens was heard and democracy won out.

July 26, the Free Syrian Army (FSA) kidnapped seven Syrian Armenians who were leaving Aleppo to resettle in Yerevan. Three women in the group were released within 10 hours, but the four men were tortured and verbally abused while being incarcerated for 45 days. One of the FSA soldiers shouted at the captives, "You [the Armenians] are all traitors! You are the *kafirs* [infidels] who support Assad! We will kill you tomorrow!" [The situation of the Armenians in Syria was extremely difficult and complicated as they wanted to maintain a neutral stance in the Syrian Civil War. They only took up arms to defend their neighborhoods, but both sides of the conflict considered this as aggression against each of their movements that made it dangerously impossible to remain in a neutral position.] The FSA soldiers continued the brutal tortures of hell repeatedly until the families were able to raise some ransom money that was demanded for each of their releases (initially it was for $60,000, but the families were only able to scrape lesser amounts). Most of the families did not have the cash, but they raised enough for the FSA to release them.

September 3. President Sargsyan announced in Moscow that Armenia will join the Customs Union of Belarus, Kazakhstan, and Russia. This was a turnaround from the thought that the country was going to join European Union Association. Vartouhi believed this was due to pressure from Russia.

October 13, Human Rights Watch (HRW) published a report on the atrosities committed by extremest groups

2014

Baroness Lady Carolyn Cox (b. 1937), past member of the British House of Lords and a leader of the Humanitarian Aid Relief Trust (HART), made her 80th visit to the Caucasus region. Vartouhi had an assignment to accompany her and her team to Nagorno Karabakh (recently officially revised her name to Republic of Artsakh). The tour met President Bako Sahakyan and other Karabakh officials, visited the new hospital in Stepanakert, Gandzasar, and several other distinguished places. Vartouhi was quite impressed with Lady Cox's vitality and energy of a 77 year old and the enthusiasm she displayed when she talked about the livelihood and freedom of Artsakh. The two also discussed of humanitarian projects Lady Cox was still working on. ["When I made my tour to Karabakh in 1997 I was lucky enough to visit the Gandzsar Cathedral where Archbishop Pargev Martirosyan (b. 1954) was presenting the Mass. My uncle claimed the archbishop had a revolver under his robe even as the Azeri-Karabakh conflict was in a truce. But the Azeris were still using snipers to kill Armenians at the border. To me it was a great honor to have attended the services of such an important person." Observation and quote by George Mouadian on his visit to Artsakh in 1997.]

The Lady Cox has cherished her visits to Armenia and Nagorno Karabakh and continues to do so. She has always encouraged and supported her quest to improve economic conditions in the country and assisted in gaining Artsakh's independence. She has labeled Azerbaijan as an aggressor nation stating, "First of all I would never say Armenians are aggressors, that is a lie – it was Azerbaijan that attempted ethnic cleansing of the Armenians from Nagorno Karabakh back in 1991-1992, it was Azerbaijan that unleashed ferocious military offensive against the civilians in Nagorno Karabakh - for instance in the capital of Nagorno Karabakh Stepanakert we observe 400 grad missiles a day fired by the Azeris on the civilians. It was Azerbaijan who committed war crimes and crimes against humanity by carrying out massacre of civilians in the village of Maraga."

When Lady Cox was asked about whether Nagorno Karabakh qualifies as an exceptional case in international law grants, she said the right to secession and independence is as it was in the case with Kosovo. She further replied, "Yes it does qualify as such. I believe the Armenians of Karbakh can never again accept sovereignty by Azerbaijan because they have been subjected to attempted genocide and ethnic cleansing. There is much evidence on this. President of Azerbaijan Elchibey has expllicitly declared, 'If there is a single Armenian left in Khabarovsk, the people of Azerbaijan can hang me in the central square.' This is a very clear and explicit policy of elimination of Armenians from Nagaorno Karabakh – that amounts to ethnic cleansing and genocide. This was against civilians which was completely unacceptable in which many atrocities were carried out. Me and my colleague made a publication way back in the 1990s giving a lot of evidence of Azerbaijan aggression against the Armenians in Karabakh in what we called 'Ethnic cleansing in progress: War in Nagorno Karabakh.' We were there as eye witnesses many times in the war and I believe,' as she said before, 'that the

Armenians have as much right for consideration of independence as the people of Kosovo."

On the team's return to Yerevan it stopped at the Mamig Babig Statue for a commemoration ceremony that was never performed when Artsakh first became independent. The "We are the Mountains" statue was completed in 1967 but was never officially recognized by Azerbaijan. Vartouhi assured Lady Cox that she would write about the whole trip when she gets back to the office.

2015

March, Armenia officially joined the European Economic Union.

March, seven people were killed in Gyumri by a Russian serviceman who was stationed at the military base near the city. Anti-Russian and anti-government rallies occurred in Gyumri and Yerevan. The assassin was apprehended by the Russian base military police and received years of imprisonment.

April 24, Armenian Genocide is commemorated world wide.

June 15, Armenian-American Kirk Kerkorian (1917-2015) died in Los Angeles, California. He was a well-known investor, businessman, philanthropist, and ardent supporter of Armenia and Karabakh. He was the recipient of the Mesrob Mashtots Medal in 2001 for his humanitarian work. Other ventures were his life as a transport pilot for the British Royal Air Force (RAF) in World War II and the founder of Trans-International Airlines. He expanded into other businesses such as the International, the world's largest hotel-casino at the time; Western Airlines; Metro-Goldwyn Mayer Corporation; the MGM Grand Hotel Casino Theme Park, that was the largest in 1994; and other casinos, hotels and movie companies. When World War II was declared, he ferried bombers across the Atlantic for the RAF. After the 1988 earthquake in Armenia Kerkorian founded The Lincy Foundation, one of the member organizations of the United Armenian Fund (UAF). In the following years he provided significant financial assistance and transportation equipment and supplies from the U.S. to Armenia. Kerkorian was honored and saluted as the "Man of the Year" by *AIM* magazine in

1993 for his unselfish and generous assistance for the Armenians. Just before his death his Survival Pictures Company released the film *The Promise*. He wanted the film to be an epic story of love, peace, tolerance, and man's inhumanity to man. In 1998, President Robert Kocharyan declared Kirkorian an Honorary Armenian Citizen. In 1995 and 2006, he made ventures into and out of DaimlerChrysler Corp. and General Motors Corp. that stirred up the auto industry. When Vartouhi heard about Kerkorian's death, she wrote in her column, "Armenia will sorely miss the man of such hign admiration. He was such a great benefactor to Armenia and Karabakh."

Summer of 2015, a British explorer, Tom Allen attempted to hike the length of the Republic of Armenia but failed the attempt due the absence of known routs and detailed maps. However what Allen did do was to sow the seeds of the Transcaucasian Trail. At a similar time, two former US Peace Corps members tried to do the same in Georgia with greater success. They mapped and connected known trails and charted what they found. Later in the year, Stone approached the British Land Rover Company and UK's Royal Geographic Society for funding a potential trail traversing the Lesser Caucasus. By the end of 2015, Allen and the American trail blazers made arrangements to eventually form a 3000 km Transcaucasian Trail extending from the Black Sea to the Caspian Sea [See Summer of 2017 for what a NGO can accomplish.]

2016

April 2, in the early morning hours of the day, fighting suddenly broke out between Armenia and Azerbaijan in Karabakh. An abrupt Azeri attack allowed the Azerbaijani forces to gain some land, but were consequently driven back to their own lines. Heavy fighting occurred for four days where both sides had heavy losses. Heavy fighting lasted for the four days until a truce was declared. Both sides unexpectedly announced a ceasefire and peace talks were again resumed. The press labeled the skirmish as the Four Day War.

July 15, rogue Turkish soldiers initiated a coup d'état to oust President Erdogan and to take over the government. Forces loyal to the state defeated the rebels and Erdogan was back in power. The reasons for the coup were the erosion of secularism, elimination of democratic rule, disregard for human rights, and the nation's loss of credibility in the international arena. The government said the coup leaders were linked to Fethullah Gulen (b. 1941), a Turkish businessman, preacher, and former political associate with Erdogan. The Turkish president labeled Gulen's group as a terrorist organization. The result of the coup was 300 people killed, and more than 2,100 were injured. Erdogan claimed the US was siding with the coup plotters of which America said we had no involvement.

Huge numbers of detentions followed the rebellion where 40,000 citizens were detained, including 10,000 soldiers, 2,745 judges, 15,000 educators, suspended, 21,000 teachers received revoked licenses. Over 77,000 people were arrested and 160,000 were fired from their jobs because reported connection to Gulen. It was a real shakedown. As a result of the coup Erdogan was granted dictatorial powers to be even more despotic.

2017

February 20, Nagorno Karabakh officially changed her name to the Republic of Artsakh and wrote a new constitution.

Summer of 2017, a long term volunteer trail building program was now in place to erect 3000 km route. Dilijan National Park in Armenia and the Svaneti region of Georgia were now a part of the corridor. More paths are planned, certain areas are forbidden and others are in military zones. However, the ultimate goal is the trail from the Black Sea to the Caspian Sea. Vartouhi, Simon, and Azad hiked on some of the routes and found the trails well marked and extremely beautiful.

2018

Starting April 13, peaceful demonstrations in Yerevan were starting to protest the election President Serzh Sargsyan to his third term as president. The protesters felt they had enough of the corruption and improper business of the government. The protests, led by parliamentarian Nikol Pashinyan, grew in numbers and spread to other Armenian cities and eventually was called the "Velvet Revolution." On April 23, Sargsyan resigned from his office, conceding that the masses were correct and that, "I was wrong, while Nikol Pashinyan was right." Vartouhi thought his statement was dignifying and noteworthy and a little surprising. An election for prime mister was held early May but he did not receive enough votes. On May 8, he was elected the new prime minister of Armenia. Countries from all over the world congratulated Armenia and Pashinyan for having such a peaceful revolution (soon called the Velvet Revolution) and wished him well in his new administration. Vartouhi was so proud of her student who she thought originally would be a leader in the future. She was confident that he would become an outstanding person for the nation because he was so firm against corruption and the massing of large percentage returns to oligarchs who demanded huge payoffs from businessmen who wanted start new enterprises.

April 24, Turkish Parliamentarian Garo Paylan (1972) introduced the Armenian Genocide Resolution in Turkish parliament calling for the recognition of the Armenian Genocide. The bill also seeked to designate April 24 the day in 1915 that the Genocide began as a national day of commemoration.

Major cities throughout the world again commemorate the Armenian Genocide.

September 22, 2018 to January 13, 2019, the Metropolitan Museum of Art of New York displayed *Armenia* to the public. It was a wonderful international exhibit of Armenian culture, art, and history. It broke all kinds of attendance records.

Yet, that has not been the only Armenian display to the world. The Smithsonian Folklife Festival celebrated Armenian artistic and cultural traditions during its annual interactive exposition on the National Mall in Washington DC, drawing record numbers. In the same year the global consortium of Francophonie, hosting hundreds of world leaders and the international media was held in Yerevan. All these events brought acclaim and honor to Armenia and to world recognition. [See

September 27, 2020, to see how the world looked the other way when the Nagorno Karabakh War started].

April 24, Prime Minister Recep Erdogan gave a speech on what he thought was a conciliatory measure on the anniversary of the Ottoman government's mass killing of the Armenians. It was the first time he had every made such a speech where Vartuohi thought in no way was it conciliatory. There was no word of apology or that the Ottomans were responsible for the tragic event. When she discussed the speech in the evening with Azad, he said, "If the Armenian Genocide was not such horrible event, I'd say the prime minister's speech was like a ghastly comedy. I don't know who he was trying to impress, but there was no sorrow or request for forgiveness in what I could see."

September 30, in the US, Garo Paylan (b. 1972) visited Soorp Khatch Armenian Apostolic Church in Bethesda, MD. The visit to Washington was also intended for meeting with members of Congress, State Department, American think tanks, international journalists, leading academics, and representatives of our civil society. Paylan is a member of the Turkish Peoples' Party and an extremely active humanist. He has given speeches in parliament where he calls for Turkey to recognize the Armenian Genocide. Paylan is one of three Armenian representatives in the Turkish Parliament. He has been called a traitor, charged with violating Turkish Law 301, insulting Turkishness, and has received death threats. When introduced to the crowd he was described as a man of courage and justice and rightly so.

2019

March 25, a surprising letter by three UN Specialists was sent to Turkish UN Representative Sadik Arslan on the promotion and protection of the right to freedom of opinion and expression and the promotion of truth, justice, reparation, and guarantees of non-recurrence in Turkey. The joint UN letter requested answers to seven questions;

1. Please provide information and/or comments on the allegations… violations attributable to Turkey in relation to the tragic events

that affected the Armenian minority from 1915 to 1923 and their consequences for the population concerned.

2. What policies have been put in place by your Excellency's Government to respond to these allegations?

3. What measures has Turkey taken to establish the facts of what occurred?

4. What measures have been taken to ensure the right of victims and society as a whole to know the truth about these events and to ensure the right of victims to justice and reparations of the damage suffered?

5. What measures have been taken to locate, insofar as possible, the bodies of Armenians who died as a result of these events?

6. Please provide information about the reasons for the adoption of the 2017 legislation preventing lawmakers from making certain expressions. Please explain how this is comparable with international human rights law, in particular with article 19 of the International Convention Civil and Political Rights.

7. Please provide information about the cases in which Article 301 of the Criminal Code has been applied to punish individuals for statement made alleging crimes against Armenians.

In addition to the seven questions the joint letter described in detail the atrocities committed against the Armenians by the Ottoman Empire and its succeeding Turkish Republic and the events that happened on April 24, 1915. The reported wanted answers to the death marches and the desert camp sites where additional thousands of Armenians perished. The report criticized "Turkey's denial" that it has continuously stated for over 100 years. More sufferings and discriminary tactics were pointed out that seeked answers.

At dinner Vartouhi mentioned the letter to her husband who more or less scoffed at the questions, "Don't expect an honest response from Turkey. We and the UN have been sending letters and communications to Turkey for over one hundred years and it's the same old bull shit answers we receive in responses. Erdogan continually denies there was a Genocide, and in other remarks he talks about reminding the

Armenians they should have learned a lesson in 1915. What lesson is he telling everyone, the one that his ancestors murdered one and half million Armenians?"

"Simon, what you're saying is true, but we and the international community have to continually put pressure on Turkey to correct the sin that she did during the war."

"I guess you're right Vartouhi, but it's like a lost cause as she continues to harass and discriminate against Christians in Turkey. What can you expect?"

"We can't give up, that's all I can say."

May 14, PM Nikol Pashinyan visited China at the invitation of President Xi Jinping (b. 1953). The two leaders talked about the relationship between the two countries and how they can be mutually beneficial to each other. Xi commented on the long history of Armenia and the great tragedy that occurred over a hundred years ago. In her report Varouhi noted that China has taken a deep interest in Armenia and has constructed the second largest embassy in the world. China is also interested in the Caucasus region due to Turkey's dream of Pan Turism and also Turkey's comments on China's mistreatment of the Uyghur Muslims. One thing Pashinyan was not too happy about was Xi's double talk; he talked about establishing great relations with Armenia. Yet when Azerbaijan president visited China about a month earlier, Xi talked about the same type of cooperation between their countries, where he mentioned that nations should abide by the international rule of "territorial integrity."

On July 10, Congresswoman Judy Chu (b. 1953) passed the Royce-Engels Peace Initiative to National Defense Authorization Act and the Congress to de-escalate the military aggression in the Nagorno Karabakh Azerbaijan conflict. The Peace Proposal called for 1) the withdrawal of all snipers and heavy arms equipment, 2) expand OSCE's role in the investigation and deployment of sensors along the "line of contact," and 3) install additional observers to monitor illegal operations. Armenia and Karabakh and the US State Department as well as 85 Congressmen and several countries endorsed the peace initiatives. Azerbaijan rejected the proposal that indicated she is not interested any peace in the region.

August 3, a legal crisis was being created in Armenia over the jailing of past President Robert Kocharyan's trial case. He originally was charged with the death of victims during the protests that landed him in jail. He was released for a while but was incarcerated again. Kocharyan has strong supporters and backers and claims he is innocent of all charges. The Constitutional Court has gotten into the picture and there is clamoring for justice. Vartouhi thinks the whole mess has turned into a real catastrophe and is not sure what the outcome is going to be.

September 19, the final trial of Aghamal Haroutiunian was held in Yerevan. Vartouhi promised herself she would follow up on the trial. She wrote in her article, "A mockery of justice" as she witnessed how Haroutiunian even after 18 years was basically a free man. He had gotten away with murder. His latest sentence was a two year suspension for manslaughter. There were several witnesses at the trial but none were actually present at the bloody scene. The full report of the key witness who physically saw the beating was denied at the original trial. A year before the second trial Stephan Newton, the witness to the beating, had sent a letter to Prime Minister Pashinyan but it was never brought up at the trial. The British man was never invited to the proceeding. Varouhi stated if the court had accepted Stephen Newton's report, the trial would have been altogether different.

About a week after the trial, Vartouhi heard from a woman who was surprised what President Pashinyan did not do to her. In an interview with the lady she asked, "What was that all about?".

"The prime minister was passing out some leaflets with a few of his assistants and gave me one. I looked it over roughly but it was on a subject that I totally disagree with him."

"That doesn't sound so bad. Did something happen then?" Vartouhi asked again.

"It was mostly about his plans to reform our court system, which I think any change is totally wrong," the woman said with conviction in her eyes. "After I scanned the leaflet I ripped it up and threw it in his face. Two of his helpers, or I believe were really his bodyguards, ran to me and grabbed me firmly on both arms. Then the PM said. 'No, no, leave her alone. Armenia is a democracy and she is permitted to do what she did.' The men released me and the PM asked me what I didn't like about the leaflet. I told him, 'You're trying to change our constitution and our judicial system.' Then one of his men interrupted me, saying, 'Did you read about the trial last week?' I told him I did."

"What did you think about it?" the reporter asked.

"I told him it was a farce and not a trial on how justice should be extended. Kocharyan's bodyguard was a murderer and he should been properly convicted for his crime. I think he got off scot-free."

His assistant then said, "Well, that's what our president is trying to change. I hope you agree?"

It was then that Vartouhi started asking questions to the woman. Names, occupation, where do you live, why you feel like you do, and other queries were asked to fill out her column. The woman then finally said, "You know I was sorry for what I did, but I was also thankful that he did not accuse me of any wrong doing."

2020

Work was started on the west-to-east road from Vardenis to Martaket linking the northern section of Artsakh to Armenia. Vartouhi reported that the completed road would be a huge economic aid to that section of Karabakh. The completion of the finished super highway and the Lachin Highway from Goris to Stepanakert and the south-north road from Martuni to Martaket would better connect Armenia to rural and small towns of Karabakh. The journalist told her editor the completion is a win-win situation for both Armenia and Artsakh.

February 19, Syria officially recognized the Armenian Genocide after 105 years. Following the Genocide, Syria was very helpful to the Armenian refugees who managed to survive the massacres. However, for one reason or another, Syria never acknowledged the horrible event until this year.

February 6, PM Nikol Pashinyan gave a speech at the National Assembly where he emphasized that Armenia has no alternative but to follow the course that he has been taking. His actions have been extremely controversial with regard to how he has been treating Armenian judges of the Constitutional Court.

February 13, an article in the Jewish Press exposed Turkish government activities to take over the Armenian and Christian Quarters in Israel. Vartouhi called the reporter who wrote the article, "Turkey Working to Take Over Armenian Quarters in Jerusalem's Old City." He pointed out that the Turks in recent years have tried to convince the local Armenians to deny the Armenian Holocaust and allowed them to purchase Armenian properties. Local Armenians have been rejecting the offers due mostly to the ongoing Turkish denial and what they did to the Armenians.

March 1, Prime Minister Pashinyan reported the first coronavirus case in Armenia. The carrier was person flying in from Iran with his wife who was tested negative. Pashinyan immediately initiated safety measures, but the virus started spreading anyway.

March 2, Vartouhi had an opportunity to conduct a telephone interview with Philippe Raffi Kalfayan (b. c. 1965) after he wrote an article on Minsk discussions. Kalfayan is a prominent French Armenian international lecturer and lawyer generally working out of Paris. In 2001 he was Secretary General of International Federation of Human Rights (FIDH). After his tenure as secretary in 2007 he continued as a dominate role in the FIDH. Among his many duties, Kalfayan has found the time to constantly concern himself with the affairs of Armenian. Vartouhi was well aware of this fact when she interviewed him.

"Professor Kalfayan how do you feel about the future of Armenia since the "Velvet Revolution?" the journalist asked after introductory remarks.

Without hesitating, Kalfayan said, "The country appears more weakened than ever. The COVIV-19 Pandemic and the political situation have been playing havoc with governance of the country and if matters do not get straightened out it will only get worse."

"Can you give me some examples?"

"Yes, of course. There has been an unjustified assault against the principles of the rule of law. The fight against corruption has garnered newly arranged confiscation of alleged 'illegal property' from some people then has aimed more at bailing out the exhausted public finances of Armenia. After the confiscation, there was an easy way to redistribute cash money to some categories of people. For the past two years, the investigation into the alleged unlawful enrichment of former politicians and oligarchs has been disappointments in term of achievements. It's gotten so bad where half the population hates the other half. I think this policy must stop."

"Oh I have noticed that half of our people are finally getting even. But how do you stop this fight for democracy?"

"You know Pashinyan made a speech last February stating that democracy in Armenia has no alternative and is irreversible. I say this great, but then he turns around and alleges that the police, judiciary, the National Security Service (NSS) and all the former executive appointees by the former government are all corrupt. And secondly, seven Constitutional Court judges should be dismissed because they are hindering the revolutionary process. We've witness two vice-prime ministers in street bawls where we don't know how to debate our issues in a civil manner."

"You know you're right, but other parliaments have fights in their chambers."

"That's true, but we are such a small country with a tremendous amount of problems we just cannot afford to have such mishaps. We have to remind ourselves that our rulers are responsible for their behavior, be it domestic or international. Their primary goals should be for the good of the country. I can give you several examples of how we are acting in an uncivilized manner."

"I think I know some myself, but I like to hear what you have to say."

"The violence is omnipresent and growing in Armenia. We have violence against women, social inequalities violence, the violence of MPs against the Catholicos of All Armenians, violence in the streets of Gavar, unexpected "suicides" of our law enforcement officials, and I could go on and on. Do you see something wrong here?"

"Yes I do, but our prime minister is trying to fulfill the mandate of the people who elected him."

"Of course however, he has to do it more democratically. I hate to say it, but Armenia will not endure this division and hate. The prime minister has to stifle this division of hate and concentrate on the economy and employment among other responsibilities."

"Do you have any recommendations on how to solve some of these problems?"

"Yes I do and I have passed these on in the past. I hope the appropriate people can do something about it. First, have President Armen Sarkissian convene a consultative meeting with the three former presidents, the prime minister, the NKR authorities, and any relevant political parties or experts in order to discuss and conclude an agreement a pact of national accord on the strategic and security issues. Second, have the former presidents and the prime minister sit around the same table. Third, have Prime Minister Pashinyan form a commission of experienced people, who offer assistance for the drafting of an emergency action plan to reduce as much as possible the effects of the pandemic crisis over the economy and avoid major social chaos and new massive emigration flow (when the border open again). In addition to the above, everything should be undertaken to the ongoing domestic self-destructive process. And on the contrary bring all political forces to agree on security fundamentals in this very troubled period.

The interview went on a while longer where Kalfayan mentioned names of possible persons who could help and those who are continually stirring the pot. He even went so far as to suggesting that the Minsk process be stopped as Azerbaijan is preparing for another war. "All is not lost, but we have to work with each other to get back on track," he concluded.

March 16, the State of Emergency (SOE) on the COVD-19 Virus was extended in Armenia but relaxed slightly to get the nation back to some kind of normalcy. Vartouhi's discussions with Pashinyan brought out the necessity to continue the policy of wearing face masks, keeping the social distance of six feet separation, staying at home, and having no social gatherings. The PM had a lot of respect and confidence in his past professor and had many talks with her on the state and condition of the nation. Other items they discussed were the continued jailing of

Kocharyan for his charge of overthrowing the constitutional order in the deadly March 2008 post-election unrest and Sargseyan's ongoing trial on corruption and embezzlement. The journalist told the PM to proceed cautiously with the trial of the two ex-presidents and to be extra careful with relations with Russia.

March 24, Armenia had now joined other countries in the world in being exposed to the corona virus pandemic and had to take drastic measures to prevent its spread. Lockdown procedures were imposed to keep the COVID-19 virus in check. Pashinyan wanted to keep the economy moving along but at the same time assure that he has some control over the virus.

April 7, the pandemic corona virus hit Armenia just as it has done to other nations of the world. The country has imposed the usual restrictions such banning travel, staying as home, closing her borders, wearing masks, expanding her health facilities, and many of the safety measures to stem the tide of virus. As of April 2, there have been 881 cases reported, 114 recoveries, and 30 deaths.

April 14, former PM Arayik Harutyuyan (b. 1973) was elected President of the Republic Artsakh. There was very little controversy on the election except from Azerbaijan that strongly condemned it and was declared illegitimate by some international bodies. However, the Artsakh and Armenia governments both hailed the election free and fair.

On the same day, April 14, Karekin II, Catholicos of All Armenians, issued a statement calling on the government to immediately release former President Robert Kocharyan from prison based on medical risks. Kocharyan was in custody pending his trial on charges of breaching the Constitution by ordering forces to fire on the crowd in the aftermath of the 2008 presidential election. Eight civilian and two policemen were killed during the incident. His Holiness' statement was a little unusual as the catholicos did not usually venture into political or civic problems as a rule, but he sent a message that has caused considerable controversy. Karekin's stirred controversy with the government in that his Holiness has no business in the government even though he had strong relationship with both Kocharyan and Sargesian.

To make matters worse the National Security Service (NSS) has accused Deputy Primate of the Diocese, Archbishop Yerevan Navasard Kachoyan of fraud and money laundering. The government claimed the archbishop colluded with an Armenian businessman to defraud another person. These issues were opening up problems between the PM and Etchmiazin that Vartouhi was not too happy about.

In the home of Vartouhi, the statement and the archbishop's problems also stirred some argument. After dinner Azad Jr. told his mother, "I read your last article on the catholicos' speech and I thought you were too easy on the prime minister."

"What did I say that you thought I was too easy on him?"

"Mother, Pashinyan doesn't have to have two ex-presidents locked up in prison. He can put them on house arrests where they still continue their trials. And another thing is the prime minister's rough treatment of our judges. I think he is way too hard on them," Azad said with a tired look in his eyes. The 52 year old son had been working 20 hour shifts at the hospital helping to cure the cordovirus victims that has beset Armenia as the pandemic has scourged other parts of world.

"Azad, I think the prime minister is doing a terrific job. Both ex-presidents abused their positions. Sargesyan is especially malicious being responsible for the eight deaths, and our judges have been much too liberal with their judgments on our questionable leaders. You don't realize how much support the ex-presidents still have even though conditions were very harsh on the general population."

"I'm sorry mother, but I don't agree with you," as the doctor said as he left the room to try to get a few hours' sleep.

What went on in the Zerouni household was not much different than what was going on in the whole country. The Velvet Revolution was not progressing as well as Pashinyan expected as there were powerful persons not agreeing with his policies. Vartouhi was continually reminding him that no matter what you do, there is always someone, or some group, who always will disagree with you.

April 21, Rouben Shougarian (1963-2020), first Armenian ambassador to the US, died in Boston. He was an outstanding diplomat and leader and did a great deal to improve the relationship between

Armenia and America. In his passing, he received a tremendous amount of accolades from politicians, scholars, and academicians.

April 21, Russian Foreign Minister Sergei Lavrov (b. 1950) made several statements regarding the Karabakh/Azeri issue. He suggested that the negotiation process of the OSCE Minsk group be stopped and that the Armenian forces in the Azeri regions be withdrawn. He also said that Russia would be increasing the price of natural gas and make changes to railway system. Both measures would be a blow to the Armenian economy.

April 24, Armenians throughout the globe commemorate the Armenian Genocide, announcing to world that Turkey is continuing her denial of her heinous crime she committed during World War I. As in many other nations, Libya's interim Government once again recognized the Genocide. This is the second year in a row for the African state. In addition to her recognition, Libya also announced that Turkish government in its new situation is committing crimes against the peoples of the world by its blatant interference in their internal affairs. Libya's statement also included how Erdogan's arrogance and his disregard for international laws and norms are added crimes against people, including women and children.

May 9, Human Rights Defender (Ombudsman) Arman Tatoyan (b. 1981) recalled that persons who hold public office and carry out relevant activities should show restraint in their political or other actions and not allow themselves words that generate hatred and cause tension. Vartouhi had an interview with Tatoyan where she learned that he had long professional career in public law and had scholarly training in several America universities including a law degree from University of Pennsylvania. He expressed his annoyance at the general brawl in parliament and the street fight between vice-president of the National Assembly, Alen Simon (b. 1980) and Deputy Prime Minister Tigranes Avinyan (b. 1989) a few weeks before. Tatoyan told the reporter, "These supposedly responsible people are not children and should behave as prudent adults. There is absolutely no excuse on how they act."

Vartouhi agreed with him, but said, "It seems to be an Armenian characteristic to want to fight and it's sad, but I really don't know what we can do about it?" She was now 71 years old and still active as a part time reporter because she enjoys her work so much. Talking to Tatoyan was like an inspiration where she felt there should be more young persons like him in the government.

May 12, Paul Goble (b. 1949), a longtime American specialist on ethic and religions questions in Eurasia wrote an article in the *Eurasian Review* that was extremely disturbing. The idea has been around since 1992 but has lately gained some background attention. His original proposal was considered ridiculous but has gained some attention in recent weeks. The plan he outlined is complex, but a simple version is "land swaps." From initial observations, Vartouhi thought none of it is, or would be, beneficial to Armenia. The Paul Goble Plan idea started in January1992 when Goble worked as a special advisor to the US Department of State on Soviet nationality problems and Baltic affairs. He was asked to prepare a background paper on the Karabakh conflict for former Secretary of State Cyrus Vance (1917-2002) who was planning to visit the South Caucasus region. In the paper, Goble described both the history of the conflict and offered some thoughts on how it might be resolved. Vartouhi thought that was really interesting that we had ideas as early as 1992 to solve the conflict, but essentially nothing has been accomplished. "We have had only talks for 28 years," she told Pashinyan at one of their meetings.

Basically, the plan called for Armenia to cede Meghri to Azerbaijan in exchange for Azerbaijan to acknowledge Nagorno Karabakh as part of Armenia. Purportedly, the plan was approved by Presidents Robert Kocharyan and Heydar Aliyev (1923-2003) at their meeting in Key West, Florida, on February 10, 2001, but was not signed by the Azeri leader. In hindsight, Vartouhi thought it would have been a disaster for Armenia. The country would have lost its border with Iran and would have gifted an open door to Turkey's age-long dream of Pan-Turkism. The idea of the plan was unbelievable at the time but strategists are reintroducing the thought again.

To make the scenario even worst, Goble sights the blog of a Turkish professor from the University of Kayseria where he stated, "The main goal the Republic of Western Azerbaijan (Irevan) is to return all the lands within the borders of Armenia." Vartouhi thought this was strictly a Turkish mentality statement and a usual twist of historical fact.

"Return what lands? Is the professor talking about the lands the Seljuk Turks occupied in the 11th and 12th centuries? Azerbaijan wasn't even a word at the time. And besides that, when the Mongols came into the Caucasus and Anatolia in the 11th and 12th centuries, they basically did away with Seljuk Turks," was Vartouhi's comment. Pashinyan nodded in agreement.

June 1, Prime Minister Nikol Pashinyan was tested positive of COVID-19 together with his wife and their three children The PM believes he contracted the disease from a drinking glass that was not picked up after one of the PM's meetings. He has put himself in self-isolation and is continuing the affairs of state from his home remotely. Pashinyan joined the list of other heads-of-state and ministers who have contacted the virus [UK PM Boris Johnson (b. 1964) was in intensive care, but fortunately managed to be cured].

June 6, ia meeting between Foreign Ministers Sergei Lavrov (b. 1950) and Zohrab Mnatzakanyan (b. 1966) the Russian Foreign Minister purportedly stated the Armenian forces would be evacuation from the Azeri occupied lands in the Karabakh region. Mnatzakanyan stated no such statement was made. Unfortunately, statements of this sort still stir emotions on both parties. Any official statements should be provided by the three chairs of the OSCE Minsk Group.

June 11, Turks held demonstrations in Muslim district in Beirut with slanderous placards and signs against the Armenians. Turkish President Recep Erdogan stirred up the Turks in Lebanon to generate hate messages and anti-Armenian sayings.

June 16, police arrested Prosperous Armenian Party leader Gagig Tsaruyan (b. 1956) for "vote buying." Tsaruyan is a government connected oligarch and former business partner with ex-president Robert Kocharyan and claims that we are at the end of the Velvet Revolution. Several days later the Armenian court rejected his arrest. Vartouhi argued with her son that the arrest was legitimate but Azad did not think it should been made in the first place.

In the following months, Inter government relations were not going too well for PM Pashinyan. He continued his contacts with the COVID-19 virus as he worked from his home. Relations with Moscow were not going well. Russian Foreign Minister Sergei Lavrov's suggestion a few weeks ago that Armenian forces withdraw from inside the Karabakh area and that Russia not lower the price of gas even though there was glut in the system.

Tigran Xmalyan (b.1963) believes the PM should be working more closely with NATO and not have a "colonial relationship" with Moscow. Many others, individually and collectively, were critical of the Pashinyan's rule that has been stressful. It has been difficulty to keep the reins of government operating smoothly with so many parties and individuals being so critical of what the My Step Party has been attempting to accomplish.

There were discussions on the dismissal of Armenian Constitutional Court. Pashinyan did not go this far but did consider some revisions. There was some discussion on the treatment business persons being arbitrarily jailed and their properties being seized. When PM Pashinyan came to power two years ago he stated there would be no vendetta, but his critics are stating otherwise. The brawls that have been taking place in parliament and on the streets should not be occurring in a civilized democracy, "but we are having them" Vartouhi wrote in one of her articles.

June 16, Turkey established a new institution to "view the various dimensions of topics, such as, history, propaganda, and law." When Vartouhi heard about it she thought it was just another rouse and detraction to douse the interest in the Armenian Genocide.

June 17, President Armen Sarkissian gave a wide ranging interview jointly to the *Armenian Mirror-Spectator, Baikar,* and *Azg* newspapers that covered his deep concerns about the spread of the COVID-19 and the loss of lives in Armenia. He pointed out that Armenia has to deal with the negative consequences of the Pandemic on tourism, international trade, social behavior, agriculture, banking, technology, and the economy. Armenia has to advance in all these endeavors in order to be constant with the world's progress. He called on political forces and leaders to be extremely responsible to the circumstances of violence, hate, curses in their own conduct, speech, and works. Vartouhi thought the interview was great, but was anyone listening and when is Armenia going to start doing the proposals the president talked about and what are the odds that his charges will be established? "The ability to work together is a tremendous asset, a characteristic that would be extremely helpful if we had it in our genes," Vartouhi said to her husband one evening during dinner.

June 22, after considerable debate and objections, the Armenian parliament voted the immediate dismissal of three Constitutional judges. The vote created quite a bit of controversy in the country. The parliament also voted to change the constitution. This could be victory for Pashinyan, yet the passages are only enraging the opposition that is becoming more demanding and verbose. The PM received 70% of the vote two years ago, promised a "no vendetta" policy, but his populous has been clamoring for more blood. He has to tread very cautiously not to make too many enemies. The "velvet" has somehow worked itself out of the revolution and it has been more difficult for Pashinyan to proceed with his popular programs.

One of the persons who has caused serious problems was former President of the Constitutional Court Hrayr Tovmasyan (b. 1970). He also was a Minister of Justice and a member of the National Assembly. Another trouble maker for Pashinyan's policies was Gagig Tsarukyan (b.1956) who was stripped of his parliament immunity but still holds powerful reins in the government and has strong ties with Moscow. Other individuals are also in the picture creating more headaches for the PM. When Vartouhi interviewed Philippe Kalfayan last March he painted a very dismal picture for the PM and the future of Armenia.

June 23, the *Turkish Harriyet Daily* reported that Turkey has strengthened the new autonomous and civil institution in order to respond to the accusations of the genocide and to develop a strategy to counter them. It will be interesting to see how much fraudulent information the newspaper generates.

July 12, Azeri President Ilham Aliyev claimed the OSCE Minsk Group peace talks have been "meaningless" and threatened to resolve the issue militarily. He then proceeded to attacked Armenia in the Tavoush Province. No assistance was received from the CSTO counties nor did Armenia request any help. To date, 16 Armenians have been killed.

July 16, Azeri forces continued their aggressive action against civilians utilizing mortars and heavy artillery in the vicinity of Avgepar and Movses villages, Armenia. There was supposedly a ceasefire, but that did not mean anything to the Azeris. The Armenian forces soundly defeated the Azeris proving that she did not require help from Russian or any of the other CSTO countries. The Azeris proved themselves again untrustworthy when they again agreed to a ceasefire; she again tried to invade the Tasush region. Her force of 100 special force soldiers were soundly repelled with heavy loses. Azerbaijan brought herself another blow when she threatened to bomb the Metsamor Nuclear Plant. Other nations clamored what a demented idea that it was as it would cause devastation in the whole area, not only Armenia. Vartouhi told her husband, "Nations carry on, or threaten to do, crazy notions when they are losing a war."

July 17, Turkish President Erdogan declared Hagia Sophia, the 6th century world famous Byzantine Cathedral, a mosque that had served as a museum since 1933. World leaders, scholars, and historians clamored that Erdogan was wrong in his declaration as the structure is far too important to not only Christian throughout the world, but also to all freedom loving people. The Ottoman Turks originally converted the cathedral to a mosque in 1453 after they conquered Constantinople. Ataturk converted it to a museum in 1933.

On the first Friday (July 24) following Erdogan's declaration, thousands of worshippers gathered at the newly converted mosque. The Turkish Minister of Religious Affairs ascended the pulpit with a sword in hand then presented his sermon followed by President Erdogan reading from the Koran. Worshippers both inside and outside the mosque were loudly shouting "Allahu Akbar." It was as if Istanbul newly conquered and the masses were glorifying in a new victory. President Erdogan followed up the sermon with his own reference to the Armenians as "remnants of the sword" and that Turkey and Azerbaijan are "fulfilling the mission of their grandfathers" against the Armenians. "This is hardly what I call a peace loving gesture by the President of Turkey," Vartouhi wrote in her column.

When Vartouhi heard about the ceremony and Erdogan's remarks, she told her husband, "It's just a renewal of Turkish oppression against Christians and non-Turks. It's Erdogan's vision to revitalize his nation to a strong Muslim state and to forget about Kemalist secularism but not about its policy of expanding the state.. All his rhetoric about the mission of their grandfathers while at the same time the denial of the Armenian Genocide all supports his hatred of Armenia. His kind words, if any, are a complete farce."

Vartouhi thought Erdogan's Saint Sofia action was not the only disapproval that could be bestowed on him. She thought he has literally become a dictator and was spreading his power, not only in Turkey, but all over the Middle East and Africa. He was even getting to the point his own people were criticizing him. His troops have invaded northern Syria almost freely ousting the Kurds who had final brought peace to the area. His troop movement into Libya has been condemned by Russia, Jordan, Egypt, France, and other countries, but ironically supported by the UN. However, so far he has gotten away with his mischief without large scale direct confrontation. He has made incursions into Lebanon stirring up the population and actually sent his mercenary forces into northern section of the country. He has aroused difficulties with Greece by proposing to drill for oil in the coastal waters of Crete and other contestable areas. Greece has naturally made objections. The problem has gotten so bad that the Greek and Turkish Air Forces and naval ships play war games with each other. Erdogan's defiance says he can do the drilling per past international agreements. Greece states "no way" can Turkey infringe on Greek territorial waters. Tension has gotten so high that both sides are talking war even though they do not want a war. When Armenia complained about Turkey's actions, her foreign minister stated that Armenians have nothing to do with the Mediterranean and that the Turks have learned nothing from their history. Vartouhi reminded the Armenian Defense Minister David Tonoyan (b. 1967) that Turkey and Greece have been at odds for centuries and have had several wars in the last century and half. Turkey is always ready to keep Armenia aware of the Genocide while at the same time deny that it happened. .

Erdogan has accused China of genocide on her 23 million Uyghurs, Moslems of Turkish origin. Vartouhi thought that was a ludicrous statement coming from the president of Turkey who is one of the greatest deniers of the Armenian Genocide and one who continues his denial state. His onslaught into northern Syrian after President Donald Trump (b. 1946) gave Erdogan the green light ended up with a near genocide of the Kurds.

Turkey has moved troops into neighboring Nakhichevan and Azerbaijan at the displeasure and disapproval of Armenia. The Armenian defense minister told Vartouhi that Turkey prompted the Azeris to start the large scrimmages in the beginning of July that turned out to be a humiliating defeat for Azerbaijan. "If Erdogan didn't prompt Azerbaijan to attack Armenia, I'm sure he at least encouraged the idea. Turkey would like nothing better than to see the annihilation of Armenia happen. She still has her dreams of Pan-Turkism (also referred to as Pan-Turanic and Pan-Turanism). "But something else has entered into the picture, Vartouhi brought up another topic when she was talking to Tonoyan.

Then Tonoyan commented, "Armenia has had a military treaty since 1992 with Russia, Kazakhstan, Kyrgyzstan, Tajikistan, and Uzbekistan called the Collective Security Treaty Organization (CSTO) where four of those countries are ethnic Turkish nations even though they're are not stout Moslems. We were able to defeat the Azeris without help from our treaty members and that was a good thing. As far as we know, those countries are not too crazy about any Pan-Turkism."

After suffering their humiliating defeat, the Azeris sent a military delegation to Ankara to discuss the conflict. President Erdogan came up with a stern warning to Armenia, "We condemn Armenia's aggression against Azerbaijan, whose territories it has occupied illegally, disturbing peace and trampling international norms." For a country that keeps losing wars with Armenia, these are strong words for a loser," Vartouhi told her husband. She had no idea what the Azeri militarty delegation did in Ankara.

"Wow, what grandiose and word mangling," Vartouhi said to her husband. "Erdogan talks about aggression. What country always breaks the cease fires and who continually uses sniper shootings of both soldiers and civilians even while cease fires are in effect? Who refuses to use international and US peace initiatives? And who is illegally disturbing peace and trampling on international norms? Erdogan has his players all mixed up. I'm positive he knows what's going on but his dictatorial mind twists facts one hundred and eighty degrees."

One other fact that should be mentioned is Foreign Minister Ahmet Davutoglu disassociated himself from Erdogan after he thought the president was going too far with his aggressiveness. In fact, Davutoglu has gone so far as to form the Future Party to oppose Erdogan. Hami Aksoy (b. 1969) who is as vociferous and belligerent as his president has taken his place.

July 18, PM Pashinyan visited the Minister of Defense Headquarters and praised the Armenian forces for repelling the Azerbaijani aggression. He told the commanders that their forces exposed the myth of Azeri invincibility and that President Aliyev's rhetoric has no meaning except to blow off hot air. Other kudos was forwarded to the troops who were told to keep on the alert and continue to do a good job.

July 20, Karen Vardanyan (1963-2020) an outstanding dedicated Armenian engineer, educator, energetic organizer, and pioneer in the high-tech industry died in Yerevan. Vardanyan's death at a young age was a blow to Armenians especially in the technical growth industry. Vartouhi noted his demise was a serious blow to the nation. Vartouhi claimed that the engineer was influential in restoring Armenia to her once highest status of the electronics leader in the Soviet Union, but he still wanted the nation to do better.

July 20, Ambassador Varuzhan Nersesyan (b. 1973), in an interview recapped much of the recent conflict between Armenia and Azerbaijan. At the latest count, 16 people were left dead including four Armenian military men and 12 Azeris. A ceasefire was arranged on July 15, primarily for the Azeris to remove their dead, but the Azeri firing started again within a couple of hours. Armenian forces destroyed two mortar firing tanks and 13 drones. The Azeri attack destroyed several civilian homes, a factory making face masks, and damaged a kindergarten school. The ambassador explained the Azeris started the clashes as usual and were continually violating the cease fire efforts. They continually refuse to have UN monitors to survey the front. Nersesyan also reminded the group that President Aliyev proclaimed on TV that the Minsk Group's activities were meaningless and threatened to resolve the Karabakh issue militarily. Aliyev went so far as to state that he would bomb the Metsamor Nuclear Plant in his war mongering rhetoric. Vartouhi thought his statement was not only dangerous to Armenia but also to the whole Caucasus region if the plant was destroyed. The journalist reminded the ambassador that Armenia could easily bomb the Minkachevir Dam in Azerbaijan that would open and destroy the flood gates to deluge two thirds of Azerbaijan including as far away as Baku. The dam is within artillery range from northern Karabakh and should give Aliyev second thoughts about a large scale war.

Nersesyan continuing his interview said, "What happens is the consequence of Azerbaijan's own actions. The Republic of Armenia is ready to immediately defend and use proportionate force to counter any encroachments on the Republic of Armenia and Artsalk. The losses Azerbaijan suffered are the results of Azerbaijan's own aggression." He concluded, "I am proud that the armed forces of the Republic of Armenia were able to fulfill their duty 100 percent.

July 23, the US House of Representatives passed powerful vote adopting a bi-partisan amendment to go on the life-saving demining assistance in Karabakh. President Donald Trump (b. 1946) originally wanted to stop the funding but congress voted to keep it going. The funding permits the HALO (Hazardous Area Life Support Organization) project to proceed to aid both Artsakh and Azerbaijan. The HALO project provides funding to find and destroy landmines that were planted during the wars between the two countries.

Belligerent Azeris attacked an Armenian protest movement in Berlin then set fire to the official car of the Armenian embassy. A few days later, 30 masked assailants raided an Armenia shisha bar in

Cologne breaking tables and chairs and throwing them through glass windows. Vartouhi said the assaults were a result of the hate messages that Presidents Erdogan and Aliyev send to their followers. Erdogan has been quoted as saying, "We have to complete the mission of our forefathers." There is no question that the statement reopens wounds of the 1915 Armenian Genocide.

July 27, Zakir Hasanov (b. 1959) Azeri Minister of Defense announced that joint military exercises will take place with Turkish forces from July 20 through August 10. This was no news to Armenia as she knew well beforehand that Turkey was amassing her regiments into Nakhichevan and Azerbaijan in an intimidation move. Armenia is well aware of what is going on and is on alert to any aggressive move by either Turkey or Azerbaijan. Russia also has her troops ready in Gyumri in the event Turkey would be soft headed enough to make any drastic moves. Vartouhi is sure no one wants a war, but the war of words is constantly going on where countries try to ply any non-belligerent victories in any way they can without actual fighting. She felt that lately Turkey has been doing a pretty good job utilizing this type of strategy (e.g., northern Syria, Libya, Cyprus, Greece, Iraq, and Lebanon). The Turkish president seems to have a knack of taking advantage of any region that is in a destabilizing state. Other nations have complained, but to date, have not yet taken any positive action. In some respect Erdogan is behaving like Adolf Hitler (1889-1945) before World War II. The notorious dictator was doing pretty much what he wanted to do before 1939. That is, until the United Kingdom and France declared war on Germany.

Erdogan has a knack of creating disorder in a region, and then impose his order to remedy the situation as if he was helping out. Example is in Syria where Turkey purportedly fought against the ISIS but only created chaos by disrupting 100,000 refugees then got the European countries to fork up of millions of dollars to care for them. Then after the Kurds brought some relative peace to northern Syria, Turkey accused them of being terrorists and forced the Kurds out of the area with President Trump's blessing. Then she goes into Iraq much to the county's displeasure on the pretense of cleaning out the terrorists.

August 4, a colossal explosion ripped through Beirut destroying much of the port buildings and causing devastation within a six miles radius, blowing out windows and doors dozens of miles away. It was as if the city and country did not have enough problems; they did not need such a disastrous calamity. The explosion was the largest manmade impact force other that a nuclear one. The Tekeyan School and other Armenian institutions were part of devastation. The prelacy buildings and the AGBU Demerjian Center in Antelias and Armenian homes and business places in Bourg Hammond were also a part of the destruction. First reports indicate over 100 people were killed with at least 4000 injuries. Several Armenians were killed including Nazra Margarian (1957-2020), secretary general of the Christian Democratic Katie Party. Authorities expect many more will be found dead and injured due to those who were caught in the debris and rubble. Some 300,000 people were displaced from their homes.

The cause of the explosion was the detonation of 2,700 tons of Ammonium Nitrate that was stored in one of the port warehouses. The horrendous blast, damage, death count and injuries definitely added to the current financial and economic problems that has been beleaguering Lebanon. There is no question that the disaster added to the agony of a nation in its worse financial crisis since its 15-year-long civil war that ended in the 1990s.

Within forty-eight hours of the blast, French President Emmanuel Macron (b. 1977) walked the streets of Beirut's damaged structures and destroyed surroundings. He consoled the people telling them help is on the way. Lebanon's politicians were too afraid to show themselves in public. Macron was like a saint to Beirut's citizens who were in anguish over the destruction and deaths. The people were also furious to their leadership for their corruption and ineptitude. They wanted to know how such a horrible accident could be allowed to happen. Macron made a promise, just as many other nations, to fund Lebanon repair and rebuilding. He will also organize an online international donor fund to accumulate more assistance. He said the funding will not be presented to the corrupt government but managed by a special United Nations Mission. Other countries used an identical approach to make their donations. Almost everyone knew about the corruption in Lebanon politics and the control by the Hezbollah. Macron got the message from the people, "Revolution, revolution, we want our crooked politicians and Hezbollah out our county." This of course will not be easy, but no moneys will be forwarded to them.

Turkey was also one of the counties that offered assistance, but much of it was on the sinister side, extensively as she has been doing to other Middle East and African countries. Recep Erdogan is concerned with the Armenians residing in Lebanon; they have been living in the country for centuries under relatively prosperous conditions. However, as with the rest of the Lebanese citizens, the devastating blast has made many of them homeless and with loss of their businesses. The Turkish president wants to make a strong presence in the country to reduce the influence of the Armenians and to get a foothold in Lebanese politics. Macron thinks this is hardly the time for such action. France has a good relationship with Turkey, but is skeptical of Erdogan's expansionist policy, especially in Libya.

For a long time Turkey has been penetrating into Lebanon through trade, so called charitable activities, and TV programs. In a noteworthy incident when popular TV host Neshan Der Haroutiounian (b. 1971) criticized Recep Erdogan's appalling policies, the Lebanese Attorney General charged him for violating the nation law that a person cannot criticize the leader of a foreign nation. Immediately after the charge, mobs formed outside the host's TV station waving Turkish flags and hurling insults to the Armenians.

One Turkish commentator was quoted as saying, "We are proud of the massacre of the Armenians. They deserved it." He added more hate and derogatory remarks to make it worse. Vartouhi wondered if Erdogan heard the remark. Haroutiounian said he is ready for the court trial that is set for October 8. As a result of this ridiculous law, 14 international organizations have formed a coalition to have Lebanon change the law to one that allows "freedom of expression" and other laws that affect freedom of speech.

Turkey is attempting to make more inroads into Lebanon by promising to rebuild the destroyed port and issue citizenship to anyone who claims to have Turkish or Turcoman ancestry. The Turkish government has gone so far as to issue cash among the Sunni community to overwhelm the Lebanese people. Lebanon army intelligence has reported that Turkey has sent arms to northern Lebanon much as she did in northern Syria before she invaded the country. Vartouhi heard from one of the older scholars that during the Syrian Civil War, Turkish mercenaries made it a specific task to bomb Armenian communities in Aleppo and completely destroy Der Zor and Kessab. If conditions get worse in Lebanon, the same measures could take place.

President Erdogan has visions of emulating Ottoman Sultan Selim I (1470-1520) who conquered Beirut in 1516. Vartouhi is sure he would like to do something similar including the expansion of the Republic of Turkey. The Turkish president has aroused the Turks living in Lebanon to form demonstrations against the Armenians living the country. The Turkish dictator is not too happy with Lebanese citizens commemorating the April 24 Armenian Genocide every year by closing all businesses and offices to remember the Genocide. He wants Turks all over the world to hate Armenians and to disrupt anything they can do.

August 9, the Armenians of Berlin decided to open an Art Exhibit to counter acts of hate messages that the Turks and Azeris are flooding anything that is Armenian. The exhibit is to run until August 30 and hopefully generate some peacefulness to the turmoil that is going on. Vartouhi told her husband, "I don't think it is going to help. The Turks and Azeris will continue to do what they are doing."

August 10, President Armen Sarkessian had an interview with the Syrian newspaper *Al-Azmenah* on the 100th Anniversary of the Treaty of Sevres that was signed by the 13 victorious countries of the Entente and the defeated Ottoman Empire. In effect the treaty dismantled the Ottoman Empire, from Armenian's point of view, to solve the torment of Armenian issues and end the sufferings of the Armenians. When asked, what did the president think? Sarkessian stated, "The Treaty of Sevres recognized Armenia as a free and independent state. Turkey and Armenia agreed to leave demarcations of the border of the countries in Erzurum, Trabzon, Van, and Bitlis provinces to the decision by the

United States (basically President Wilson's proposal) and accept this decision immediately and all other proposals."

*Al-Azmenah.*questioned, "But the Treaty of Sevres. remained on paper...?"

"I would rather say that the Treaty of Sevres was not fully ratified (which means it remains perfected and it is true that when it comes to Armenia its decisions were not implemented because the international political situation had changed, but at the same time, it never denounced the treaty either). The Treaty of Sevres is a legal, interstate agreement which is defacto still in force because this document became the base for other documents for determining the status of a number of Middle East countries after WW I or more recently, among them Syria, Mesopotamia, Palestine, Hejazi (Saudi Arabia) Egypt, Sudan, Cyprus, Morocco, Tunisia, and Libya.

"Among with all this, the Treaty of Severs could have promoted three resolutions of Armenian issues and unification of the Armenian nation on its historical lands. It could partially mitigated the losses inflicted on the Armenian people by the Genocide of 1915 and thus create conditions for the regulation of the relations between Armenian and Turkey and establishment of a lasting peace among the peoples of our region."[More was discussed with regard to the Lausanne Treaty not containing any words of annulment of the Sevres, thus it should still be in effect. The two treaties are separate legal documents. The Lausanne treaty came much later.]

On the subject of the recent Azerbaijan attacks into Republic of Armenia, President Sarkessian said, "These days when the entire world and we are fighting against our common enemy, the corona virus pandemic, and regardless of the fact that conflicts all over the world have been halted, our neighboring country – Azerbaijan tried to take advantage the situation and use it in the negative sense this 'window of opportunity' to unleash aggression on the Armenian border." Sarkessian then talked about Armenia's readiness to thwart the Azeri attacks with an embarrassing defeat for Azerbaijan. He talked about President Erdogan's aggressive and hate rhetoric and never mentioning the Genocide done 105 years ago. He also mentioned Azerbaijan's threat to hit the Metsamor nuclear plant. Sarkessian told the reporter, "That's a menacing remark, 'nuclear terrorism' and God forbid if it happens one day, we all will have a Chernobyl." Vartouhi thought the interview covered a lot of territory and explained how Armenia related with current affairs. Ironically while all the above was going on, the Azeri snipers are still busy doing the evil task of trying to kill civilians and soldiers at the LOC (Line of Contact).

August 20, scores of demonstrators from the Armenian Environmental Front (AEF) and Save Amulsar movement assembled in front of the Armenian National Academic Theatre of Opera and Ballet to raise awareness of the environmental threat from the Amulsar goldmine and to protest government inaction. A British mining firm, Lydian International Limited, discovered gold in Amulsar in 2006 and has been trying to construct a mine ever since, but has encountered local protests and blockades. To date, it has been a complicated mess with PM Pashinyan first supporting the protestors then the mining company. Vartouhi's investigation and interviews indicated that operations are in limbo, but from observations and analysis it does not look like any significant work will be started at the mine.

August 23, Armenia reported the capture of 2nd Lt. Gurgen Alarerdyan (b.1989) by the Azeri forces and his sentencing to life imprisonment. The Azeris claimed the capture was a result of a botched commando raid. The Armenians claimed Alarerdyan mistakenly ventured a little too far into the LOC. He is charged with espionage and other violations. In any event, he should be considered a POW and treated as such and not subjected to a life in prison verdict.

September 1, French President Macron returned to Beirut with great hope from the Lebanese people. Macron met with some of the new officials of the government assuring them that they would not be receiving any funds if there is any sign of corruption or if there are questions about reforms made in the banking system. If the funds are not used directly for the people there would be no funds. The same policy is also utilized by other countries sending aid to Lebanon. The French president discovered that there had not been much clean up in Beirut except for volunteer clean-up crews opening up the roads. There was a tremendous amount of more work to be done. He was not too happy with what he saw. He also received the latest count of death at about 200, but still counting. One member at the meeting told him 13 Armenians were found dead. Macron told the members that he would be returning in October to assess how the recovery work is going. "I expect to see great improvements," he assured them.

Vartouhi who was assigned to report on what was going on was surprised that she did not hear much about Hezbollah in this whole scenario. She had a lot of high school friends she wanted to see, but did not have time for that. She interviewed pedestrians in the streets, local journalists, community leaders, and a few politicians. There was tremendous animosity against Hezbollah who had enormous power in the country. There was a general feeling that the bombing was due to Hezbollah's activities, not that they had anything directly with the explosion, but they were the ones who wanted to keep the massive tons of Ammonium Nitrate in the port warehouse. Many leaders said it was much too dangerous and should have been stored in a more remote place. Hezbollah won the argument. As it turned out, Vartouhi found out by interviewing a few leaders who knew what was going on that some portions of the Hezbollah controlled stockpile of fertilizer were shipped to Belgium then to France, UK, Switzerland, Greece, and possibly to other countries. She was a little surprised to discover that a few people actually though some Hezbolla personnel have helped Lebanon. The EU classifies the Hezbollah military group as a terrorist organization, but not its political arm. The US State Department believes all Hezbollah groups should be categorized as terrorist and should oversee what Hezbollah ships into their countries. Vartouhi was hopeful all the EU nations take heed to assure no Ammonium Nitrate is transferred into their countries and to ban all Hezbollah organizations.

Vartouhi did not have time to visit any of her past friends, but she remembered how beautiful Beirut was such a wonderful place back in the 60s; "Paris of the Middle East" it was rightfully called. There were well over 200,000 Armenians living in the country at the time, but due to the long civil war and later disruption of foreigners, corruption, and the slowdown or loss of business many Armenians left the country. She found out there were only 156,000 living there now, but many were leaving. She also heard the Turks in Beirut had a demonstration against the Armenian in the Muslim section of the city. They were carrying placards, signs, and other derogatory phases against the Armenians. Even worse were death threats to some of the Armenian leadership and slaughter to the Armenians residing in Bourj Hammoud. Some messages included provocative statements in justifying the Genocide and calling the Armenians insidious and deserving of the murders they received. All this from Turks who their leader continues to deny that there was a Genocide. She remembered how her grandmother told her how Lebanon opened her arms welcoming and supporting Armenian refugees during the Genocide. Most of the Armenians were happy in Lebanon, that is, until the civil war where it turned bad for the whole country.

Vartouhi returned to Yerevan with prayers in heart for Lebanon. She prayed that the new leadership was capable of repairing the horrible damage that was bestowed on their country. She prayed that the Armenians and all the Lebanese people return to good health and to regain their homes and businesses as rapidly as possible. She prayed that the vast funds that are being donated to the nation be utilized wisely and effectively.

September 4, Armenian Defense Minister David Tonoyan made some significant and political statements at a joint Moscow session of the defense ministers of Commonwealth of Independent States, the Shanghai Cooperation Organization (SCO), and the Collective Treaty Organization. Tonoyan's main concern was Turkey's aggressive moves in the last few months. He talked of Turkey's regional geopolitical ambitions by using a full range of destructive approach fueled by an expansionist ideology. To counter Turkey's dangerous moves in the region, Tonoyan added, the Russian presence in the region, as well as the deepening of military-political cooperation between Armenia and Russia are the most important deterrents contributing to the preservation of regional stability and security."

"Unfortunately, there are two schools of thought in Yerevan on how our relations with Russia should be. One, we should work closely with

Russia and other is to break off interactions with Moscow," Vartouhi told her husband when she heard about the meeting. "The dilemma puts our prime minister in a difficult position. However, I don't think he has a choice because of the manner Erdogan is behaving."

"You know, I think you're right Vartouhi, Erdogan has a tremendous ambition to restore the glory and expanse of the Ottoman Empire and he sure is working hard to get to that status. France is about the only country that's giving him any obstacle. I think the Turkish leader is living in a dream world when he makes statements like, 'Turkey is helping the international arena by fighting terrorism.' He's become a terrorist himself. I notice he also likes to intimidate nations by conducting war maneuvers with Azerbaijan and send Turkish citizens to countries like Syria, Libya and Lebanon. " Simon added.

The reporter did not know what kind of agreement the meeting ended up with and would have to wait until Tonoyan gets back to Yerevan.

September 10, Baroness Caroline Cox sent a letter to Azerbaijan Ambassador to the UK Tahir Taghizade in response to a letter he sent to her on September 7. The ambassador's letter outlined the Azeri biased side of the war situation describing the rightful occupation of Nagorno Karabakh.

In a response letter back to the ambassador, Cox provided a concise and detail account of the history of Nagorno Karabakh and Nakhichevan that Vartouhi was sure the ambassador was aware of but choose to distort the facts. Cox pointed out four main areas that she felt the ambassador was way off base. First was Nagorno Karabakh. She pointed out Karabakh was 95% Armenian when Stalin detached the enclave to Azerbaijan. She reminded Taghizade how Azerbaijan initiated a war against the Armenian population living in Nagorno Karabakh - in breach of international- recognized conventions. She was in Stepanakert when the Azeris used cluster bombs and 400 GRAD missiles a day to fire on the civilians of the city. She also witnessed the massacre in Maragha and saw decapitated civilian bodies and homes still smoldering from the military attack. She wrote Taghizade that she believes the Armenians of Nagorno Karabakh have the same legal right to self-determination as the people of Timor Leste, Eritrea and Kosovo.

The baroness mentioned the occupation of Shushi that was occupied by the Azeris for decades as part of the Nagorno Karabakh Autonomous Oblast. The city was originally recognized of Armenia culture in the Caucasus second only to Tbilisi in Georgia, that is, until thousands of Armenians were massacred in March 1920. The archbishop at the time was decapitated and his head was put on display on a pole.

The third point Lady Cox explained was the enclave of Nakhichevan [that had more than a majority of Armenians in 1923] was made an Autonomous Republic in Azerbaijan which had no land connection and was fully attached to Armenia. Azerbaijan carried out an ethnic cleaning until there were no Armenians left. The Azeris have destroyed tens of thousands of UNESCO protected ancient stone carvings and other Armenian sites and artifacts.

Lady Cox believes the Armenians have a right to recover Nakhichevan. Or perhaps Azerbaijan would offer an honorable alternative: the right for Nagorno Karabakh to be recognized as Armenian land; and the Armenians to concede Azerbaijan's occupation of Nakhichevan?

The last point the baroness wrote was the pardoning, rewarding and glorifying an Azeri army officer who hacked to death a sleeping Armenian colleague in Hungary in 2004. According to a recent judgment by the European Court of Human Rights, Baku's actions amounted to the 'approval' and 'endorsement' of the 'very serious ethnically-biased crime.'

Lady Cox also mentioned Azerbaijani aggressiveness. Over a four day period in April 2016, Azeri forces launched an offensive into the territories controlled by Armenian forces in Nagorno Karabakh, resulting in many deaths. In July of this year, Azerbaijan deployed artillery batteries close to the civilian population of Tavoush that targeted a face mask production factory. What was worse was the bombing of a kindergarten in the village of Aygepar. Also in July was the pro-war demonstrations held in Baku. Thousands of protestors demanded the Azeri Government to fully deploy the army, chanting 'Death to Armenians.'

The last words Lady Cox mentioned were the hate messages that are generated against the Armenians. This is provoked in the government and taught in schools that claim Armenia is the 'Number One Enemy.' [This policy is identical to what is propagated in Turkey]. To top the protestor's shouts, the Azerbaijan Foreign Minister made a recent statement, '*The Armenian side mustn't forget that the state of the art missile systems our army has are capable of launching a precision strike on the Metsamor nuclear power plant.*' Such statements support the fact that Azerbaijan is committed to war and cruelty rather that peace.

After reading Cox's letter, Vartouhi thought she said it like it is. The reporter deemed everything Cox said, but believed the words went in one ear out the other of the ambassador. She still thought the Turkish and Azeri leaders will make up stories to counteract the truth of history. Vartouhi thinks the Azeris do not have any intention for peace.

September 16, angry protesters in Yerevan demonstrated against Minister of Education, Science, Culture, and Sport Arayil Harutyunyan (b. 1979) carrying signs "Education is our Right" and "Arayik Resign." Demonstrators protested against what they saw as extreme reforms by the Minister of Education. Claims were made that personnel in the ministry were inexperienced and were compromised by foreign powers. They accused him of attempting to institute "anti-Armenian material into the curriculum and was called a "Parade of Failures." Harutyunyan who was an advocated and member of the Velvet Revolution claimed he was only doing what the people wanted.

September 24, a huge explosion of a Hezbollah stronghold occurred in the village of Ain Qana, Lebanon, just north of Sidon. The cause of the blast was unknown and fortunately there was no loss of lives. The latest count on the August 4 bombing is 220 dead with 650 injuries and 300,000 without homes.

September 21-26, Russia launched a military exercise that Armenia joined with China, Myanmar, Belarus, and Pakistan to take place in the north Caucasus. On the 25th Armenia and Russia had large scale joint coordinated counter-terrorist warfare exercises including 1,500 soldiers, helicopters, aviation and air defense, and all types of war equipment. After the maneuvers the forces returned to their home bases not knowing what was going to happen in two days.

September 27, Azerbaijan initiated a full scale surprise attack on the Republic of Artsakh. The Azeris launched fighter planes, drones, artillery, and rockets across the whole LOC and attacked Stepanakert with large scale artillery bombings. Karabakh and Armenia immediately called up their reserves, proclaimed martial law, and prepared buses to carry thousands of Armenians volunteers to aid in the defense. Diaspora Armenian organizations generated petitions condemning the attack and Turkish involvement. Funds were raised to support Artsahk, and calling for volunteers to join in the defense. Other measures to assist Karabakh included mobilization for mass protests in front of Azeri and Turkish institutions and diplomatic offices, news coverage to sensitize public opinion, and call to action for statesmen and legislators around the world to condemn the Azeri assault. Azerbaijan falsely claimed Artsakh started the fighting, but the enclave would have no reason to do so. Varouhi was sure the international community was well aware of this deception.

Following the day of the attack, Armenian Ambassador Varuzhan Nersesyan announced the Azeri offense was much larger than the April 2016 and July 2020 clashes and that the responsibility for the current attack was the reckless natures of the dictatorships in Baku and Ankara. He also claimed that it is possible that the violence could spread into Armenia. He stated that he thought the surprise assault was well planned and was being accompanied by Turkish military supplies and weapons and had large scale war drills just weeks ago with Turkey. The aggressive rhetoric by the two dictators also was a part of the scenario.

Initial reports from the field stated that 100 people have died, including 11 civilians. Nersesyan further stated that during the July clashes, he noted that Azerbaijan openly disregarded and refused the proposal of the co-chairs of the OSCE's Minsk Group to establish a mechanism to monitor ceasefire violations and discover which party was responsible each time. When Vartouhi heard that statement, she thought this was nothing new as the Azeris for decades have violated every ceasefire that had been agreed to and they never approved to have monitors stationed along LOC. Connecting the dots, Nersesyan concluded, "The current attacks are nothing but the implementation of a decades-long policy of aggression on the part of Azerbaijan. It is on the record and the responsibility cannot be avoided."

President Erdogan claimed the war was first initiated by the Armenians. This is double talk by the dictator as he also said at the same time, "Azerbaijan had to take matters into its own hands whether it likes it or not." This was after he remarked that the OSCE Minsk Group had failed to resolve the conflict for more than 30 years so Azeris had to do what they did. It also was obvious that Turkey has been supplying major weapons to the Azeris with strong indications that that she pressured them to initiate the attack. Statements from foreign countries said the fighting should stop and a ceasefire should be initiated. This was fine Vartouhi thought, but none of them stated that the Azeris were responsible for starting the war.

French President Macron who is extremely concerned about the attack said he would call presidents Putin and Trump to discuss the situation to determine if they could do something to stop the carnage. He accused Turkey of not only bringing in Syrian mercenaries, many of them former ISIS warriors and jihadists into the fight. Turkey also supplied the Azeris with Turkish weapons and advisors. Their numbers reached as high as 4,000 and their earnings would be $1500.00 or more a month. Macron expressed "deep concern" to Turkey. The Russian Foreign Minister demanded the "immediate withdrawal from the region." Message from Putin's spokesman advised avoiding "further undesirable escalation of the situation." The US called for "immediate halt to the deadly hostilities" and warned against "external parties' participation." Artsakh President Arayik Harutyunyan, stated, "Our forces are fighting against Turkey." Erdogan and his supporters have all confirmed that that they are supporting Azerbaijan 100 percent.

September 28, President Sarkissian delivering opening remarks at CYBERSEC200 Conference with NATO started with a talk on cyber threats from Azerbaijan and NATO partner Turkey but soon talked about the Azeri large scale military attack on Armenia yesterday. Sarkessian declared, "NATO member Turkey is fully in supporting now Azerbaijan through its electronic drones through cyber-attacks. But it's not only that. Turkey is supporting Azerbaijan also through their personnel, advisers, mercenaries and also with their F-16 fighter aircrafts. For every Armenian living worldwide that's sort of a return of the ghost. Why I say ghost, because that's the ghost of the Ottoman Empire, that 105 years ago masterminded the Armenian Genocide. There's no way that we can allow that this genocide happen again." The president presented additional information on the assault where in one incident a mother and child were killed. He received a count of 200 military and 14 civilians have already been killed. Schools were also were bombed. He concluded his talk by saying that the Turkish government now has 360 decrees of complications around them [Greece, Libya, Iraq, Syria, Lebanon] and are still creating problems everywhere.

September 29, on the other side of the world, Ambassador Armen Baibourtian (b.), Consul General of Armenia in Los Angeles, held a press conference to express concerns from the Armenian Diaspora. He wanted to let the press know about the unprovoked attacks on Karabakh, and to let Diaspora Armenians how they can help. He expressed that Armenian Fund is the only official organization accepting donations on behalf of the governments of Armenia and Artsakh. He commented that it would be safe for tourists to visit Armenia, but Vartouhi did not think it was a good idea, at least at the present. He pointed out that Azerbaijan has been preparing for this attack for a long time. Foreign countries such Turkey and Israel have been selling weapons to the Azeris for years and that Turkey has gone further by bringing mercenary such as such jihadists troops from Syria while conducting military maneuvers with Azerbaijan.

Baibourtian stated that since the May 12, 1994, where all parties agreed to the ceasefire arrangement, Azerbaijan has constantly broken the agreement. He mentioned that Prime Minister Pashinyan has said, "The Armenian side is dedicated to reaching a solution that is favorable to the people of Armenia, Artsakh, and Azerbaijan. When Vartouhi heard about the PM's remark, she said that's fine except Azerbaijan does not have the same dedication to a peaceful solution. When the ambassador was asked about the CSTO assisting Artsakh in the conflict, he remarked, "When and if Armenia decides there needs to be help from the CSTO, have no doubt that this is a powerful union of military power and will come Armenia's aid." Vartouhi again thought, "I hope this not wishful thinking because the CSTO did nothing to help when the Azeris attacked Tavoush Provence [Armenia did not ask for aid], however during the July brief war they did not even condemn Azerbaijan for assaulting Armenia. We'll just have to wait and see what happens."

On the same day Vartouhi and her former student, Anna Hakobyan Pashinyan visited the hospital, hopefully, to hearten wounded soldiers to health. The prime minister's wife is a strong advocate for peace, yet has also been criticized for being a war monger because of photos of her and other females in military uniforms. There is also a painting of her in uniform with a palm branch between her teeth and holding a Kalashnikov AK-19 assault rifle. She would like to see all Armenian and Artsakh females have a rifle and be trained to use it. Vartouhi wrote in one of her columns, "The "First Lady" is criticized for advocating peace while holding a rifle and recruiting other females, including Azeri females, but no one says anything about Mayr Hyastan holding an unsheathed sword. I think it is something akin to what President Theodore Roosvelt (1858-1915) of America, 'Walk softly, but carry a big stick.'" Vartouhi was happy being with her former student, but sad due to the war. Her job now was being a war correspondent that kept her pretty busy. The job was tough and could be dangerous, but she at least was able to see Azad once in a while because he was taking care of the wounded from the heavy fighting.

September 29, as a result of the aggressive action by Azerbaijani forces, there was a call for the United Nations Security Council (UNSC) to take some action, but none was forthcoming. Yet, as usual there was a call to stop fighting, initiate a ceasefire and return to the negotiating table with Minsk Group. There was no statement on Azerbaijan aggressiveness or of Turkey's participation in the fighting. Vartouhi thought this emboldened Aliyev and Erdogan even more as there was no chastising or condemning of their hostilities.

September 30, a Turkish jet fighter F-16 flying from Azerbaijan attacked an Armenian Sukhoy aircraft flying 60 km inside Armenian air space. Turkey denied the involvement. How can Turkey lie when it is so obvious?

Observers noted that Turkey hired Syrian mercenaries purportedly to protect the Azeri oilfields, but were sent directly to the front.

It did not take long for Azad to sign up to assist in the field hospital. He made weekly trips back and forth to the front to restore the wounded soldiers.

French President Macron condemned Turkey for attacking Armenia; he was one of a few national leaders to do so.

September 30, the Yazidi (also spelled Yezidi) celebrated the opening of their new Seven Angel Temple on the skyline of Aknalich village in Armenia. The Yazidi shrine is the largest one in the world and befitting that it was constructed in Armenia where they are the largest minority in the country. Previous to their habitant in Armenia they had a sizeable population in norther Iraq and Syria. However, during the mid-2000s the ISIS killed, kidnapped, or displaced thousands after which many migrated to Armenia. The ancient religious group did not have a homeland, but they now feel safe in Armenia.

October 1, Congresswoman Jackie Speier (b. 1950) introduced HR 1165 condemning the Azerbaijan military operation against Nagorno Karabakh and denouncing Turkey's interference in the conflict. It did not take but a few hours for the Azeri propaganda machine to spew out their falsehoods and deceits on who started the war, who is the aggressor in this conflict, who is bombing civilian structures, who is continually breaking the ceasefires, who is wrongfully occupying the enclave of Nagorno Karabakh, and any other statements that ridicule against Armenia. Vartouhi's rebuttal is to look at satellite records and the clarifications of independent observers to see the truth in what is occurring to determine how the Azeris lie.

October 1, the European Research Council (ERC) awarded a major research five year prestigious grant for the "Study of Medieval Armenia History grant is for two million Euros and is headed by Dr. Zara Pogossian who has a long list of academic achievements, awards, and experience. The project will be a huge first time study of Armenia and her relationship and contacts during the 9th to 14th centuries medieval Eurasian identities such as; Crusades, Byzantines, Georgians, Islam, Arabs, Persians, Mongols, Seljuks, the Ottomans, and any other culture impacting group on Armenian history. A working staff of nine scholars will be assisting Pogossian and will be mainly operating out of the University of Florence but also going to other locations when necessary. When Vartouhi heard about the project her investigation indicated that this is an unheard of great project for an Armenian study. She was sure the resulting endeavor will expose Armenian experiences to a huge group of scholars, academians, and other interested parties.

October 2, sixty US Congressional leaders called the Secretary of State Mike Pompeo (b. 1963) to take decisive action to condemn Azerbaijan and the Turkish-led offensive against Artsakh urging sanctions on both countries. Congress passed House Resolution 1165 condemning the Azerbaijan coordinated offensive on Nagorno Karabakh and denounced Turkish interference in the conflict. All military aid is to be cut off and Presidents Aliyev and Erdogan were condemned by Congressional and Senate members.

Starting on the week of the initial assault major cities all over the world conducted demonstrations condemning the Azeri onslaught and Turkey's desire to initiate Genocide. Hundreds of signs stating, "Turkey author of Genocide," "Artsahk wants Freedom,"

October 3, in an address to the nation PM Pashinyan stated the following, "The objective of the Azerbaijani-Turkish bandits is not about claiming territory. Their objective is the Armenian people. Their objective is to continue their genocidal policy." Vartouhi was sure the Armenian people were aware of the Turkish-Azeri policy, but is the international community aware of it? Armenia should hammer this point out to the world to let it know what the true purpose is of the Turkish mentality.

October 3, Azeri rockets and drones from Ganja continued to bomb Stepanakert targeting civilian and blocks of apartments. The Artsakh forces attacked Ganja airport to ensure the F-16 fighter planes could not be utilized so conveniently.

October 3, away from the battle scene but still a problem area for Armenians was a letter that Garo Paylan, an Armenian member in the Turkish parliament and Peoples' Democratic Party (HDP), wrote to the Turkish press. With all kinds of threats and being called a traitor he accused the government of war propaganda and openly supporting Azerbaijan. He called for negotiations to settle the dispute by de-escalation rather than to keep fighting. He wrote on the discrimination and hate speech propagated by the government. He mentioned that his party (HDP) and he have been targeted for calling for peace by an organization called Eurasian Strategic Research Center (ASAM) that through ads in some newspapers. He has accused of "Insulting Turkishness."

Soon after his letter was published, Turkey again reinitiated intimidation and harassment pogroms against the Armenians, Greek, Assyrians, Jews, and anyone who was not Turkish. The government supported the ASAM in the organization's attempt to silence the Armenian PM and targeted him with hate speech. Paylan filed a criminal complaint against the ASAM responsible members for accusing him of treason and other charges. Relentless smear campaign was set up accompanied by intimidation and wide spread arrests of her non-Turkish citizens, mostly on pent up charges. Vartouhi said this was nothing new for the Turkish government as she did this every time there was some issue Ankara pursued

October 4, news agencies such as CNN, CNBC, REUTHERS, and several others started presenting the news from the Azeri/Artsakh front. Heavy fighting was occurring along the LOC with artillery fire from both sides. Azeri artillery has been hitting Stepanakert very hard causing deep civilian casualties. Karabahk has bombed the military airport in Ganja, Azerbaijan's second largest city. Both sides calm heavy civilian losses, but Karabakh at least sent warning to Ganjan telling them to leave the city because they will be bombed. For the first few days there were no major changes on the battlefield although the Azeris claimed they captured a few small villages; Artsakh claimed they recaptures some. There were a lot of claims and counter claims in the reports. Karahakh was ready for any peace settlement but Ilham Aliyev said there will be no peace, professing that Karabakh will be completely retaken. Turkey said there would no peace talks until Armenia removes all her forces from the occupied territory and Karabakh. And that she continually would support Azerbaijan, in effect, no matter what. PM Nicol Pashinyan stated they will destroy Azerbaijan so that she will never be able to fight again. One of the news agencies reminded readers that 30,000 people were killed from 1990s war. Vartouhi thought that did not make any difference to the Azeris as they were using mercenaries anyway. It also reported that casualties so far have been 158 military deaths and 11 civilians. Azerbaijan did not report her deaths.

October 4, news agencies such as CNN, CNBC, REUTHERS, and several others started presenting the news from the Azeri/Artsakh front. Heavy fighting was occurring along the LOC with artillery fire from both sides. Azeri artillery has been hitting Stepanakert very hard causing deep civilian casualties. Karabahk has bombed the military airport in Ganja, Azerbaijan's second largest city. Both sides calm heavy civilian losses, but Karabakh at least sent warning to Ganjan telling them to leave the city because they will be bombed. For the first few days there were no major changes on the battlefield although the Azeris claimed they captured a few small villages; Artsakh claimed they recaptures some. There were a lot of claims and counter claims in the reports. Karahakh was ready for any peace settlement but Iham Aliyev said there will be no peace professing that Karabakh will be completely retaken. Turkey said there would no peace talks until Armenia removes all her forces from the occupied territory and Karabakh. And that she continually would support Azerbaijan, in effect, no matter what. PM Nicol Pashinyan stated they will destroy Azerbaijan so that she will never be able to fight again. One of the news agencies reminded readers that 30,000 people were killed from 1990s war. Vartouhi thought that did not make any difference to the Azeris as they were using mercenaries anyway. It also reported that casualties so far have been 158 military deaths and 11 civilians. Azerbaijan did not report her deaths.

October 4, news agencies such as CNN, CNBC, REUTHERS, and several others started presenting the news from the Azeri/Artsakh front. Heavy fighting was occurring along the LOC with artillery fire from both sides. Azeri artillery has been hitting Stepanakert very hard causing deep civilian casualties. Karabahk has bombed the military airport in Ganja, Azerbaijan's second largest city. Both sides calm heavy civilian losses, but Karabakh at least sent warning to Ganjan telling them to leave the city because they will be bombed. For the first few days there were no major changes on the battlefield although the Azeris claimed they captured a few small villages; Artsakh claimed they recaptures some. There were a lot of claims and counter claims in the reports. Karahakh was ready for any peace settlement but Iham Aliyev said there will be no peace professing that Karabakh will be completely retaken. Turkey said there would no peace talks until Armenia removes all her forces from the occupied territory and Karabakh. And that she continually would support Azerbaijan, in effect, no matter what. PM Nicol Pashinyan stated they will destroy Azerbaijan so that she will never be able to fight again. One of the news agencies reminded readers that 30,000 people were killed from 1990s war. Vartouhi thought that did not make any difference to the Azeris as they were using mercenaries anyway. It also reported that casualties so far have been 158 military deaths and 11 civilians. Azerbaijan did not report her deaths.

October 4, news agencies such as CNN, CNBC, REUTHERS, and several others started presenting the news from the Azeri/Artsakh front. Heavy fighting was occurring along the LOC with artillery fire from both sides. Azeri artillery has been hitting Stepanakert very hard causing deep civilian casualties. Karabahk has bombed the military airport in Ganja, Azerbaijan's second largest city. Both sides calm heavy civilian losses, but Karabakh at least sent warning to Ganjan telling them to leave the city because they will be bombed. For the first few days there were no major changes on the battlefield although the Azeris claimed they captured a few small villages; Artsakh claimed they recaptures some. There were a lot of claims and counter claims in the reports. Karahakh was ready for any peace settlement but Ilham Aliyev said there will be no peace professing that Karabakh will be completely retaken. Turkey said there would no peace talks until Armenia removes all her forces from the occupied territory and Karabakh. And that she continually would support Azerbaijan, in effect, no matter what. PM

Nicol Pashinyan stated they will destroy Azerbaijan so that she will never be able to fight again. One of the news agencies reminded readers that 30,000 people were killed from 1990s war. Vartouhi thought that did not make any difference to the Azeris as they were using mercenaries anyway. It also reported that casualties so far have been 158 military deaths and 11 civilians. Azerbaijan did not report her deaths.

October 4, news agencies such as CNN, CNBC, REUTHERS, and several others started presenting the news from the Azeri/Artsakh front. Heavy fighting was occurring along the LOC with artillery fire from both sides. Azeri artillery has been hitting Stepanakert very hard causing deep civilian casualties. Karabahk has bombed the military airport in Ganja, Azerbaijan's second largest city. Both sides calmed heavy civilian losses, but Karabakh at least sent warning to Ganjan telling them to leave the city because they will be bombed. For the first few days there were no major changes on the battlefield although the Azeris claimed they captured a few small villages; Artsakh asserted they recaptures some. There were a lot of claims and counter claims in the reports. Karahakh was ready for any peace settlement but Iham Aliyev said there will be no peace professing that Karabakh will be completely retaken. Turkey said there would be no peace talks until Armenia removes all her forces from the occupied territory and Karabakh. And that she continually would support Azerbaijan, in effect, no matter what. PM Nicol Pashinyan stated they will destroy Azerbaijan so that she will never be able to fight again. One of the news agencies reminded readers that 30,000 people were killed from 1990s war. Vartouhi thought that did not make any difference to the Azeris as they were using mercenaries anyway. It also reported that casualties so far have been 158 military deaths and 11 civilians. Azerbaijan did not report her deaths.

October 4, President Armen Sarkessian in an address to Diaspora Armenians praised them for being the nation's second army. He said, "This time it was not only Azerbaijan we have to confront but also genocidal Turkey with its arms, servicemen and mercenary terrorists, with hateful words and anti-Armenian propaganda against us and against the freedom-loving people of Artsakh. This is the same Turkey, which perpetuated ethnic cleansing and Genocide against the

Armenians 105 years ago in the Ottoman Empire. This time this will not pass; we will not allow genocide to happen."

October 5, Amnesty International's Crisis Response identified and condemned the Azeri use of cluster munitions.

October 6, the Armenian National Committee of America (ANCA) sent a letter to the Israeli Ambassador to stop sending lethal weapons to Azerbaijan. ANCA Chairman Raffi Hamparian wrote, "Israel should immediately halt the sales or transfer of lethal or dual-use material or technology to Azerbaijan. Insure that Israel will never be complicit in a second Armenian Genocide." ANCA further wrote to US State Department, "This [Azeri/Turkish killings] represents a new low for the State Department, worse even than their shameful record acting as open denier to the Armenian Genocide and outright apologist for Turkey and Azerbaijan's anti-Armenian violence instead of making excuses for Ankara and Baku, the State Department should be imposing sanctions and preparing criminal indictments against Recep Erdogan and Ilham Aliyev."

October 7, Turkey launched an air and extensive bombing campaign into northern Syria followed by a land invasion a few days later that forced more than 275,000 people from their homes and killed 45 Kurdish civilians and several journalists. Under attach were ambulances, health facilities, and a medical point belonging to the Kurdish Red Crescent. Vartouhi also received reports that indicted the Turkish forces exercised serious human rights violations. She told her husband that Turkey probably would not have made the invasion if President Trump had not more or less given Erdogan "the go ahead to do what you got to do." She thought it was a stab-in-the-back to the Kurdish forces that had fought so valiantly and destroyed the ISIS forces. She was also surprised that Russia did not do anything or say anything about the invasion.

October 8, US House Representative Adam Schiff (b. 1960) in a statement with Armenian Ambassador Varuzhon Nersesyan said, "I believe the United States should make clear to Azerbaijan and Turkey that if they persist in this violence instead of embracing a peaceful settlement to the conflict, we are prepared to recognize the Republic of Artsakh as an independent nation." Varouhi thought these were extremely strong words coming from a Congressman, however she thought encouraging. She prayed that they result in a fact that it happens.

Congressmen and women from both sides of the isle made statements condemning Azerbaijan and Turkey for their aggressive action and the killing of so many civilians. Most of them, as several countries, called for a return to a ceasefire and resumption of peace talks. A few called for a declaration to declare the Republic of Artsakh an independent country. There was a call for President Trump to pursue an immediate cessation of hostilities and facilitate a peaceful settlement of the dispute. Some Congresspersons called for an immediate suspension of all military assistance to Azerbaijan and Turkey. There were more remarks and demands where most of them were for Azerbaijan to stop the killing of civilians and for Turkey to get out of the action. Vartouhi noted a lot of these Congressional actions, but were totally ignored by the two aggressors.

October 8, Armenia accused Azerbaijan of shelling the Ghazanchetsets Cathedral in Shushi that had a direct hit by a shell that penetrated the dome and did considerable damage inside. Minutes later the bombardment continued causing more damage. The Azeri defense minister denied attacking the cathedral. Vartouhi told her editor, "How could the Azeri defense minister deny that they did not bomb the cathedral? Does he think the Armenians would bomb their own holy edifice? The statement was like most of the fabrications the Azeris make," Fortunately, there were no deaths, but there was a lot of destruction. She hoped the Russian journalist who was wounded in the attack reports the storming in Moscow and they do something about it.

October 9, Armenia accused Azerbaijan of shelling the historic Holy Savior Ghazanchetsots Cathedral in Shushi. The Azeris denied the accusation but the evidence is in the bombing. Vartouhi asked her husband, "How can they deny that they didn't do it? Do they think the Armenians would destroy their own church?"

"Of course not, but we all know the Azeris are super liars and they don't seem to care that it's an international crime to target religious sites during a war," Simon responded.

October 9, Philippe Raffi Kalfayan the prominent French Armenian international lecturer and lawyer [see March 2, 2020] gave a lengthy special narrative on Azerbaijan and Nagorno Karabakh to the *Armenian Mirror Spectator* outlining the pros and cons on the principles of self-determination and territorial integrity. At the concussion of the report he had four suggestions to solve the conflict problem:

- The Republic of Armenia must call for the international recognition of Nagorno Karabakh independence by other Nations.
- The National Assembly of the Republic of Armenia must call for the international recognition of Nagorno Karabakh independence by national parliaments.
- United Nations' members must consider that the prevention and repression of genocide is *jus coens* (peremptory) *and erga omnes* (universal obligation) whether their country ratifies the Convention or not.
- All diaspora individuals and significant concerned organizations must advocate their respective governments and parliaments for recognition of Nagorno Karabakh independence.

October 9, there was no report of a trial of Nishan Haroutiouian, the Lebanese-Armenian TV celebrity and announcer who ridiculed Turkish President Erdogan on the air. Vartouhi thinks it may have been postponed again.

October 9, Vartouhi ran across a *Newsweek Magazine* article by Gavin Wax (b. 1994) that was a real eye opener as what is going on in the sub-Caucasus region. He pointed out that Islamic aggression and expansion into lands of Christian people should not be a reality of the 21st century. But it is. He states that it is time for the United States to responds to the attacks of Azerbaijan and Turkey on Armenians. Vartouhi showed her editor some significant excerpts from his writings, "Hundreds of people, including civilians, have been killed as the second week of heavy clashes between Armenian and Azerbaijan potentially turns into a third....The Republic of Artsakh is almost totally Armenian, about 99 percent. Part of the oldest Christian states in the world, it remains a front line against encroaching Islamism. A war over the land has been officially ongoing since the fall of the Soviet Union, but a 1994 ceasefire deal maintained a relative standstill until major escalations from Azerbaijan on September 27. Thomas de Waal (b. 1966), an expert on the region, has identified Azerbaijan as the aggressor in this most recent flare up." He points out that Turkey; a strategic NATO partner for the US, is leading most of the onslaught and is consistent with Erdogan's effort to build a neo-Ottoman empire, leading offenses against Kurds in their territory as well as Greeks in the Aegean and Cyprus. Wax discusses hired Syrian and Islamic fighters and the support the US taxpayers give Turkey in the sum of $153 million and Azerbaijan $14 million. "Keeping those dollars home would be the easiest thing to do," Wax wrote. Vartouhi thought the US should do much more than just stopping funds to the two aggressors.

Wax further wrote, "The US should not be expected to be the policeman of the world, but there should be an interest in preserving of Christianity in the Middle East. But it must do right by the American taxpayers who are footing billions of dollars in foreign aid to countries that wish to destroy the Christian way of life." He advocates removing Turkey from NATO and also for the US to recognize the Republic of Artsakh [the US Congress is discussing that issue now although President Trump has been silent on the issue]. Vartouhi thought the proposals and ideas from Wax and Waal have a lot of merit and should be pursued by not only the US but also other democratic nations.

October 10, NBC News and BBC declared Azerbaijan and Armenian agreed to a cease-fire today through the efforts of the Russian foreign minister together with the Armenian and Azerbaijani foreign ministers. The main purpose purportedly was to exchange prisoners and gather their dead. Vartouhi was sure the Azeri main purpose was to prepare their forces for the next huge assault and before she completed her statement the Azeris started shelling Stepanakert again. In a sense, the ceasefire was a farce because Azerbaijan is not ready for one while at the same time President Erdogan said, "We will not have a ceasefire until Armenian forces completely move out of Nagoro Karabakh." That does not sound like he is ready for any ceasefire. In addition she found out the Azeris did not even gather their dead; they just wanted to prep for the next assault. Muslims are supposed to bury their dead within 24 hour of their dying, but President Aliyev, not being a devout Muslim, chose to ignore that staunch rule.

Also on October 10, but far away for the battle scene was the US Library of Congress correcting its "Armenian Massacres" to "Armenian Genocide." The correction was long overdue but it now more truly describes what occurred in 1915-1923.

October 14, PM Pashinyan spoke on national TV to the Armenian people telling them on the progress of the fighting and how important it was to keep up their spirts. He told them to remember our fight at Sardarabad over 100 year ago where we defeated the Turks and we can do it again. He thanked the countries for requesting a ceasefire to stop the bloodshed. He reported about 523 have died since the hostilities had started. He asked everyone to pray with him for the deceased and their loved ones. He asked all Armenians to pray with him for the brave fighters to keep our freedom.

On the same day, the State of Michigan passed a resolution recognizing the Republic of Artsakh and condemning Azerbaijan's and Turkey's aggression against the Armenians of Artsakh and to recognize the Republic of Artsakh as an independent country.

October 15, the United Nations Human Rights Office stated that Turkey could be held accountable for possible war crimes, including the execution of captives and death of a female Kurdish journalist in her invasion of northeastern Syria. The statement included attacks on medical facilities, the bombing of a convoy of civilians and journalist during its now weeklong offensive in Syria. The UN did eventually impose sanctions on Turkey but Erdogan still went about his aggressive moves.

October 17, a second ceasefire was declared by Azerbaijan and the Armenia initiated by the US, France, and Russia through the Minsk

Group. Vartouihi wondered how long this one would last. Reported deaths of Armenians totaled 633; the Azeris did not report a count. The truce was violated by the Azeris a few hours later.

October 18, President Donald Trump during his campaign rally in Carson City, NV, praised the Armenians as good people and good businessmen. When asked about the situation in Nagorno Karabakh, he said, "We're looking into it." When Vartouhi heard about the remark she told her editor, "Don't count on President Trump to help the Armenians. He's much too buddy, buddy with Erdogan to do much for the Armenians. We thank God for US Congress for seeing what Turkey and Erdogan really are and passing the resolution recognizing the Armenian Genocide and the Turkish involvement in the Artsakh war."

October 22, Australia's most populous state of New South Wales recognized the independence of the Republic of Artsakh in a 61-2 vote. Huge groups of demonstrators throughout the globe are condemning Azerbaijan and Turkey for their humanitarian attacks on civilians and showing signs that ask nations to recognize the Republic of Artsakh, inforce sanctions on Azerbaijan and Turkey, and protest against Israel for selling lethal weapons to Azerbaijan.   In connection with the Israeli supplying arms to the Azeris, Israeli scholarly groups have called for the cessation of Israeli arms sales to Azerbaijan. Other Jewish organizations did the same. Hebrew leaders, such as Profs. Israel Charny (b. 1931), Yair Ajruon (b. 1945), Noam Chomsky (b. 1929), and many other scholars also joined in raising their voices against Israel's action.

October 22, at a US State Department press conference, Secretary of State Pompeo said, "All countries supplying weapons and support to the sides in the conflict [Azerbaijan and Armenia] should cease." He also talked about keeping the ceasefire and returning to negotiating table just as numerous other countries are doing likewise. Three key mandates were presented to the secretary; 1) Recognition of Artsakh as an independent country, 2) Cutting off all military supplies to Azerbaijan, 3) Empose sanctions on Aliyev and Erdogan for killing of civilians and crimes against humanity.

October 23, Human Rights Watch again reported several instances of Azeri cluster munitions being utilized demanding an end to the use of banded weapons. Vartouhi saw these reports and commented in her column why no nation or the UN did anything to force the Azeris to cease using them.

October 23, over 50 US House members called for crippling sanctions on President Aliyev and the country's top military leaders for war crimes committed against Artsakh civilians during the ongoing Turkish and Azeri attacks. Secretary Pompeo met with Azeri minister and Congresspersons called on the Trump Administration to "impose significant, tangible consequences on the individuals responsible for Azerbaijan's continuous campaign of aggression against civilians in Artsakh." President Trump did nothing about the proposed sanctions.

October 24, In Washington, DC, the Library of Congress formally announced that it is correcting its reference to "Armenian Massacres" to "Armenian Genocide." This is a long overdue correction that should have done years ago, but diaspora Armenians were glad it is now properly named.

October 25, President Trump again made complimentary remarks about the Armenians during his rally in New Hampshire. The next day he congratulated President Aliyev and PM Pashinyan for initiating a ceasefire.

October 26, a ceasefire was announced by the US, Armenia and Azerbaijan. Vartouhi wondered how long this third ceasefire would last?

Vartouhi's question was answered before the day ended as Azeri troops were focusing their sights on the second largest city in Artsakh, Shushi, and the home of the famed Ghazanchetsots (Holy Savior) Cathedral. Heavy intense fighting with casualties in the hundreds took place for the Azeris to get within three miles of the city. The situation was extremely critical for Artsakh. President Arayik Harutyunyan was immensely concerned about the possible fall of the city. He broadcast, "The one who controls Shushi controls Nagorno Karabakh. We must realize that and take part in defending Shushi. We must reverse the situation."

November 6, Reiters reported the Azeri denial that they were shelling Stepanakert. Vartouhi pointed out the ridiculousness of the statement to her husband. "One only has to look at what has gone on in the city. Who has done the destruction? The Armenians? The Azeris lie so much that every time they open their mouth, falsehoods pour out."

Reports indicate 1,177 troops have already died since the war started. Azerbaijan does not report their deaths, but the Russians have estimated more than 5000 of Azeri soldiers have been killed. The battle for Shushi has intensified where the Armenians so far have held their own. The Azeris believe Artsakh's second largest city is a key goal and they are putting everything they have into the assault. So far, multiple attempts to take the city have been repelled. The Azeris have also put pressure on Lachin to close the access route from Armenia into Nagorno Karabakh and continuing their bombardment on Stepanakert.

October 30, Prime Minister Pashinyan conducted a press interview with reporters from Great Britain, USA, Belgium, Austria, and Italy. In answer to their question he told them about Turkey's involvement with her American war planes, lethal arms, mercenaries, and jihad fighters. He explained that the West will have to meet Turkey in Vienna if they do not stop her current exploitations in Syria, Libya, and here in Artsakh. He told the reporters, "A non-shooting war was going on in Europe and they do not even know it. Europe has been living in prosperity for about 60 years, and opulence prevents them noticing the war that is place." He elaborated on this theme with, "Vienna's security is not in my working portfolio. I can only warn you against the imminent threat."

When asked, "What do you mean?"

"Look at what has happened in France. Look at the tone in which the Turkish President speaks of the French President. Could you ever conceive of any country's official representative possibly speaking about the president of another country with such admonishment? Who could have conceived it 15 years ago? … If you continue to ignore the ongoing war, it will become more and more visible over time. People are being beheaded in the streets of Europe [Azerbaijan has stated it will give of each of her soldiers $100. for every head he turns in]." In effect, what the prime minister was trying to get across to his audience was that Europe was having the same problem Armenia was having and not knowing it.

The radical Muslim groups were pressuring Europeans to cater to their whims and culture not what the laws of the nations are.

When asked about having a diplomatic solution to the war, Pashinyan told them, "How you can have a diplomatic solution when you cannot have a ceasefire? We,ve had three of them, none lasting over one day." He also talked about Azerbaijan always starting the fighting and not Artsakh or Armenia. "It does not make sense for a country to start a war when it is trying to build schools, churches, and public structures."

November 4, a press conference was held with President Armen Sarkessian that included foreign political and public figures and representatives from various countries. When questioned about the aggression against Artsakh and who started the war, Sarkessian's response was, "Armenia did not start this war. They did not start shelling civilian settlements. There is no need for Armenia to start a war. How can you build schools, hospital, roads, and churches and start a war? Is this logical? It is obvious that Turkey and Azaerbaijan started this war and should be no question in anyone's mind that they did." They also discussed the unnecessary killing of Hrant Dink that occurred years ago and why it's rational tor Artsakh to become a free reality. Other issues were conversed such as Turkey's involvement in the conflict and ambition to expand influence and control into the region.

November 7, President Putin telephoned President Macron where both expressed concerns over the large scale clashes and the involvement of the fighters from Syria and Libya. Putin said he was taking steps to implement another ceasefire. Macron has his problems in France with the Muslim uprisings, but he still is interested in suppressing the Karabakh war. Backing from the French president's clampdown ranged from trying to receive commendations from the Muslim countries, but Varouhi thought he had enough problems with the Muslims in his own country. Support for the French president's clampdown ranged from support to commendations from the Muslim countries. President Erdogan publicly declared, "Macron needs mental treatment." He then called for the boycotting of French products. Vatouhi claimed Erdogan is the one who needs mental treatments.

November 8, Dr. Tanner Akcam (b. 1953), the acclaimed Turkish scholar, author, and lecturer, answered several questions at a PAREV-TV news conference. Vartouhi listed the answers to the questions in the order that he responded;

- Turkish President Erdogan got involved in the Karabakh war because he wanted to expand his influence and control into the South Asian region.
- The cancer growing in Turkey is due primarily to Erdogan's lust for power and his dreams of becoming another sultan. Not only is he looking at the Turkish states in Southern Asia but also the Middle East.
- Artsakh is Armenia not Azerbaijani. It always has been regardless of what the Azeris say.
- When looking at the conflicting international rules of "territorial integrity" or "self-determination" one has to research the history of the area, the population living in the area, and the desire of the people living in the region. The international community has a blind eye to fact because Artsakh was assigned to Soviet Azerbaijan for seven decades.
- I think the Minsk Group has not researched the illegal designation Nagorno Karabakh when Stalin ceded the enclave to Azerbaijan in 1923 when it was 95% Armenian. The same could be said for Nakhichevan when its population was 75% Armenian.

November 8, Azerbaijan claimed she captured Shusha where the Armenians claimed she had not. There was heavy fighting around the city. Hundreds of Armenians began to leave Karabakh for Armenia.

November 9, Armenia and Azerbaijan again agreed to a Moscow brokered truce in the Nagorno Karabakh war. Presidents Putin and Aliyev signed the agreement while awaiting PM Pashinyan's signature. He did later in the day announcing it was an "extremely painful decision." The signing initiated protests and riots in Yerevan where the violence expanded to Government House and to the prime minister's residence. The rioters vandalized the inside of the government structure and after not receiving an audience at the prime minister's residence they broke windows and furniture in the house. Thousands in the mob shouted for his resignation and called a traitor by many. Pashinyan said he would not resign and later said, "It's not a victory, but there is no defeat."

Vartouhi obtained a copy of the agreement that she was disappointed in but still wanted to report a summary truce provisions.

1. A complete ceasefire and end of all hostilities is to be enforced. All Parties are to stop at their positions. There was no mention of Karabakh's future in the truce.

2. The Ahgdam and Gazakh regions shall be returned to Azerbaijan until November 20, 2020. Shusha (Shushi is Armenian spelling) is to be under Azerbaijan's control.

3. A Russian peace keeping force shall be deployed along the line of contact and the Lachin corridor. Armenia will provide a corridor from Nakhichevan to Azerbaijan that is to be protected by Russian peace keepers.

4. The Russian peace keeping mission shall be deployed in conjunction with the withdrawal of the Armenian forces. The duration of the Russian peace keepers shall be five years. There will be an option at the end of five year by the involved parties.

5. A peace keeping center will be deployed to control the ceasefire. Turkey is to have some involvement in this center.

6. Armenia is to return the Kelbaja region to Azerbaijan November 15, 2020 and the Lachin region by December 1, 2020, leaving behind the Lachin corridor (5 km wide) and at the same time develop a construction plan for a new route from the Lachin corridor to Stepanakert. Azerbaijan will guarantee traffic safety along this route and deployment of Russian peace keepers to protect this route will be determined.

7. Internally displaced persons and refugees who are returning to the territory of Nagorno Karabakh and adjacent areas shall

be under the control of the Office of the United Nations High Commissioner for Refugees.

8. There is an exchange of prisoners of war and other detained persons and bodies of the dead.

9. All economic and transportation links in the region are unblocked. Armenia provides transport links between the western regions of Azerbaijan and the Nakhichevan Autonomous Republic

Vartouhi thought there were a lot of questions both Parties would be concerned with because everything was not real clear. She analyzed two different documents that were not the identical; she consolidated her report from the two. She also did not trust Azerbaijan keeping the truce, although the fact that Russia would be maintaining a peace keeping force would help. She hoped that she was right.

November 9, during one of President Putin's telephone conversations with President Aliyev, the Russian president emphasized that Christian churches and monasteries located in the region should be handled with care. Azerbaijan must ensure that these Christian edifices be protected and not be harmed. Aliyev assured Putin he would abide by his request. When Vartouhi heard about the request and acknowledgement that it would be taken care of, she almost threw-up, "I don't believe it," she gasped at her editor.

November 10, the protests outside and in in parliament continued. One group looking for the prime minister found the President of National Assembly Ararat Mirzoyan (b. 1979) severely beaten. He required two surgeries to regain his health. Seventeen political organizations that did not have a member in the parliament blamed the PM of all the problems demanding his resignation. Another aspect of the mass protest was the resignation of several of Pashinyan's ministers and other government officials, but the PM held his ground.

It did not take long for the blame game to start as different bodies began accusing each other of all kinds of wrong doings. Government officials accused protesters for not joining the war effort and not going to the front. Pashinyan accused the previous government leaders for the bribery and corruption that ate the resources that would have strengthener the military. Some people accused the government of not negotiating seriously and appearing anti-Russian and the accusations went on and on. Vartouhi thought it was sad that so much blame was going on because none of it will bring back the thousands of young soldiers killed during the war. Little did they realize if Turkey had not gotten into the war, we would not have all these problems because Azerbaijan by herself never could have won the war.

November 11, the very next day of the truce signing, Pashinyan admitted he made a mistake. After looking further into status of the negotiations, he had to tell the people the Armenian side was to return five districts without specifying the status of Karabakh or there would be war. There were massive protests of thousands in Yerevan calling for the prime minister's resignation. He made some additional statements on the logic of the situation and what would have happened if the war had happened earlier. However, at this point Vartouhi did not know what her former student could do. She understood the prime minister had no choice in signing the painful document after the Armenian commanders told him, "We had no choice because we would have lost more territory if we kept on fighting and lose many more soldiers." The president of Artsakh carried the same sentiment.

However, what happened is done. Vartouhi in discussions with several militay and civilian experts thought all Armenians should cooperate together to work matters out. There is no room for blame or arguments. Most people should realize the conditions for peace are very vague and that there is still room on the negotiating table. Artsakh is presently under Russian and Armenian control, but people have to return and reoccupy the enclave and encourage more Armenians to inhabit the land. Armenia should try to work more closely with Russia and develop strong diplomatic relations with other nations. The Armenian military has to modernize with more effective weaponry (easier said than done but it is crucial). Armenia has to build alliances with other nations. This was evident when no nation did anything to assist during the war. Russia did after hostilities ceded, but that is not enough. Armenia should realize Diaspora's strength and try to work more closely with it. Most Armenians throughout the world love their mother land and are willing to help. Three hundred million dollars was been raised during the war and the journalist was sure more would be coming when necessary.

November 12, PM Pashinyan addressed the nation again on TV. He again iterated the sorrow in the events of the last few days. He again repeated how the General Staff of the Armed Forces and the president of Artsakh kept reporting every minute counted the war had to be stopped as soon as possible. He elaborated on the battle conditions were at the time and could have got the worse if the fighting continued. He explained the agreements made on the corridors that were opened and guarded by Russian peacekeepers. He talked about the security of Artsakh and the good possibility of the country being recognized internationally. He covered several others topics but ended with a request for unity in the country. He felt this was critical for the nation to go forward. He could not emphasize this enough.

November 14, an assassination attempt was made against PM Pashinyan but was stopped by the Armenian National Security Service (NSS). Several people were arrested. The protests continued on a large scale with PM stating that he will not resign.

November 14, it did not take long for Russian peacekeeper to start moving into Artsakh and with heavy military equipment. Vartouhi thought it looked like an army preparing for battle but she thought it was better to remain silent on this one because she and a lot of other people did not know the intent of the Russians. [At this point I do not think anyone knows the intent of the Russians, even the Russian don't know their own intent right now!].

In any case, the Russian peacekeepers are also camped outside Shushi blocking any entrance or exit from the city. Five hundred Azeri soldiers are already in the city where they have requested a corridor into the city. To date the Russians have not replied. The next day, General Rustam Muradov, commander of the Russian peacekeepers in Artsakh, met with President Arayik Harutyunian that infuriated Azerbaijan and raised concerns about Russia's future role. Vartouhi was sure Shushi was one of the cities that were supposed to be turned over to the Azeri, now she was not sure. In fact, she like everyone else in the region was not sure what was going on. Yet, she did not think the situation could get worse at this time due to Russian peacekeepers being present. She was very confident that many changes would be coming the next few days or weeks. Currently there are all kinds of speculation.

November 15, Armenian cultural, art, and science figures sent a united message to President Putin, President-elect Joseph Biden (b. 1942), President Marcon, UN Secretary Guterress, and UNESCO Director-General Azoulay stating that numerous Armenian historical-cultural monuments of Artsakh are under serious danger. The letter stated, "During these 45 days of war, the Azerbaijani armed forces have deliberately targeted the Armenian historical-cultural monuments. Shushi's Ghazsanchechots Cathedral has been deliberately bombarded with UAVs….Meanwhile the Armenian side has not only preserved, but also renovated the Islamic people's historical monuments both through state, individual and public efforts…." The message continues on to describe what has occurred in Nakhichevan in last few decade where the Azeris have destroyed all vintages of Armenian culture and history. There are no 5840 Khatch Kars, 89 Armenian churches or 22 tombstsones in Nakhichevan, or evidence of the Old Julfa Cemetery that was razed to the ground in from 1998 to 2006. Vartouhi explained that nothing was done to save these treasures of history. The Armenians of Artsakh have been well aware of Moslem destructions and have fought to keep them preserved, but they could use some help.

November 16, "The war is over but the conflict isn't." This was a statement by Jirair Tutunjian (b. c. 1948), an Armenian Canadian journalist, lecturer, and editor who was born in Jerusalem. In an interview with World Geostraegic Ensights, he elaborated on the Azeri Karabakh war and covered many issues that were explained by other experts. He explained how the Azeris were humilitarily defeated three times until President Aliyve went whimpering to Ankara for help. Now the war became a different contest. President Erdogan offered to help by taking over the military operations against the Armenians. Modern lethal weapons, American built F-16 Fighter planes, and Turkish trainers, mercenaries and jihadist from Syria, and high tech killer drones were now utilized in the battle field. The huge input of weapons and illegal manpower was too much for the ethnic Armenians to defend their land. Russia intervened with a peace pact that was literally a crushing defeat for Armenia. In any event, the bloodshed stopped.

The initiation of peace threw Armenia into turmoil. There were clamors for PM Pashiinyan's resignation, accusations of treachery, charges of incompetence, and military unpreparedness. There was a call for unity but no one seemed to be listening. No one can say what is happening in Armenia, or what is going to happen in the near future. Right now, the imposed peace leaves Armenians resentful. That cannot be a recipe for a permanent peace. There has to some recognition of the international community of the history of Artsakh and her rightful place in nations of the world, however small a country she would be.

However, Turkey is now in the picture where European nations and NATO kowtow to Turkey, as Tutunjian points out. He comments, "I really do not understand why the Western nations and NATO are so sympathetic of Turkey. I feel without Western support Turkey would collapse before you could spell Caliph Erdogan. That huge Turkish army would be useless without the economic and military support of the West...and yet Europeans do nothing despite Turkey's insults and threats of the Europeans. Of course, Azerbaijani oil and gas are important to Europe. However, the international community and media remained deaf to Armenia's plight for several reasons. The international public is unfamiliar with the conflict. They framed the conflict is akin a squabble among Lilliputians whose petty affairs had no impact on the world." France is probably the only country that understands all this, but to date she has not been much help.

One other issue is Israel that is also a part of this equation... Azerbaijan has bought close to five billion dollars' worth of armament from Israel including the deadly drones that were so devastating to Artsakh. Israel has also trained Azeri soldiers and Aliyev's bodyguards. Israel also uses Azerbaijan as a window to spy on Iran. Israel gets 40% of her energy from Azerbaijan.

When any country and world scholars bring up the Armenian Genocide, Israel turns her face and caters to the Turkish denial. Israel is buddy-buddy with Turkey except when some question comes up on the Palestinians. She also forgets the riots and protests the Turks have against the Jews and Christians. Turkish mobs go crazy and wild when they have an opportunity to bash and destroy Armenian and Jewish shops whenever they can. Israel takes the position that that Jews have been the only people who have had such a devastating history. Many Jews in America and in other countries do not recognize Israeli policy on the Genocide much to Israel's displeasure. But that's another story.

Another Armenian Canadian Dr. Arshavir Gundjian (b. 1936), prominent scientist and Armenian community leader, researcher and inventor, retired professor of Electrical Engineering at McGill University, and high powered laser technology also has some comments on the war. He believes the main cause of losing the war is the lack of highly sophisticated modern military weaponry. The Turkish/Azeri war literally was much too overwhelming against the Armenians. Gundjian believes if we had the necessary lethal weaponry, the outcome would have been altogether different. He points out a few other concerns as some of the have done and are continuing to do.

Gundjian believes all is not lost. He thinks Armenia could and should regain the Soviet Union status of what it was in that period [Armenia was the known as the Silicon Valley of the USSR], but lost that prominence due to neglect or the nation just thought she had too many other problems to solve. Now we have seen the outcome. Regrettably, Armenia was one of the leaders in lasers (light amplification by stimulated emission of radiation), far ahead of any of her neighbors that went ahead with the technology. Armenia has the brain power to regain her eminence in this knowhow but has to have the determination to develop it. If Armenia had it, she could have blown the Turkish and Israeli drones out of sky and in their initiating positions. Gundjian goes on to explain the mechanics of lasers and how they can be use in almost any industry. Vartouhi wanted to point out that Armenia currently has had promoters who have stressed teaching and development of the electronics and lasers, but were not strong enough or convincing enough to get the government to work in this direction. Maybe the "Fourth Republic" will see its potential.

November 17, in an interview with President Putin, a question came up on the issue of Turkish participation the peacekeeping operation, he remarked, "As for the peacekeeping mission, it is true that Azerbaijan and Turkey kept speaking about the possibility of Turkish involvement in peacekeeping operations. I believe I eventually managed to convince our Azerbaijani colleagues that we should not create conditions or motives for undermining our agreements which could provoke the parties to take extreme measures or actions. I am referring to the bitter legacy of the past, the tragic and bloody events that took place during the First World War, the Genocide." Vartouhi saw where Putin visualized the political potential of the "Genocide" to convince Azerbaijan not to involve Turkey. Could he do the same with Erdogan? Vartouhi doubted it. Putin has stated several times that they still have much work to do and Foreign Minister Livor has indicated the Minsk Group would be finalizing the peace agreement.

As far as the internal situation in Armenia is concerned, Putin stated that it is necessary for the country to unite, not to divide. He thinks accusations against the prime minister is baseless. "There are no grounds for treason."

November 18, the Turkish parliament granted President Erdogan permission to send a force of peacekeeper to Azerbaijan. There was some question about the use of soldiers as monitors of cease fire and that they had to be Ankara appointees. Vartouhi thought this was only one of the many provisions of the truce that was nebulous. However, she was thankful the provision for 2000 Russian peacekeepers was clear.

November 18, following the devastating defeat of the Armenians from the war, PM Pashinyan presented a six-month roadmap if he still remains in power. He outlined 15 steps that follow:

1. Restart the Nagorno Karabakh peace process in the format of the OSCE Minsk process.
2. Return the people of Karabakh to their homes and help them in the restoration process.
3. Provide a provision of social guarantees for the families of killed servicemen and citizens.

4. Restore residential and public structures and infrastructure damaged during the war in the territory of the Republic of Armenia.
5. Provide social guarantees, prosthetics and professional training for servicemen with disabilities.
6. Provide social guarantees for the families of "soonest return" of captured soldiers and civilians and quick clarification of the fate of missing soldiers.
7. Provide a system of psychological rehabilitation of the individuals who took part in the war and society in general.
8. Approve and launch the Reform Program for the Armed Forces.
9. Overcoming the corona virus pandemic and eliminating its consequences.
10. Restore the environment for economic activity.
11. Revitalize programs for solving demographic problems.
12. Amend the Electoral Code and adopt new a law on [political] parties.
13. Introduce the institution of professional judges as the first step in establishing an anti-corruption court. Implement the law of confiscation of illegal property.
14. Hold regular thematic consultations with representatives of the Armenian political community and civil society.
15. Hold regular thematic consultations with Armenian organizations and individuals of Diaspora involvement of the above processes.

Vartouhi thought these 15 undertakings were simple enough but still required a tremendous amount of work and cooperation. She felt the prime minister had to convince the public that these procedures are feasible and if carried out would benefit the nation and citizens. Azad thought Pashinyan was too late for him to bring these about. "He should have thought about these a lot earlier," he said to his mother. Simon agreed him and thought PM should resign.

November 19, Vartouhi read an article, "Artsakh's Military Disaster and the Writings All Over the Wall," by Konstantin von Eggert (b.

1964), a well-known and respected Russian journalist, political analyst, and communications consultant. She was intrigued by his knowledge of what has been going on and the potential future. She felt she had to call him for an interview. His first comment was, "Russia and Azerbaijan were in full agreement dismembering Artsakh, but dividing the spoils of war will inescaply pave the way for more military hostilities." It was a disturbing introduction but she continued asking questions

She asked "Did Russian intelligence know about the impeding attack and why didn't Putin say anything to Baku about what his intelligence knew?"

"Yes, they knew about the impending attack and knew Turkey and Israel were to be a part of it [Israel by training Azeri fighting personnel and providing all kinds of lethal military equipment]. Their combined military maneuvers were signs that they were preparing for war."

"Didn't Armenia and Russia do the same?" Vartouhi asked.

"Yes, but it was a big pretentious farce. They did nothing to ward off the Azerbaijani/ Turkish surprise attack"

"Couldn't the Armenians defend themselves from the Azeri/Turkish "blitzkrieg" surprise attack?"

"Under the circumstances and the intelligence that was deprived to the Armenians, no, they had no hope for any kind of victory. Your Head of Defense Forces HQ of Armenia Colonel-General Onik Gasparyan (b. 1970) determined what was going on and that he also saw that the Armenian forces were inadequate to fight off the combined Turkish and Azeri attack even though Armenian soldiers were brave and courageous fighters. The Turkish and Israeli drones were free to execute the high destruction because the Russian electronic defense mechanism systems were not adequate enough to knock them all down. The President of Artsakh also saw if they kept on fighting, more land would be lost and more of your soldiers would be killed."

"Wasn't Prime Minister Pashinyan aware of all this?"

"Yes, because Col. Gen. Gasparyan told your PM and others in the government, but nothing much was done. In fact an actual quote was, 'Our opponent is no longer only Azerbaijan, but also Turkey. Therefore, Armenia cannot effectively confront the joint military potential of these states and it is necessary to direct all the political and diplomatic potential to avoid, or at least postpone the war.' I think the general's warnings were quite clear but no one seemed to be listening or they were just ignoring what I told them." Another significant issue that von Eggert brought up was the use of Asymmetrical Warfare that Vartouhi was not familiar with. She asked, "What is Asymmetrical warfare?"

"Basically it is warfare used by a less powerful force against a power that is more formidable, or guerilla warfare. Armenians have used the technique many times in the past to fight off more commanding armies. Gen. Gasparyan could have utilized the principles of Asymmetrical Warfare, or at least thought about it. But he did not and we all know the outcome." Other issues were discussed allowing Varouhi to understand that the war in the beginning was rather useless because Turkey now had a strong input to the operations. The reporter made a mental note to herself that she would talk to warfare experts to learn more about Asymmetrical Warfare.

November 20, Azeri forces occupied Aghdam after Armenian troops left the city. Plans were in place for the other Azeri forces to do the same to other agreed upon cities. However, there was about how the Russians and Turkish peacekeepers were fulfilling their assignments. Vartouhi this was only one problem on the overall picture.

November 21, Additional news from Washington was the call for $100 million in US assistance to prevent humanitarian disaster, reengineer the OSCS Minsk Group negotiation process, and end the sale of arms to Ankara and Baku. In addition some members of Congress have called for more sanctions against Turkey and Azerbaijan. Vartouhi thought it was great what the US Congress was doing in contrast to what President Trump has done. She was well aware that the president owned several large pieces of property in Istanbul and Baku so that may have something to do with reluctance to help Armenia and Artsakh.

November 21, Vartouhi was assigned a follow-up to interview some Armenians in questionable Artsakh zones as a part of the truce agreement. She was hoping it was clearer in what was known in Yerevan. But she discovered it was just as bad because many of the Armenians who remained in Artsakh had no idea if the land they occupied still belonged to them or was to be transferred to Azerbaijan.. Questioning the leaders of the local communities was in the same predicament. They had no idea what they could tell their citizens on what the status of the provisions were. There was a great deal of confusion and anxiety over the new borders.

November 25, French Senate voted 305 to 1 to adopt a resolution calling for the recognition of the independence of the Republic of Artsakh. The resolution not only declares Artsakh independence, it condemned the military aggression of Azerbaijan against the people of Nagorno Karabakh and that Azerbaijan has been supported by the Turkish authorities using jihadist and mercenaries. The resolution also called for the withdrawal of Azerbaijani armed forces from the territories occupied after September 27, 2020 and for providing massive humanitarian aid to the civilian population of Artsakh. Other measures called out included an international investigation into the war crimes against the civilian population including weapons prohibited by international law. Other condemnations were specified that Azerbaijan denounced as a "piece of paper adopted to serve narrow political ambitions."

November 28, the Army Science Board Military (ABS Military) reported some startling and disturbing news that Vartouhi ran across. The ASB Military is a highly respected and edifying US government organization that provides information to the army with advice and recommendations on matters relating to the Army's scientific, technological, manufacturing, and logistics, as well as any other information the Secretary of the Army deems necessary. In this case, the data Vartouhi discovered was "what's going on in the Karabakh/ Azeri War." First of all, the document reports that 87% of Google search results show misinformation and propaganda. It reports one video of an Armenian soldier killing a captured Azeri soldier on the battlefield. There was nothing else in that area that was caught on camera.

Looking at 40 videos of Azeris committing war crimes was another story. They were mostly videos of war crimes that included executions of civilians and soldiers, decapitations, torture, mutilations, abuse, humiliation, and cluster bombings of civilian settlements. One video that was extremely upsetting was the beheading of an Armenian civilian and placing his body on a dead pig. The Azeri soldier approached the body and placed his boot on the civilian's stomach pressing down to cause blood to squirt out the man's decapitated neck. Another soldier picked up the head and also placed on the pig adjusting it to get desired camera angles. Other Azeri soldiers were laughing while all this was going on. The horrible act that took place was a common occurrence against civilians and soldiers. The scene was sickening when Vartouhi saw it on tape.

More wide spread than the inhumane tactics of the Azeris were the interaction and complexity among the USA, Turkey, Israel, Azerbaijan, and Iran. These countries were a part of the inclusive action in one way or another. The report asked, "How was the US involved?" The complex answer starts with – "the USA's current Number One enemy is Iran. It is a well-known fact that Turkey was directing the Azeri Army, the jihad mercenaries and terrorists telling President Aliyev what to do. President Erdogan got the green light from President Putin and the US did not tell Turkey not to have maneuvers with the Azeris or to stop American arms shipments to Turkey. The thinking - Turkey is a NATO ally and we should help her with war material. NATO is led and is largely financed by the US. Other not so well-known facts are that Azerbaijan has assisted the US and Israel with espionage campaigns on Iran and has allowed Israel's Mossad permission to run operations from Azeri territory. This relationship has further allowed either Israeli agents or paid mercenaries to sneak into Iran and assassinate Mohsen Fakhrizade (1958-2020), the "Soleimani of Iran's nuclear sector" and the top scientist in the nation.[Oasem Soleimani 1957-2020) was another Iranian major general who was killed by a US drone on January 3, 2020)]. Fakhrizade was considered the most prominent and important Iranian nuclear scientist in the region.

In the evening Simon and Vartouhi discussed much of the above scenario and how it was related to Israel's involvement and major weapons support to Azerbaijan and the country's closeness to Iran. Simon pointed out that Israel also ignores the Armenian Genocide and does not concern herself over the Genocide that Turkey and Azerbaijan are transgressing today. Israel wants oil and Azerbaijan is an opportune launching pad where she can conduct espionage operations into Iran. He told his wife, "No one is interested in Armenia; nations are only interested in their own welfare. You think Russia is concerned about Armenia? She is more disturbed about Turkey getting a better foothold in our sub-Caucasus and has managed to do that by aiding Azerbaijan. Russia has succeeded in getting her peacekeepers involved, but I don't think we have seen the end of that intricacy. At the overall cost of hurting Iran, the US, Israel, and Turkey has enabled Genocide against the Armenia people. I'm afraid to think what is going to happen next even though we have a peace pact now?"

December 1, by the beginning of December Russian peacekeepers and Azeri soldiers were occupying their relative assignments. However it was not clear for every position. It was especially difficult for civilians because they had no reliable information as to what is going to happen in each of their villages. Thousands burned their homes and left Artsakh. The same was true for the Azeris as many of them left Azerbaijan and returned to their past residences. The situation in Shushi was particularly questionable because the original agreement stated that the city would be occupied by the Azeris. Five hundred Azeri soldiers are there now, but they cannot leave the city or no one can enter unless they were approved by the Russian peacekeepers who are camped outside the city. Catholicos Karekin II (b. 1951) is especially concerned because the Ghazanchetsots (Holy Savor) Cathedral is in Shushi and the Azeris have not displayed any respect to Armenian sanctuaries. In fact, they have bombed the cathedral twice and have done worse by making it a practice to destroy whenever they have the opportunity to do so. Supposedly President Aliyev told President Putin his troops would be careful regarding churches and monuments. Vartouhi did not believe his words and the evidence showed it.

On December 1, Azeri troops entered the Lachin District that Armeia surrendered to the Azeris but soon left due to the peace agreement. Russian peacekeeper would assure the 3.5 mile corridor remains open. A few villages near the corridor would remain Armenian.

December 3, the French National Assembly joined the Senate to call for the recognition of Artsakh independence. Hopefully, other countries would be following suite.

Last month US Congressman Adam Schiff (b. 1960) stated that we (Congress) are prepared to recognize the Republic of Artsakh as an independent nation if Azerbaijan and Turkey persist in violence instead of embracing a peaceful settlement. Vartouhi did not know if the congressman introduced any bill to congress even though the Azeris and Turks disdisplay the violence and more the congressman was talking about.

December 3, Azerbaijan reported at least 2787 soldiers were killed in the 44-Day War with ethnic Armenians in Artsakh. Another 100 are missing. This the first time the Azeris reported their battle deaths. Armenia believes the number is more like 7630 Azeri and mercenaries deaths. The Armenian defense minister reported the loss of 2996 troops. Vartouhi pointed out that both sides undermine the numbers because they do not like to report casualties.

December 3, Philippe Raffi Kalfayan, the expert on international law, wrote an article that addressed much to what has been occurring. Vartouhi got a hold of the document so that she could write an article on it. The first thing she noticed was that there was a lot of finger pointings as to Armenia's loss from the war. Of course, this was true of many other people who now were smarter than before the war. But she wanted to see what the expert had to say. He claimed that he talked to PM Pashinyan several months ago when Armenia had the upper hand in her relationship with Azerbaijan. Kalfayan asserted that Armenia was in a position where she could have returned the captured territories to Azerbaijan and that she would regain her independence and the free passage through the Lachin corridor. Pashinyan did not care for the idea.

Before Russia initiated the peace pact, Kalfayan came up with another idea. He sent an October 30 letter to Pashinyan that include three main points;

1. Stop the war as soon as possible.
2. Visit Moscow as soon as possible to request President Putin to intervene between Armenia and Azerbaijan.
3. Install a war cabinet of a small team of experienced people from different political forces until the war and negotiations end up.

All these sounded simple enough, but maybe too simple. How come the Minsk Group did not think of these ideas? He claimed Armenia was too confident that they could hold off an Azeri attack and they did very well for a while, but she never anticipated that Turkey would be taking over the reins of an Azeri offensive, which the Turks did. Armenia was no match for Turkey's contribution to the war. Vartouhi was glad Russia at least stopped the carnage. Another point Kalfayan made was that Armenia should have recognized Artsakh's independence long ago, but Armenia said it would have interfered with the Minsk Group Process. Putin said why would other countries proclaim Artsakh independent when Armenia did not? Good point the reporter thought.

December 5, Prime Minister Pashinyan gave a speech telling Artsakh Armenians they would be receiving financial aid to return to their homes and compensation for veterans who served during the war.

December 10, Russian peacekeepers reported a violation of the cease fire in the Gadrut region. The Russian defense minister did not assign blame, but the Armenians claimed the Azeri military launched the attack. Other attacks were reported in additional areas. The confrontations did not surprise Vartouhi because the Azeris were usually the ones who broke the ceasefire agreements in the past, but this may be a different case due to the Armenians countering Azeri aggression on civilians. The situation as it now stands is extremely vulnerable due to how the peace agreement was established. As mentioned previously, civilians know very little if they can stay in their own homes or feel to villages that are to be occupied by only Armenians. The Armenian military is not much better situations where they may be occupying village, but the town is surrounded completely by Azeri forces. We are yet to see how the Russian peacekeepers are going to cope with this serious dilemma.

One other problem Russia and Turkey have is the installation of a Turkish military post in Azerbaijan. The two powers already agreed to set up a joint center in the region to monitor the ceasefire, but Turkey also wants its own independent post for influence in the region. Russia thinks it is unnecessary. Both parties agreed to continue the talks in Moscow. Vartouhi thinks Turkey wants to get a stronger footing in the region. "There's going to be a lot more disagreements between Moscow and Ankara before this whole mess is straightened out."

December 10, Baku had its victory parade today where President Aliyev brazenly called out Yerevan (Iravan), Zangezur (Zangazur), and Sevan (Goycha) historical Azerbaijani lands followed by President Erdogan praising Enver Pasha. Vartouihi was not surprised by the speeches as the continuous fabrications flowed from their lips. Aliyev especially blatantly talking like he was responsible for the victory where he never would have won if Turkey did not take over the Azeri military and Erdogan bragging about Enver Pasha who was one of prime perpetrators of the Armenian Genocide. But the falsehoods continued; Vartouhi told her husband, "I guess it was the Nazi who said, 'If you tell a lie long enough and with strong conviction, people will believe what you say.'"

After the parade ended, Erdogan claimed the Armenians burnt down their own churches. Vartouhi could not let that wording pass, "How ridiculous can you be to make a statement like that. Who would believe it? Yes, the exiting Armenians burnt their homes because they didn't want the Azeris to live in them." Another fairytale the Azeri president came up with was, "Create a six state grouping for peace in the South Caucasus and Armenia could join it alongside Russia, Turkey, Azerbaijan, and Georgia, but only if Yerevan fulfills its responsibilities related to such a platform." When the journalist heard this remark, she just made a disparaging look.

One other concern is the concluding remarks by the two Muslim presidents when they implied a Genocide may be on the way. Our journalist thought this may be a test to determine what the international community would think. She was confident if an added Genocide was started, there would be a huge clamor, but not by the two cocky leaders implying Genocide. She was not sure. Armenia should go on a diplomatic and educational campaign to alert the international public about the potential deadly disaster. Currently, the only nation in the way of Turkey's dream of her Turian state is Armenia.

December 11, Azeri forces as customarily again, broke the ceasefire and attacked the southern Hadrut villages of Hin Tagher and Khtsabert injuring three Armenian soldiers and taking one civilian captive. "Why are they taking civilians captive?" Vartouhi asked the Armenian defense minister.

"I have no idea except, I do know they sometimes take prominent civilians captive and ask for huge ransoms. It's a common practice with them," was his response.

December 13, Armenia and Azerbaijan finally started their prisoner exchange. A Russian plane carrying 44 Armenian prisoner landed in Yerevan's Erebuni airport. It was not clear if the cargo included both soldiers and civilians, but the Armenian defense minister stated that additional information would be forthcoming. The Azerbaijan government agency did not report on the number of Azeris who were returned home.

December 14, the United States imposed sanctions on Turkey for the acquisition of the Russian S-400 air defense systems further complicating the already strained relations between Washington and Ankara. Turkey refused for over a year, pleas from the US to reverse the decision but continued to ignore the Washington requests. The US had no choice but to impose the sanctions. Both parties in the US Congress hailed the sanctions with many members stating the step should have been taken long ago. Turkey condemned the sanctions as a "grave mistake" and urged Washington to reverse the "unjust decision." Ankara in its usual response to similar problems suggested forming a joint working group with the US and NATO to resolve the issue. The US did not comment on the suggestion.

Vartouhi in an interview with the Armenian defense minister both agreed that the sanctions should have been imposed months earlier when Azerbaijan starting using American built F-16 fighter planes in the Turkish Air Force in the war assisting Artsakh. The defense minister told the reporter that was not the only reason for the US to impose sanctions; Turkey hired mercenaries, jihadists, and used American built munitions to support the Azeri battle against the Armenians. The US congress saw a lot of these transgressions, but the US administration had a blind eye to the aggressive actions and the use of US arms.

December 14, on the very same day, Washington imposed sanctions on Turkey. Ankara again condemned the penalties threatened to retaliate over the move. Turkey repeated the action would harm ties between the NATO allies a "grave mistake." Turkey's foreign minister again brought up having a joint working group to allay the US concerns. Vartouhi told her husband, "What's there to discuss? Turkey violates the trust America gives to her then purchases weapons that can be utilized against US allies. Turkey further said she required the arms to fight terrorism. What terrorism? The terrorists and jihadists Erdogan brought into Azerbaijan to fight the Armenians? No, I don't think Turkey has much to condemn."

December 17, President Putin announced at a news conference, "The next stage in the armistice is normalization of the entire region." Vartouhi did not think the extent of the normalization was not clear as many of the conditions and statements in the peace pact. There are all kinds of ideas floating around, yet many of them are nebulous. "We have a lot to be determined, understood, and then eventually agreed to.

December 21. Vartouhi ran across a PBS Newshour report by journalist Simon Ostrovsky (b. 1981) who wrote on the Artsakh conflict. It was an interesting account, especially because he is a dual Israeli American citizen. He wrote about an Azeri soldier desecrating the body of an Armenian soldier and how destructive the Azeri military was. This was nothing new to Vartouhi because she heard it many times from the Armenian soldiers. Ostrosvsky did not see any Armenian soldiers dismembering any Azeris. He reported that the Turkish drones played a big part in fighting. He wrote nothing about the numerous Israeli drones. He noted the speeches by Aliyev and Erdogan where they spewed out their hate messages and Azeri president word that all people will be able to live in security. Vartouhi thought this statement was a farce due to their history on how they treat Armenians.

December 21, PM Pashinyan made a visit to Syunik Provence but was cut short by protestors. He was able to pay tribute to the soldiers who were killed during the war and buried in a cemetery in Sisian. The protests forced the prime minister to shorten his visit. Armenia army units withdrew from the area west of the border despite protests from by local residents. The locals believed the Azeri troops were much too close to their towns. There also was a question about the road from Goris to Kapan where a few sections straddled into Azeri territory. The Armenian Defense Minister and National Security Service (NSS) assured the locals the road would remain open. The Armenian Defense Minister also made a statement that Russian border guards deployed in Syunik will guarantee its security. All of this sounded great to Vartouh,i but interviews with the locals indicated they were not comfortable with what they were hearing. Pashinyan cancelled other visits he was planning to Goris, Kapan, and other Syunik towns, because the protest movements were too strong so he returned to Yerevan.

Novemberk 23, grandmaster Levon Aronian (b. 1982) won a playoff chess match with India's top player to win the presistigous Tata Steel Blitz. He dedicated his victory to Armenia, to all compatriots who fell on the battlefield and to all who struggle for the Armenian nation. Unfortunously, he was unable to attend the European Team Championship held at the same time. Unfortunously, the Armenian team members did not walk off with any championship, but they won quite a few of their matches.

December, 25, PM Pashinyan invited parliamentary members and an extra parliamentary force to hold consultation on the issue of holding a snap election in 2021. He said he was ready to step down only on the decision of the people. He also said he was prepared to continue to lead Armenia in case the people reaffirmed his trust in this hard period.

Chapter 10

Armenia and Artsakh Start Rebuilding, 2021 to Present

2021

January 1, Armenia would love to erase the horror of 2020 and put it to bed. The country would like to look forward to 2021, but at this point the situation does look bleak. Armenian lost the war with Azerbaijan and Turkey and the peace process is in turmoil. Armenians have no assurance of what is going to happen next or what they can do now. There are numerous protests calling for PM Pashinyan's resignation, but he refuses to do so, "Let the people decide," is his answer. Many called him a traitor, which Vartouhi did not think was fair. Maybe it could be called incompetence, but he did get rid of the oligarchs and corruptors of the republic. He did chase the oligarchs out of the country with their capital, yet with nothing coming in to replace the resources they possessed.

The corona virus has played havoc in Armenia just as it has in other nations in the world. Armenian opposition political forces continually claim that Pashinyan did not manage the proper conditions to stem its spread. Many believe the Armenian healthcare system has collapsed. There is confusion and anxiety over the new borders. Inhabitants of Artsakkh do not know if they can remain in their homes or have to move. Another item the PM has learned during all this chaos is that it's a good idea to work closely with Russia. He realizes that the country is pretty well divided on this issue, but he now feels that it is imperative to keep good relations with the "big brother" in the north.

Currently, what does all this mean for Armenia? However in the confusion, finger pointing, the blame game, and allegation conditions continue. Armenia could be in a worse catastrophe than she is now. There is no question that Armenia did not have enough military strength to fight off the Turkish/Azeri blitzkrieg. [Who knew Turkey would be one of strong participants?] The army has to regroup, acquire more modern weapons, and the government has to start functioning again with sturdy relations with helpful countries. Let them realize what Turkish full aims are and inform them how much participation they had in the war. Russia has her own goals in this overall scenario, but we have no choice to work closely with her. The citizens have to realize that they have to have the will to work together. The question of Turkish peacekeepers in the area is still in limbo; Turkey thinks it's okay. Russia says no. What is going to happen there?

With regard to suggestions on what to do about the future, Raffi Bedrosyan (), a Toronto civil engineer, concert pianist, and writer endorsed several ideas. His main theme was to strengthening Diaspora's role in its relationship with the motherland. The war demonstrated how much financial and humanitarian aid can be generated. He feels that the Diaspora can also supply technical, scientific, and economic resources. Diaspora communities conducted massive demonstrations and protests in major cities all over the world, denouncing Azerbaijan and Turkey for their aggressive and inhuman actions. A few of the measures he proposed were to have diaspora Armenians even in the government, re-establish a Ministry of Diaspora, have an exchange program of high school and college students emphasizing cultural and technical interactions, and other programs. Vartouhi thought other experts also proposed ideas that Armenia should at least think about.

January 5, another faultfinder in the loss of the war was Tatul Hakobyan (b. 1969), journalist, lecturer, author, and analyst, who added his name to the list of the critics on the conflict. He thinks Nikol Pashinyan is the primary cause of losing the war but he also blames many others, past and present personalities. These included cronies, political supporter, cheerleaders in the Diaspora, and the Armenian Apostolic Church. He even puts blame on Artsakh President Arayik Harutyunyan and a few of Armenia's past leaders who in hindsight had opportunities to establish winning situations but did nothing. Hagobyan talks about the myth of victory in 1994 and the mismanagement of how we abused that victory in thinking that Armenia was undefeatable. The journalist talks about corruption in Armenia and Karabakh as contributing to losing the war. Another report claims Pashinyan did away with corruption. Who is one to believe when we have conflicting reports? He does not say anything about Turkey's entrée into the war and the real cause of the defeat. He thinks the trilateral agreements of November 6, 2020, will help to fathom the depth of our own ignorance and eventually pave the way for a more equitable solution to the nations of the region. Vartouhi hopes he is right but he does not have the confidence that the present administration will turn out favorably for Armenia.

January 11, following talks in the Kremlin, Presidents Putin and Aliyev, and PM Pashinyan signed a joint statement on the development of Karabakh. Both Pashinyan and Aliyev received hugs from Putin as they entered the room where the two sub-Caucasus area leaders only nodded to each other. According to Putin, the plan for the implementation of the agreement will be presented by the deputy prime ministers of the three countries. This will lead to a trilateral working group that will deal with the restoration of economic, trade and transport links, as well as the opening of borders. The three leaders declared the following (Vartouhi summarized the information):

- A tripartite Working Group would work to unblock all economic and transportation routes in the region.
- The Working Group will hold the first meeting until January 30, 2022, based on the progress that is being made and monitoring its headway. Agreement among the Republic of Azerbaijan, the Republic of Armenia, and Federation of Russia is hereby referenced as the Parties.

- In order to implement the directions of activity, the–chairs of the Working Group will approve the composition of the expert subgroups and will present a list of projects with the approval of the Parties.
- The Working Group by March 1, 2022, will submit for approval at the highest level by the Parties a list and a schedule for the implementation of measures involving the restoration and construction of the new transport infrastructure facilities between Armenia and Azerbaijan.

Pashinyan thanked Putin for the effort he is investing by restoring the stability and security within the region and in resolving the Nagorno Karabakh conflict. He stated there are still many issues to be solved mainly are the status of Nagorno Karabakh and the exchange of war prisoners. He further stated that Armenia is ready to continue negotiations within the frameworks of the OSCE Minsk Group. Near the end of the meeting Pashinyan said, "I hope that we will continue to advance. I would like to emphasize once again that the most important issues for us at the moment are humanitarian issues, concerns of exchange of prisoners of war, which are provided for in paragraph 8 of our joint statement of November 10."

On the issue of POWs, Pashinyan brought up that Azerbaijan has been delinquent on this concern and has come up with all kinds of excuses that really deny the intent of the original agreement. Aliyev, in his usual arrogant character and conceit, has gone so far as to make a ridiculous claim that the Armenian POWs are like terrorists. It probably is a good thing he did not make that claim in front of Pashinyan. The PM is sure the Azeri president is trying to fabricate an excuse or formulate a justification for not returning the POWs. Pashinyan did not say anything about the cruel and inhuman treatment, and even torture, the Azeris exert on prisoners and civilians. Maybe it would be appropriate to throw these facts into the face of Aliyev, but the PM was sure the Azeri dictator would deny it.[Azerbaijani treatment is not only cruel, inhumane, and illegal but also cannot continue to be tolerated in the 22nd century by civilized nations.] The Geneva Convention III has a lengthy document on the POW issues where all nations are expected to comply. Azerbaijan has not been adhering to it.

Aliyev's concern is the construction of the road that is to be routed between Nakhichevan and Azerbaijan through southern Armenia. This of course in the eyes of Turkey is the initial start of a Turian state across southeastern Asia. Armenia before the war was the only country that was in her way. There is even talk about the construction of additional railways in the region. Pashinyan thought the POW issue should have priority over the road issue. Vartouhi thought the PM should have emphasized the POW issue more strongly. Other issues as well are still unanswered or solved. She also said they discussed the transportation and road issue with no clear determination, but with a lot of potential ideas. Vartouhi thought Edmond Azadian (b.), a well-known and prolific writer on the Armenian and Artsakh issues and concerns, summarized the meeting fittingly. Azadian commented, "The speeches following the signing of the document sounded like three deaf people had spoken to each other."

January 11, President Putin called for a trilateral meeting among PM Pashinyan, President Aliyev, and himself in Moscow. He wanted to discuss the solution of humanitarian problems, and the protection of cultural heritage sites. Azerbaijan admitted that she had taken 62-"terrorist" prisoners, but Armenia disputed that claim. There are no Armenian terrorist; they are all Armenian soldiers. Pashinyan made it a point that Azerbaijan has not returned the POWs as agreed to at the November 9 meeting. There was talk on the establishment of automobile and rail communication to ensure international shipping across Armenian and Azerbaijan. There was no talk of a "corridor" between the two countries nor the status of Nagorno Karabakh..

January 11, in Armenia on the same day as the tripartite meeting, President Armen Sarkessian penned a fresh article about the inevitability of building a substantive state and the way to restore the country's strength. He dealt on the nation's past, its glories and tribulations and that we still can overcome the current situation as we have done in the past, "Today, we are experiencing yet another moment of all-national psychological depression. We will be able to overcome it and establish new principles to build our future depending on us only." He thinks we all are accountable for our problems…"Just like before, we are looking for special footholds and 'rescuers' – individuals or countries who will be able to take us in the right direction which will ultimately lead to prosperity and security. In this frantic search, we completely forget that this path is in front of our eyes and is called the independent Republic of Armenia." He explains how we obtained our independence after five centuries but we did not lay the foundation of public administration among the executive, legislatives, and judicial branches. He also pointed to other anomalies.

"In 1994 Armenia liberated Artsakh. Within a nearly two decade period, she failed to negotiate a permanent independence. She did not pay enough attention to Artsakh's developement and growth, strengthening military operations, and acted like there were no serious challenges ahead. Armenia felt like it was a victorious nation. Now they ask, "Who am I now?" Sarkessiam continued, "We had only managed to deceive ourselves, and thus had already signed the defeat statement. Our government has to acknowledge we have a deep political, economic, social and psychological crisis. Citizens have every moral right to demand concrete, meaningful answers on the way-out of the crisis. The president called for the amending the Electoral Code and Constitution and balancing the three branches of government." He called the "Third Republic of Armenia" a thing of the past, and that we are facing a new reality that forces us to be very sober, accountable, and purposeful. "We can call reform a 'New Pages start,' 'A New Beginning' or 'The Fourth Republic.'"

Sarkessian continued, "The change of power in 2018 could have been a new phase of our history. We had sufficient ground for people's unification, enthusiasm, and support, but no offering of a new ideology. The 'Fourth Republic' must become the new ideology. Emphasis will be placed on the quality of the state, which requires a radical overhaul of the system of interrelation without compatriots among the world. Geopolitical, perceptions, politics, economy, security, military-industrial complex, medicine, science, and education are created by people, and today we are in dire need of the best specialists."

After dinner last night, Simon and Vartouhi were discussing the president's report. Simon said he didn't think it was much different than others who analyze "after the fact." [It's called Monday morning quarter backing in America.]

January 18, at a Moscow press conference with Russian Foreign Minister Sergei Lavrov, he stated the status of Nagorno Karabakh remains unresolved. It must be subject of future Armenian-Azerbaijani negotiations and the OSCE Minisk Group accords. In the meantime, he stressed, the territory will be protected by Russian peacekeepers. The issue of POWs came up again where Armenian human rights activists accused Azerbaijan of refusing to cooperate with Russia and the International Committee of the Red Cross (ICRC) in the process of exchanging POWs. Whenever the question comes up Azerbaijan always has some kind of ridiculous excuse.

Three day earlier in a related manner, Armenian Foreign Ministry spokeswoman Anna Naghdalyan asked whether there are prerequisites for humanitarian programs? She commented, "The Armenian side has always supported humanitarian contracts between the societies of the region, which should be based on mutual respect and tolerance and be aimed at creating mutual trusts. Certainly, relevant prerequisites should be established for such a program." She noted that the Azeris have not demonstrated a willingness to follow such a program by creating obstacles of the repatriation of Armenian POWs, issuing a stamp glorifying the ethnic cleansing of Armenians, as well as President Aliyev's threats attesting to the fact Azerbaijan is challenging the trust building efforts of international mediators. She also questioned Aliyev's provocative statements declaring a "war prize and symbol of victory" after considerable damage to Shushi's Holy Savior Church. There were no reported answers to her questions.

Associated with the POW issue is the humanitarian violations that Azerbaijan has been practicing with Armenian captives. There is increasing evidence of gruesome atrocities including murder, torture, mutilation, and other cruel treatments being committed by Azerbaijani forces against prisoners as well as civilians. There even have been video news releases of Arzeri soldiers bragging and laughing as their fellow comrades were killing, torturing, and mutilating prisoners. There is no question that these atrocities are illegal, but are grave violation of international human rights law and international humanitarian laws. To date, the Azeri soldiers have gotten away with these barbarian tactics, but hopefully; there will be a judgment day. There is no question that Baku should be held accountable for these violations.

January 19, the trial of President Robert Kocharyan and three other former officials facing coup charges resumed today. The trial was delayed for four months due to the Karabakh War.

January 22, the European Parliament strongly condemned Turkey's "destabilizing role" in the Karabakh conflict. The EU accused Ankara of sending thousands of "jihadist and terrorist fighters" to the conflict zone and called for an end to Turkish military aid to Azerbaijan. The parliament passed two resolutions; one called for the continuation of the Karabakh settlement peace accord of the Minsk Group and stressed the "urgent need" to ensure the security of the Armenian population and its cultural heritage in Nagorno Karabakh. The resolution also deplored "the transfer of foreign terrorist fighters by Turkey from Syria and elsewhere to Nagorno Karabakh, as confirmed by international actors including the OSCE Minsk Group Co-Chair countries." Turkey as usual denied sending members of Turkish–backed Syrian rebel groups and Azerbaijan have done the same for the presence of mercenaries. Vartouhi does not see how the two aggressors can deny such claims when the Armenians have actually captured such belligerents. Turkish denials are literally insulting when it is so evident she is not telling the truth. She wondered how the EU comes up with all these accusations but really does nothing to punish the belligerents.

In addition to all the above, Azerbaijan violated some of the Minsk Group's core principles. One was, there is to be no military solution to the conflict, but the Azeris sure demonstrated some violent military actions, and the other was for the Azeri aggressiveness_not to assume that "territorial integrity" is the answer to the Nagorno Karabakh question. The Minsk Group is accertain of that decision.

Other events are currently occurring in America that certainly will affect Armenia. Joe Biden (b. 1942), the new US president, has a different look toward Turkey than the one Donald Trump had. His policy sounds more like the EU resolutions that were just initiated. Biden has already stated that he will support the US accepting the recognition of the Armenian Genocide and he will be a more "human rights" president than Trump was. Even better was congressional support that recently bestowed towards Armenia such as passing the Genocide resolution, humanitarian assistance, and sanctions on Turkey.

The reconvening of the OSCE Minsk Group should also affect the potential of what could happen in Armenia and Artsakh. The human rights violations against soldiers and civilians, the destruction of Armenian churches and homes, the use of cluster munitions, the hiring of mercenaries and jihads, and all the other atrocities and exploitation Turkey and Azerbaijan during the war should affect any new rulings the Minsk Group comes up with. Turkey has already made some serious change in her aggressiveness by soft toning her actions. President Erdogan has stopped calling offensive names to President Macron and is willing to work with him, the Turkish president is now willing to talk to Greece and Cyprus rather than make aggressive moves in the Mediterranean, and is now showing a little respect to the EU concerns. Vartouhi again said, "We have to see how this all turns out, but it may open up some diplomatic opportunities for Armenia."

January 20, Vartouhi received a report written by Stepan Piligian, the well-known *Armenian Weekly* columnist, that summarized up-to-date events together with some of his comments. He is a leader in the Armenian New England community working with political persons and organizations. He believes there are three attributes of leadership that are necessary for an emerging democracy. These are integrity, political will, and competence. He does not think Armenian leaders have experienced these characteristics. The "Velvet Revolution" ushered in a period of hope but the war shattered that hope. There were some signs of progress, but PM Pashinyan's refusal to compromise on the diplomatic front was his downfall. Former President Ter Petrossyan tried 27 years ago but he had to resign due to the lack of support. Piligian points out other problems and comments, but he thinks some place in this small nation of Armenia there has to be someone who fits the role of a good leader.

January 25, thirty Armenian Trucks were reportedly attacked in the Georgian area populated by Azeris who resided in the neighborhood. After the attack, Georgian police escorted the trucks to the Armenian border and are conducting a criminal investigating the incident.

January 28, an opinion piece was written in the *Washington Post* by Turkish journalist Asli Aydintasbas (b. 1973) on President Erdogan's charm measures to President Biden and European leaders. The comments softened the rash rhetoric he had in the past as he is well aware of Biden's feelings on the Armenian Genocide and the measures he has taken in Artsakh, Syria, Greece, Libya, Cyprus, and other countries. The Turkish president has also has made an attempt to make amends with President Macron who was "advised to get his head examined" after some disputes in France over Muslim infractions. The new Sultan of Turkey thinks he has a good relationship with France now. He has also made it clear to the leaders that Turkey has improved her foothold in the Caucasus and the Middle East and that she does not need help like she used too.

President Biden who up to the present has refused to answer calls from Erdogan, has "warned Pashinyan to stay away from negotiations with Turkey. If any process of Armenian –Turkish relations is initiated, Biden will refrain from recognizing the Armenian Genocide and that's's what Turkey wants." Armenia should not fall for the lies again, because that has been an Ankara tactic for many times so that the US would avoid using the word Genocide. Yet even with all the friendly aspirations Erdogan is sending out, the Turkish dictator still needs friends so he has to be careful of what he does. Aydintasbas did not say anything about Turkey's financial condition that is in a chaotic state. .

Ankara has signaled that it is "ready to normalize relations with Armenia."

"But don't believe it," was Vartouhi's response when she read it in the February 1 *Washington Post*. She finds it extremely difficult to believe how Turkey can make such a statement after decades of abuse, harassment, hatred, massacres, and destruction. "One cannot change its attitude or belief by merely making a declaration. Even today she still thinks Genocide. If Turkey was genuinely sincere about improving relations with Armenian, the first thing she should do is acknowledge the crime that her ancestors committed and make amends for their sin." Biden so far seems to be alert to Erdogan's rhetoric and has gone so far as to warn Pashinyan not to believe everything you hear from the Turkish sultan.

January 30, a trilateral group of Armenians, Azeris, and Russians met for the first time to lay- out the transport links among the three countries. Azerbaijan and Turkey will be connected through MerghrI in Armenian's most southern province of Syunik. Armenia will be connected to Russia through Azerbaijan. There are advantages and risks to lay-out of the route, but they were agreed to back at the November 9 trilateral settlement. There was also agreement on the return of POWs that was accomplished to a minor degree. There is no question that more should be returned.

February 1-12, Turkey and Azerbaijan started large scale joint military exercises in Kars region of Turkey. Vartouhi told her husband, "It's just another intimidation move on Turkey's part to upset the situation in the Caucasus region." The winter war games are near the Armenian border and only a few miles to where Russia has a military outpost in Gyumri.

February 3, Vahan Zanoyan (b. 1951), a well-known retired global strategist and advisor to numerous governments and corporations, and a writer, addressed the right and wrong lessons for the Artsakh War. He elaborated on the large number of finger pointing, controversy, and blames and counter blames that followed after the war ended. He discussed Levon Ter Petrossian's role in trying to find a long range peace solution back in 1994 when Armenia was the winner at the time. Then, the Armenian thinking was that we were invincible and lacked the vision to strengthen the country militarily. In what Zanoyan calls Static Mindset, he thinks Armenia was not realistic when she believed she could appease Turkey and Azerbaijan with mutually neighborly relations. Armenia did not think there was going to be a war. Under the circumstances at the time, Armenia could not have won a war and if the overall situation does not improve, Armenia could lose again. It does not sound good. Zanoyan thinks the war could have been avoided if we were truly ready for it.

Vartouhi thought Zanoyan's presentation was fine except he did not cover the real reason Armenia lost the war. This was also true of the many other critics and "Monday morning quarter backs" who have answers for the loss. It's relatively easy to dig up causes after one observes exactly what has happened. The reporter believes that if Turkey had not entered the war, Armenia would have won just as she did in the earlier struggle of the April 2016 Four Day War. She mentioned this notion in her column where many of her readers agreed with her.

February 4, Turkey's Interior Minister Suleyman Soylu (b. 1969) renewed an old accusation that the US was behind the July, 15, 2015, uprising where rogue Turkish soldiers attempted to overthrow President Erdogan and his government. Ankara has blamed Turkish preacher Fetuillah Gulen (referred to as FETO) for the rebellion and has been asking the US for his extradition since 2016. America has refused to send Gulen back to Turkey because there was not enough evidence to show that the preacher was involved. The US State Department has called the accusation "wholly false."

February 6, President Aliyev accused Armenia of "obstructing the creation of the Zangezur Corridor [the tentative passageway through Southern Armenia connecting Nakhichevan to Azerbaijan]" and once again using threatening words against Armenia. "We [Azerbaijan] are ready to collaborate with Armenia. How many times have the deputy prime ministers of the two countries met already? Armenia refuses to collaborate." And as usual he has to add, "…that Zangezur is historic Azerbaijani territory." When Vartouhi heard that, "Yeah, maybe for a year or two! Armenia eventually will be opening a passageway, but probably wants to give Aliyev a hard time."

A little later in the month, Artsakh authorities introduced a bill to add Russian as an official language as well as Armenian. Aliyev again came out with his belligerent tone hinting toward the region heading for a new round of escalation. He again used harsh rhetoric against the Russian peacekeepers and that "Nagorno Karabakh does not exist."

"These are hardly the language of a man looking for peace!" commented Vartouhi in her column.

February 13, the new Foreign Minister of Artsakh David Bakayan (b. 1973) in an interview with the *Armenian Mirror-Spectator* declared that the republic must remain a geopolitical actor. He discussed the prevailing conditions and stressed that Artsakh must understand internal political issues and must have a crucial political voice. He said a majority of Artsakh's population has returned, but there are about 45,000 who are still in Yerevan. In his interview he declared, "Artsakh is like a wounded person who has lost one of its legs, one of its arms, one of its eyes, and whose heart is wounded. We are in a kind of emergency department. Every day we get up and look at Shushi. We need some time to create appropriate conditions, construct houses for our people and provide them with jobs and other opportunities for living." With regard to the POWs, he said, "Artaskh unfortunately doesn't have enough resources to do it alone (bring back prisoners), but we are communicating with international organizations and peacekeepers. Unfortunately, international law and institutions cannot guarantee the return of these people because Azerbaijan violates international laws, norms and conventions, including the Geneva Convention." With regard to Armenian monuments, churches, and museums, he said, "The Azeris are destroying our culture and heritage. We are going to struggle to preserve our heritage, which has been destroyed systematically." Other issues were discussed indicating a lot of hard work laying the burden ahead for country.

February 14, Turkey announced the arrest of hundreds of people due to the Kurdish Workers Party (PKK) execution of 13 Turks in northern Iraq. The US sent condolences and condemned the killings. Garo Paylan, HDP representative and MP, stated that overnight over 150 party members were arrested including the detainment of Kurdish mayors from cities and towns. During the past five years Ankara has accused the HDP to have links with the PKK and have jailed more than 10,000 members. Paylan thinks the aim of Turkey is to reduce the number of Kurdish voters so that their parliament membership is reduced.

February 15, Vartouhi heard about a billboard all the way from Philadelphia, PA that was quite surprising. The ad read:

AZERBAIJANIS [AND TURKS] ARE READY TO LIVE IN HARMONY WITH ARMENIANS. "HOW ABOUT ARMENIANS?"

PAID FOR BY MUSIAD USA

When she mentioned the ad to Simon, he too was surprised, especially coming from a Turkish organization in America. The members personally may feel that way but Turks in the US have for decades demonstrated hate toward the Armenians by attacking cultural and religious institutions and demonstrating against them at every opportunity. MUSIAD USA is a Turkish American Businessman Association made up of Turkish American businessmen and industrialist. The organization was established in 2013 and is an offshoot of MUSIAD TURKEY.

February 16, Yerevan acknowledged that the Russian peacekeepers in several incidents where foreign journalists were initially denied entry into Artsakh, later they were allowed "after the situation was clarified." It is a well-known fact that Azerbaijan would like a ban, however, Armenia and Artsakh have always welcomed, and still welcome, tourist, journalist, and most everyone else to visit Karabakh.

February 18, Paul Goble, the journalist and political expert who came up the controversial land swap ideas in the early 1990s and now residing in Azerbaijan, has gotten into the picture again. One of his ideas such as in his Meghri Plan that some people thought was ridiculous at the time is presently near an actuality. Turkey still dreams of having a corridor into Azerbaijan through southern Armenia. Goble points to the idea that Azerbaijan is now a new power in the region and has become a partner with other nations. Vartouhi wrote in one her other columns that Azerbaijan would be "a nothing" if Turkey was not by her side, but unfortunately for Armenia, Ankara is a strong supporter for the Azeris.

In any case, Goble thinks there is the potential for new alliances among the countries in central Asia that winning the war permits an east-west bridge among the Muslim nations, in a sense, cutting off a south-north bridge between Iran and Russia. Turkey, Azerbaijan, and Pakistan already have a January 14 joint declaration supporting each other both economically and militarily. However, Russia has a huge fleet in the Caspian Sea so she cannot be too concerned about that problem. Goble also mentioned that Pakistan supplied both troops and arms to Azerbaijan during the Karabakh War and that she never acknowledged Armenia's independence after the fall of the USSR.

Goble did not say anything about how Iran and Israel ties in with this mishmash where Iran was also a loser besides Armenia and she had nothing to do with the war. There is no question about Israel helping the Arzeris during the war and now getting a foothold with an apparent border with Iran. Israel now has direct link to Iran that allows her to conduct stealthy operations and in the event of a clash there are no other countries between them. It is not an ideal situation for Iran.

February 22, Armenian Defense Minister Vagharashak Harutyunyan (b. 1956) made a statement that would welcome an expanded Russian military base closer to the Azerbaijan border. He stated that he did not see a need for it to be a formal base, but deployment of a military unit would probably be adequate. The statement did not say anything about PM Pashinyan, but it is a well-known fact that in the past he was not amenable to the Russians in Armenia, but now he is in a welcoming mood. This was true except he criticized Russia the next day (see February 23).

February 23, PM Pashinyan made a statement that insulted Moscow by complaining about Russian Iskander-M short range missiles that did not explode, or that only 10% of them exploded. He also criticized the Kremlin for waiting too long in the war until Armenia was weakened. That together with his strained relationship with President Putin and his controversy with his own military personnel brought about an attempted coup to promote his resignation.

February 25, General Onik Gasparyan (b. 1970) and forty officers issued a statement calling for the prime minister to resign from the government because he was no longer capable of leading the country and for his dismissing of Tigran Khachatryan (b. 1977), Deputy Chief of Staff from his position in the army. On the same day PM Pashinyan announced the nation's military attempted a coup yesterday. Some people in the government believed President Putin may have triggered the strived coup due to Pashinyan's criticism of the Russian missiles and her waiting game to help Armenia until she was weakened in the conflict. On the same day the PM issued an executive order removing Gen. Gasparyan from his position in the army. This was after the army issued the statement calling for Pashinyan to resign.

February 27, President Armen Sarkissian refused to sign off on the Gen. Onik Gasparyan's removal declaring the action unconstitutional. Pashinyan retaliated by reminding the president of his decree on the removal of the general. Vazgen Manukyan (b. 1946), former PM, defense minister, and potential interim PM, stated the army would never allow the government to sack the general. He thought there would be a rebellion.

Adding more fuel to the fire, former President Robert Kocharyan voiced support for the military by stating, "At this critical moment, we call on the people to stand by the Armenian Armed Forces. The government that ceded land and lost the war must leave." Vartouhi was not sure what the outcome of this debate was going to be but she thought it was a part of a gigantic mess for Armenia. The situation was getting so bad that arguments were initiating within families. Even in her own family, Azad thought Pashinyan should resign where Vartouhi thought he should remain. Simon thought the PM should remain in power, but he was the man in charge when Armenia was delivered the disastrous peace pact. Yet, he did stop the killings and possibly stopped more loss of territory. The situation was a real dilemma, but was tearing the country apart. In one manner, there were no clashes between the two idealogies, but the situation still was not good.

March 1, PM Pashinyan addressing a large crowd in Republican Square stated, "If a parliament quorum could be assured, his party was ready to call a vote. The only way to change the composition of the current government is through legal, free, and fair elections. You elected me, and the only thing you can do is to have another election." Vartouhi thought the demonstration was more like reelection campaign speech. The PM did not say anything about the return of POWs, the quandary of the wounded, his relationship with the military, or the defense of the Armenian borders. Other political activist Armenians such as Edmond Marukyan (b. 1981), leader of the Bright Armenian Party, and Vaszgen Manukyan (b. 1946) contested the prime minister's statements that the election process is much more complicated. Edmon Marukyan would only greenlight an election if Gen. Gasparyan was reinstated. Other rival protests were carried on in other sections of Yerevan. Vartouhi told her husband, "We are yet to see how this all phases out."

March 2, the Berlin International Film Festival was planning to present the film *Black Bach Artsakh* at its 2021 festival. The film depicts some of the events that occurred in Artsakh during the war, but has been criticized as being biased. Berlin did not contest the non-showing of the film at the festival but plans to present the film at another time.

March 3, Officers of the Anti-Smuggling Department of the State Revenue Committee (SRC) of Armenia discovered the largest case of heroin smuggling since 2014. The storage had an estimated market value of $45,000,000, which is unprecedented in the whole region. The warehouse in Yerevan had 33 boxes of heroin labeled as yeast that came from Iran and were scheduled for Western Europe. Six people with different citizenships were arrested where others were investigated.

March 3, Boston Mayor Marty Walsh (b. 1967) announced in a letter addressed to the Greater Boston Armenian community that he was rescinding the proclamation issued by his office for Khojaly Commemoration Day at the end of February, and apologized for its promulgation. The issue in the letter concerned the "so-called massacre or genocide" of Azeris in Khojaly in 1992.

Similar letters in other US cities occurred where they also wrote proclamations. When the Armenians of the community heard about the Azeri Khojaly proclamation and the mayor's response to it, they immediately informed him as to what happened on that February day 29 years ago. There is still a dispute that ex-Azeri President Ayaz Mutalibov (b. 1938) claimed the massacre was organized by his political opponents to discredit him. Other major cities are having similar problems as the Azeris and Turks are taking more aggressive stands trying to offset the impact of the Armenian Genocide.

March 5, US Secretary of State Antony Blinken (b. 1962) spoke with PM Pashinyan emphasizing the importance of the US–Armenian bilateral partnership. The secretary stressed the significance of respect for the rule of law and democratic institutions. He expressed the continuing support for the development of democratic processes and institutions in Armenia. Both men highlighted the need to resume the peace process through the Minsk Group.

March 9, thousands of protestors of opposition supporters blocked the Armenian parliament building demanding that the prime minister step down. Most of the demonstrations have been peaceful, but occasional scuffles with the police occurred. There was incident with this one. Fortunately there were no reports of serious injuries.

March 11, as if Armenia did not have enough troubles, Health Minister Anahit Avanesyan (b. 1981) announced that a new wave of COVID-19 virus is invading Armenia. This is not much different than other countries in the world where strict measures were not taken. The third wave is rapidly filling up hospital beds, creating more cases and deaths, and the request for additional vaccines is being shouted. The health minister stated that the total count of deaths from the virus was 3416 with 187,441 cases. To contain the virus, citizens are reminded to take the necessary precautions as noted previously. Steps are also being taken to acquire additional vaccines.

March 13, the *Armenian Weekly* reported the publication of Israel Charny's new book, *Israel's Failed Response to the Armenian Genocide*. Charny together with numerous other Jewish scholars have continually rebuked Israel for not recognizing the Armenian Genocide. In 1999, Charny was creator and editor of the *Encyclopedia of Genocide* that included almost 100 experts and details on the genocides in several countries. He dedicated one chapter in the encyclopedia to the Armenian Genocide.

March 16, the European Parliament, citing the OSCE Minsk Group, passed a resolution condemning Turkey for using Syrian terrorist mercenaries in the Karabakh War. The resolution also called for Turkey to withdraw her troops from Northern Syria because of her violation of the Geneva Convention. Turkey just ignored the resolution.

March 18, in meeting with Prosperous Party leader Gagik Tsarukyan (b. 1956), PM Pashinyan agreed that they would have early snap parliamentary elections on June 20. The PM wrote, "The best way out of the domestic political situation created was special parliamentary elections." It did not take long for the different parties to dispute the proposed election and come up with their own ideas. The debate has been ongoing. From what Vartouhi has analyzed, there is not any party strong enough to change what is occurring. Even if Pashinyan wins in the election, he will have to improve his performance, which does not appear to be likely. The problems probably will still exist. The general public is watching to see what happens.

March 18, Russia and Turkey celebrated the Centennial of Moscow Treaty that had formalized the border between Armenia and Turkey. As usual, Armenia had no input to the treaty and had no choice in the harsh agreement. Today, there is a question about the legality of the Moscow Treaty and the Kars Treaty. Vartouhi thinks even if the two treaties are declared illegal, what would the international community do about it?

Treaty of Moscow and the following Treaty of Kars may have been a "love affair" between Mustafa Kemal and Lenin, but the situation is now different. Turkey did not have permission to attack Northern Syria but she did anyway killing thousands of Kurds. However, the Russian stance on Crimea may be quite different. Turkey thinks the strategic peninsula really belongs to the Tartars even though the headland contains only 12% of Muslims. Turkey is now also supplying arms, especially the deadly drones, to Ukraine that is in contention with Russia. Moscow probably is not too happy with Turkey now having a direct link to the southern nations of Asia. Vartouhi thinks the talk of brotherhood is nice, but that the two countries have interests that are not compatible.

March 19, a bipartisan letter led by Foreign Relations Committee Chairman Senator Robert Menendez (b. 1954) and signed by 37

Senators calling for President Biden to acknowledge the Armenian Genocide just as the House and Senate passed resolutions in December 2020. Two weeks before, 180 House Representatives called on the Biden administration to take a harder line against Turkey.

March 23, Armenian health officials reported an alarm in the start of a rise in a third wave of COVID-19 cases. The second wave that ran from July 2020 to January 2021 resulted in 4505 deaths and appeared that the disease was under control even with the Azeri attack of September 27. But new cases and deaths resumed in February 2021. Some critics have claimed that Armenia's management of the virus has been a disaster. Health officials again stressed that all citizens get vaccinated.

March 29, Foreign Minister Ara Ayvazyan (b. 1969) made a statement that Turkey must end its "hostile" policies toward Armenia if it wants to contribute to peace and stability in the region. Speaking in the Armenian parliament, he noted that Ankara has never reciprocated Armenian attempts to improve bilateral relations. There were considerable comments on Ayvazyan's comment, both pro and con, but it remains to be seen how Ankara remarks to the message. Vartouhi told her husband, "Don't expect much. Turkey is so full of hate and so afraid to admit her role in the Genocide that she would never look for a peaceful protracting with Armenia even though she says she does. And right now, she is pretty much in her glory with her potential gateway to Central Asia. I don't think she has any concerns on how to get along with Armenia."

March 30, Vartouhi ran across a report by Col. Scott Shaw of the US Army's Asymmetric Warfare Group that was a little startling news. The report, "The U.S. Army Goes to School on Nagorno-Karabakh Conflict" is a real eye-opener with regard to modern warfare. Shaw claims that with inexpensive combat–ready drones have initiated a new kind of fighting. He points-out situations where Turkish Bayarajtar TB2 drones and loitering munitions, many of the Israeli-made, played havoc on the battle field. Actual reports of how serious the damage was has to be confirmed, but is what is known, is that the destruction was overwhelming and deadly. In a closing statement Shaw said,

"The Army, which has long enjoyed a firepower advantage in static positions, will now have to think about reinventing the wheel to be a constantly moving force, avoiding detection and incoming fire." Other organizations have generated similar reports.

April 1, Portland, ME, became another city that rescinded and apologized for the Mayoral proclamation of "Khojaly Remembrance." After the Armenians of Portland discussed the issue with Mayor Kathleen Snyder (b.1970), she rescinded the proclamation. She understands now a little better on what the situation is in Artaskh and the matter of Genocide.

April 2, Armenian Ambassador to the US Varuzhan Nersesyan (b. 1973) in an interview with the *Armenian Mirror Spectator* highlighted the problems of Azerbaijan illegally retaining and abusing Armenian POWs and destroying Armenian cultural monuments. He emphasized that Armenia had returned all Azeri prisoners but Azerbaijan has not. He claims that only 75 captives have been returned where they are still holding 200 war and civilian captives. The ambassador said, "The reason why Azerbaijan is not returning them is clear: Azerbaijan keeps them as hostages trying to gain advantage in other matters."

In another criticism, the ambassador has seen horrendous videos of Azeri military abuse on Armenian soldiers and civilians. The Azeris are proud of the fact that torture, beatings, and even beheadings are common practices. Azeri soldiers proudly show their faces on the internet videos when performing these dreadful acts. Azerbaijan claims she is investigating these charges but at the same time is promoting abusers to higher ranks.

Another Azeri attitude is the destruction and desecration by the Azeri military on Armenian cultural and religious monuments. This is not a new claim as it has been presented hundreds of times, yet the Azeri and Turks are continually doing their destructive abuses. Vartouhi thinks there should be some form of punishment on the perpetrators of these damaging acts. Nersesyan claims these destructive undertakings deserve the full condemnation by the international community and immediate action to stop any further attempts at devastation, desecration, and destruction. There have been some statements to stop the abuses but both Turkey and Azerbaijan continue the destructive practice.

April 6, a judge in Yerevan threw out the court charges against former President Robbert Kocharyan that the Armenian's Constitutional Court had in 2018 declared unconstitutional. The trial has not yet ended and there is still a lot of charges and debate as to what is supposed to follow.

April 7, in a meeting between PM Pashinyan and President Putin, they agreed that the Russian president would pressure President Aliyev to release Armenian POWs. The next day, Russian Gen. Ruslan Muradov (b. 1973) flew to Baku with an apparent mission to release the prisoners. It turned out to be an extremely disappointing venture. There was high level anticipation, but it did not happen. News from Baku indicated that Azeri president was angry because the Karabakh authorities had not delivered maps of current minefields and by problems he was having to construct his hankered corridor through the Syunik region. Vartouhi was not surprised, because she was sure the president would come up with some excuse for not delivering the POWs. Aliyev also came up ridiculous and nefarious comments like some of the prisoners were "terrorists" and would be tried in by Azeri officials.

Needless to say, there were a lot of embarrassments why the request for releases did not go through. Armenia followed her November 9 responsibility by returning prisons but the Azeris have not. PM Pashinyan believes he made a big mistake when he returned the Azeri prisoners where Aliyev is not following the rules. Vartouhi's comment was, "What do you expect from Azerbaijan and Turkey that believe they are doing the correct thing."

April 13, an emboldened President Aliyev announced the opening of "Millitary Trophies Park" in Baku boasting to the world the Azeri victory over Armenia and Karabakh. The park displays dehumanized Armenian soldiers, the helments of killed Armenian soldiers, and their mannequins where Azeri children are encouraged to choke them. "What grotesque way to generate hate among children," was Vartouhi's comment when she heard about opening. Other displays show the conquests of destruction.

April 19, President Aliyev again threatened to establish a "corridor" in Southern Armenia by force at an Azerbaijani Public TV broadcast. The corridor would connect western Azerbaijan with the Autonomous Nakhichevan Republic. The comment was met with outrage in Armenia. There has been considerable discussion on this issue where Foreign Minister Anna Naghdalyan has stressed several times that Article 9 of the November 9 trilateral statement does not mention the establishment of a corridor.

April 21, PM Pashinyan made an unexpected visit to towns of Meghri and Agarak where some angry residents greeted him with catcalls and insults, accusing him of surrendering Artsakh and intending to sell Syunik. The result was a hasty retreat back to Yerevan.

April 21, Armenia launched her COVID–19 vaccine campaign after receiving her first distribution of 25,000 doses of Oxford-AstraZenica's vaccines. Armenia has blood cloting reports of the vaccine but manages to get 173,017 doses administered. However, Armenia continued to have problem because there was a huge lack people getting the vaccines.

April 23, three major southeastern Michigan cities and the State of Michigan signed proclamations declaring April 23, 2021 as "Turkish Sovereignty and Children's Day." The three cities were Southfield, Ann Arbor, and Warren. The proclamations sent shock waves throughout the Armenian community in that the mayors of these cities and the governor could issue such documents on the eve of Armenian Genocide Remembrance Day. The result of the protests ensued apologies and disclaimers on the proclamations. (Also see end paragraph of April 24 to see how other Turkish denialism propaganda works.)

April 24, major cities throughout the world venerated the 106th commemoration of the Armenian Genocide. US President Joe Biden recognized the Genocide with many leaders calling the statement a historic event. The US now becomes the 30th country to have formally recognized the Armenian Genocide. The UK and Israel have not. Biden statement included the mass murders committed by the Ottoman Turks and the disaster they brought upon the Armenians. He talked about the human rights abuses that Turkey has been committing and believes Turkey should be adhering to the NATO and EU standards. Ironically,

Turkey has not recalled her ambassador as she usually does, possibly because she needs the US more that the US needs her. Turkey stated that she would comment on the Biden's statement at a "time of its choosing."

Time Magazine, May 10-17, 2021, also acknowledged Biden's remarks on the Genocide and further pointed out the history of the Ottoman murders and atrocities. The magazine also mentioned that the wounds of the past will only be fully healed after Turkey acknowledges the Genocide. Other newspapers and magazines all over the world acknowledged Biden's comments; most thought the recognition was overdue.

The government of Armenian sent a thank you communication to Biden, "Your message brought to completion the process of recognizing the Armenian Genocide in the United States." Prime Minister Pashinyan also sent a letter to the President thanking him for recognizing the Genocide and setting an "inspiring example" for those hoping to see a just and tolerant world. He hailed Biden's statement as "a powerful step on acknowledging the truth, and bringing justice to the victims of the Genocide and their descendants."

As expected Turkey made threatening remarks that Biden's statement would create problems in Turkish-American relations and also deteriorate relations between Turkey and Armenia. Vartouhi thought the latter statement was a farce because there is no amicable relationship between the two countries, especially after Erdogan made his speech where he said, "Maybe it's time for Turkey not to take NATO and America for granted." Vartouhi stated that people should keep in mind that Turkey celebrated the centennial of the Gallipoli Campaign victory during the same time in an attempt to downplay the Genocide.

In other methods of disavowing the Armenian Genocide is for Turkish lobbies to issue proclamations to individual communities or to place large displays on billboards. The Turkish American Cultural Association of Michigan (TACOM) and sister groups in other states, under the umbrella of the Assembly of Turkish American Associations (TAAA), are typical of the organization that promote ads, proclamations, advertisements, sponsoring publications and academic centers, and other public presentations. This is fine and good, except Turkey and her lobbies do it during April 24 every year to water down the veneration and remembrance of the Genocide.

April, 25, Prime Minister Pashinyan officially submitted his resignation where it was accepted by President Armen Sarkissian. This is the first step in triggering the process to hold snap parliamentary election by June 20. According to the Constitution, Pashinyan will remain as interim PM although with some political debate.

May 3, the Human Rights Watch submitted a list of names for 12 civilian and seven soldiers who are being held by the Azeri government. A previous confirmation sited 31 other cases of execution of civilians while in Azerbaijan captivity. Dozens of cases of missing civilian hostages remain unconfirmed. The Azeri government has continually abused and persecuted both civilian and military personnel and confronted responds with flimsy and inappropriate answers.

May 9, former President Robert Kocharyan announced that he decided to return to politics to rectify what he believes are great threats to the country's long-term security and stability. Kocharyan said, "Our goal is to establish a dignified peace." Other detractors accuse Kocharyan of undermining Armenia's statehood, both at home and abroad, favoring a culture of entrenched corruption, selective clientage, nepotism and brutal repression and murder. He still faces charges of bribery but nonetheless is thinking of being a candidate in the upcoming snap election.

May12. Acting PM Pashinyan held a Security Council meeting where he discussed the border situation in Sev Lich in Syunik Marzx. Two hundred and fifty Azeri soldiers just strolled 3.5 kms past the borders of Syunik and Gegharkunik provinces into Armenian territory. Among Pashinyan's several statements he said, "I wish to reiterate that a piece of information about shootings, hostilities, injuries and casualties has nothing to do with reality. On the other hand, it should be noted that the situation is a least near-critical, if not critical. Were it not for that, we would not have to convene a Security Council meeting. Anyway we need to keep calm in this situation. On the other hand, we need to be consistent in terms of defending our state and national interests, and make decisions about steps to take and the tools to use."

Earlier he said that Armenian forces responded with appropriate tactical maneuvers and other necessary measures, but he did not say what the end result was.

Vartouhi believes Pashinyan's concern is valid. Azerbaijan has begun war games on the Armenian borders with 15,000 troops and heavy weapons. Vartouhi thinks Aliyev is just trying to instigate another war. Several countries have objected to the buildup, but Russia has remained disturbingly silent. Some analysts claimed Armenia can resort to the Collective Security Treaty Organization (CSTO) to help, but request for assistance has been worthless according to the journalist, "The CSTO can even be a negative influence when some of its members actually sent congratulations to Azerbaijan after the 44-Day War. Belarus was one of those countries," she remarked to her husband. Simon responded by just nodding sadly.

May 20, interim PM Pashinyan confirmed the authenticity of a "so called" secret document that had been circulating online since the previous evening. He did not disclose the details of the draft, except that he called it a "preliminary agreement" that were "100 percent consistent with national interests of Armenia. If Azerbaijan implements the agreements that are stipulated in the document, then I will sign the document," he told a government session. There was considerable debate as to what the document contained, and was yet to be confirmed by Azerbaijan. Vartouhi thought it was too early to comment on the redacted document that was still incomplete.

Later meetings and disclosures revealed many ramifications that came to light. Some of these included, 1) the document was kept secret because all the details were not worked out, 2) the documents contained an addendum to another document, possibly an agreement between Pashinyan and Russia or Azerbaijan, 3) Aliyev supposedly has made some promises, but no one seems to know what those promises are, yet almost everyone knows the Azeri president has made numerous statements that the Karabakh issue is a non-issue because he has settled it by military action and that Armenia itself is in danger not only Karabakh, 4) it is not clear how Turkey and Russia fit into the "secret" document, and a few other question marks.

Other concerns included the relativity of CSTO that has not done much in the past, but could be involved and the fact that President Putin warned the parties if they did not carry out the November 9 agreements, it meant suicide to the non-conformist. President Aliyev is currently holding 200 POWs who are still alive. Iran may be getting involved with what has been occurring now that President Biden has more or less opened the door for her. Iran certainly is not happy about Turkey's expansion in the area so it is questionable what steps she will be taking. Another question is what will be the future developments between the US and Turkey and how that relationship will affect Armenia?

May 20, Phillippe Raffi Kalfayan wrote another article on the perils of Armenia, "Now is the time for a statesman in Armenia." The article joined the other "experts and criticizers" on the nation's situation. He discussed the futility of the 5000 dead and 10,000 injured as if nothing has happened and the mistakes of our leaders in the past. He claimed there has been no ideology or platform offered from the present administration and that there has been plenty of fragmented, incomplete, partisan, and finger pointing, slander, and insults from accessors. He proposes that Armenia act now to mobilize and dedicate intelligence and resources to a few objectives. He claims Armenia should have the security and diplomatic strategy in both short and long term and put aside personal conflicts. Vartouhi again wrote in her column, "Sounds great, but how do you go about doing all this?"

May 20, while all the above was going on, Azeri soldiers crossed into the provinces of Syunik and Gegharkunik without firing a shot. Armenia appealed to Russia for more troops in the area and to CSTO that made an obligatory response to the call, but did nothing to remove the troops. Legal protection means nothing as the Azeris violate the international laws that are in effect. Amnesty International has recorded numerous Azeri human rights violations but have been ignored by Baku.

May 27, Interim PM Pashinyan made a proposal for Armenian and Azeri troops to move to their original positions or have observers from Russia or the OSCE Minsk Group states be deployed in the area. The proposal followed the infiltration of several hundred Azeri soldiers who crossed the international border of Armenia in Syunik province before being stopped by Armenian forces around Lake Sev. A similar intrusion was also halted south of the village of Verin Sjprja in the Gegharkyunik province. Also before the PM's proposal, Foreign Minister Spokeswoman Ana Naghdalyan insisted that in addition to the Azerbaijani withdrawal the process of border delimitation and demarcation should be a part of the comprehensive peace settlement. All this sounds great, except it falls on President Ilham Aliyev's deaf ears, who continually holds Armenian POWs and threatens Armenia and Karabakh with wild intimidations. To show his arrogance on the very next day, he gave a speech in Aghdam declaring that Azerbaijan will continue to strengthen her borders. He said words from European Parliament are all meaningless. During his speech he outlined 12 theses that basically stated there was no hope for Armenia and that Azerbaijan acted with dignity during the 44-Day War. He completed his speech by claiming that both the previous and current Armenian governments are to blame for not being able to defend their borders. Vartouhi thought the Azeri president may be correct on his last statement, but was entirely incorrect on his soldiers acting with dignity. "They were worse than wild animals. Beheadings and tortures were common practice for Azeri soldiers and they still are when the opportunities arise," she wrote in one of her columns.

With all the discussions that are going on, two things that Armenia has insisted on before border demarcation talks are, the release of POWs and the Azeri forces pulling out of Armenian territory. The arguments include the formation of a committee of Russian, Armenian, and Azerbaijani representatives to iron-out the border positions. Vartouhi said "good luck" on this one too. Aliyev may agree to such a move, but will find a way to botch-it-up when it is ready to be enacted.

May 27, Armenian Foreign Minister Ara Ayvazyan (b. 1969) resigned from his position only after six months on the job. He later said he resigned in order to "make sure that there are never any suspicions that this ministry could take some steps or agree to some ideas or initiatives, which are against our national and state interests."

May 28, Vartouhi came across an *Armenian Mirror Spectator* article written by Dr. Arshavir Gundjian that was a real eye-opener regarding the potential future of Armenia. Gundjian is a distinguished and award winning retired professor of Electrical Engineering from McGill University of Montreal. He pointed out, quite accurately, the mishmash and turmoil in the country just as many other political and military analysts have also done, but he also noted the danger of the present situation. The article, "We Need to Get Ready for New Battles of Sararabad," discusses the non-readiness of Armenia today and what we have to do to prepare ourselves in the event our enemies look forward to another Genocide (he does not mention Turkey and Azerbaijan, but our reporter and readers knows who they are). Among many scenarios he mentions a need for introducing a fresh political, diplomatic, economic, and military strategic ideas. To date, Pashinyan nor Kocharyan have not produced any designs or thoughts in this regard. The professor further explained not to expect any assistance from our so called allies or friendly large states if any catastrophe occurs.

Sadly, if the regular Armenian army based on today's authoritative calculations, will still be prevented to intervene. There remains no other alternative but for civilians and volunteer groups to create human barriers to the enemy advancing into Armenian lands. Armenian civilians should be permitted to arm themselves to protect themselves and their families and properties. Present day Armenia does not allow this. We have to be ready at the entire Armenian border. Readers should recall a fiery and forceful warmongering speech a few months ago when the arrogant and cocky Aliyev talked about fighting in the streets of Yerevan. Our finger pointing political leaders should keep this in mind. Vartouhi can not figure out how PM Pashinyan talks peace with Azeri dictator who uses such language.

June 1, acting PM Pashinyan and President Macron met in Paris where the French president insisted that Azerbaijani troops withdraw from Armenia's border areas. He also called on the two countries to demarcate their border through negotiations and without "any fait accompli on the ground." The US State Department urged similar measures two weeks earlier accompanied with a statement, "pull back all forces immediately and cease further provocation." As usual, Baku maintained that its troops took up new positions on the Azerbaijani side of the frontier and did not cross into Armenia. The fact that the Azeri forces are physically present on Armenia lands only proves that Baku is playing a fictitious role. To make matters worse, Azerbaijan claims it captured six Armenian soldiers on the Azeri side of the border. In a joint statement the following day, the triparty Minsk Group representatives backed the proposed troop disengagement, but did not specify that their respective countries were ready to send observers. "So what does this all mean, when Azerbaijan still keeps her troops on Armenian soil, and continues to perform aggressive acts against the Armenians?" she asked Simon at dinner.

"It means that Azerbaijan agrees with a lot of statements, but does what she wants when the time comes for action," Simon answered. Vartouhi nodded in agreement.

With the upcoming snap election in three weeks, political groups are starting to form. Twenty-six have registered, 22 political parties and four alliances. The groups vary in looking for support from Russia to ignoring or refusing to relate with Putin's influence. One issue that was coming on strong was the Azeri desire to open the corridor through Zangezur. Pashinyan has managed to procrastinate on the concern, but Aliyev insists that there is no way Armenia can reject her November 6 agreement. As for the election prognosis, anything is possible with so many parties participating. Hopefully, some kind of national unity will result, we have to wait and see.

June 1-2, a surprising announcement was made by Armenia on the upcoming large-scale CSTO military drills to be held in Armenian territory. The six member-states, including Armenia and Russia confirmed that the exercise will take place this year. Vartouhi was especially surprised because the CSTO has rendered no support, militarily or even verbally, to Armenia throughout the 44-Day War or during its aftermath. "It's going to be extremely interesting how the operation turns out," she wrote in her column.

June 11, former President Robert Kocharyan held a press conference on his candidacy for the upcoming election. Over 100 participants from various parts of the world attended the Zoom conference in Watertown, MA, where many questions were asked. Topics included; the economy, relations with diaspora, the future of Armenia and a way out of the current crisis, the increase in political tension, polarization of the Armenian society, the increase in emigration, and his past record of corruption. Businessmen who participated in the meeting agreed to visit Armenia following the June 20 snap elections to discuss a road map for investing in Armenia. The Azeri demand for an access through southern Armenia was not discussed.

June 11, Tatul Hakobyan (b.1969), journalist, writer, coordinator at the Ani Armenian Research Center, and political analyst made a presentation on the reasons we lost the 44-Day War. "I can give you 100 reasons. But there was one main reason we lost the second time in our history. The first time was in 1920 when our American friends, one of the main allies at the time, were telling us to find a common ground with our neighbors and not to rely on them. …Instead, we were determined that the future of Armenia will be decided in Sevres or other places, and not with our neighbors. We went to war and lost much of our territory." Vartouhi thought he was so correct on that point.

Hakobyan continued on to say, "I think the main reason for the recent defeat is that we didn't estimate our strengths correctly. As a political principle, we chose not realism, but a dream of having a big and biggest Armenia. We didn't listen to friendly countries who were telling us to speak with Azerbaijan and to accept painful but dignified compromises." He states, as many other analyst, Armenian has to strengthen her military. Vartouhi agreed, except he said nothing about building a defense against the deadly drones and also to use drones as an offensive weapon. Hakobyan is also wary of the upcoming election, but is hopeful he wakes up to a peaceful Armenia on June 21.

As for Diaspora, he thinks that it is now in a confused state with everything that has happened and is still going on. He believes that Armenia should try to ensure the presence of the Diaspora in her political life and to make new talking points with the diaspora organizations even though there may be differences in the organization policies and opinions. He believes we should stay away from the "toasts and wishful thinking" mentality.

June 14, Presidents Biden and Erdogan met at a side meeting of the NATO Conference with no apparent worldly news. Biden said, "We had a positive and productive meeting, much of it one on one. Our teams are going to continue our discussions and I'm confident we'll make real progress between Turkey and the United States." Erdogan echoed that optimism saying that areas of cooperation between the nations are richer and larger than the problems. However, neither of the presidents provided any details on how they would cut through existing tensions nor did they discuss anything about what is going on in Armenia and Artsakh, as far as Vartouhi knew. Many questions from reporters after the talk were ignored by the two.

June 15, acting PM Pashinyan promised to "cut off the hand" that would try to oppose the southern province of Syunik to the rest of Armenia as he campaigned in Sisian. During his speech he displayed a hammer tied with three-colored ribbons which he symbolized as to what he called the "steel revolution" as follow-up to the "velvet revolution." He further explained that the hammer is a symbol of construction and the rebuilding of Armenia and the need to establish a dictatorship of law and order. Vartouhi thought the word "dictatorship" came on a little strong, but she understood there has to be some strong measures to overcome the crisis within Armenia. She was not sure how the word would affect the voting in five days.

June 16, Armenian and Russian defense ministers spoke to each other by phone on the possible deployment of more Russian troops along Armenian's borders with Azerbaijan. There was no commitment from the Russian minister at this time.

June 18, hardliner Ebrahim Raisi (b. 1960) was elected president of Iran, one of the few countries that have befriended Armenia in the recent past. Rasisi has indicated that he will continue to do so. He publicly warned Russia, Turkey, and Azerbaijan to tread cautiously in their relationship with Armenia. In the throes of the US sanction release, she has been flexing her muscles in the area. Raisi has made it clear to Russia, Turkey, and Azerbaijan that she will be one of the countries involved in the concerns of Armenia.

June 19, on the eve of the snap elections violent rhetoric dominated the atmosphere. The ongoing campaign that started June 7 has been overwhelmed by dissemination of hateful and violent rhetoric by the candidates. There was a lot of vile, hateful and insulting words, used in their speeches. Former President Levon Ter Petrosyan warned that the upcoming election might be the "most dangerous in the Armenian history." Candidates were extremely loose with their speeches and did not hesitate to criticize almost brutally. Vartouhi did not think it was a pretty picture.

June 19, Edmond Azadian, author and Senior Editorial Columnist of the *Mirror–Spectator* interviewed President Armen Sarkessian on issues plaguing Armenia, mainly that there is a disconnect between the presidential office and the executive branch of the government. The president was one of the prominent leaders who had called for Pashinyan's resignation and is now advocating formation of a government of technocrats with himself as a head of a tech cabinet. He pointed out that Armenia was a failure in world diplomacy even though he had made recent trips to Georgia, Kazakhstan, and Moscow. As for the exchange of POWs, he acknowledged that it was a bad deal because Azerbaijan did not abide by the November 9 agreement. He recommended that Armenia develop a strong diplomacy. He acknowledged that Armenia had many talents and resources that are not being utilized due to constitutional constraints. He believes this should be changed to permit better association. When asked about the relationship between the church and state he thought it was excellent, but emphasized the state should not interfere in church affairs, nor vice-versa. At the end of the interview, the president had a previous agreement with Pashinyan to hold a referendum in October on a new constitution.

June 20, the snap parliamentary elections resulted in the projection of PM Pashinyan to retain a reduced parliament majority following a bitterly contested electoral campaign. Pashinyan received 53.92% of the vote followed by former president Kocharyan with 21.04%. Most observers thought the balloting went smoothly, although there were some comments from several candidates. Kocharyan did not reject the results, but cast doubt on the preliminary figures calling them "highly controversial." Other observers declared the voting "free and fair" despite some violations. Even before the final results were counted, congratulatory messages were received from the European Union, France, Russia, and other countries.

Pashinyan has recognized some of his shortcomings in the past, and has opened the door to some of his adversaries. He has thoughts about hiring expert diplomats, having better relations with Russia, and he promised to look for qualified people outside his administration to help him in his relations with others and the Catholicos that has not been the greatest. However, Pashinyan is looking into it. Vartouhi thinks it is a little ironic that Arayik Haruytunyan (b. 1973), is both one of his policy advisors and also the same to the Catholicos. The journalist remarked, "You'd think a person in that capacity could bring people together."

June 29, the Baku Court on Grave Crimes resumed the illegal trial of 14 Armenian POWs accused of terrorism. The prisoners were charged under four articles of Azerbaijan's Criminal Code and had no attorneys in their defense. Many experts, American and European lawmakers have urged Azerbaijan to end the sham trial of Armenian POWs. Vartouhi noted in her column what a farce the trials were, but also noted that with all the criticism and illegality of the hearings nothing was being done to stifle the absurdity of them.

June 30, the State of New Jersey became the 10th state to recognize Artsakh as an independent country. The resolution includes many paragraphs on what Ottoman Turkey did during April 24, 1914, and what Azerbaijan is doing in the present and what she has done in the past. When Vartoouhi read the document she thought New Jersey did a complete job of declaring independence of Artsakh, and also what the Turks accomplished during World War I and the illegal and inhuman Azeri actions now.

July 5, the Armenian Americans for Human Rights (AAHR) group issued a press release requesting that Secretary of State Antony Blinken and President Biden to impose sanctions on Turkey and Azerbaijan for using terrorists on Armenians during the 44-Day War. David Boyajian, spokesman for the AAHR and author of many articles on civil rights, reported Turkey's supply of jihadists and terrorists to the Azeri army and asked why the US did not impose sanctions on the two Muslim states? Boyajian also asked why the US is continuing the funding to

Azerbaijan when she is utilizing terrorists and has plenty of money from her oil reserves.

July 5, Azerbaijan initiated the trial of 14 Armenian POW on assumed charges of treason. Dozens of other prisoners are being held awaiting decisions from the Azeri government while protests are being issued by human rights groups and democratic countries. Azerbaijan just ignores the requests stating they are true claims of treason. Vartouhi wrote, "Treason against whom?"

July 9, European Union Commissioner for Neighborhood and Enlargement Oliver Varhelyi b.(1972) announced in Yerevan that the EU has offered Armenia an aid package of over $3 billion, 62 percent more than previously promised. The fund was bestowed due to the fair elections and a support to help recover from the 44 Day War. Parts of the fund are to be used to support small and medium sized enterprises and for transportation infrastructure that includes a new north-south highway to the Iranian border. At the joint meeting with Pashinyan, Varhelyi said, "I hope that Armenia will soon have a strong government, a strong parliament, and a strong parliamentary majority because we have a lot to do." Vartouhi made a silent prayer for the commissioner's hope to become a reality.

In addition to the above, Iran has also expressed an interest to the road and has agreed to set up a joint working group for Iranian companies to participation in the construction of planned roadworks.

July 14, Azeri forces continued their attacks into Armenia. One Armenian serviceman was killed with a mayor and several soldiers being wounded following a battle near the strategic border of Yeraskh in southwest Armenia. Other areas were also under intense fighting.

Arshak Karapetyan (b. 1967) was appointed Deputy Defense Minister a few weeks earlier. It was reported that he has strong relations with the Russian authorities.

July 14, Azeri President Aliyev came out with the following ominous treats. "We will return there and we will be returning there. Nobody can stop us. We will definitely return because there is no other way. After the opening of all transportation links, we will, of course, return to the land of our ancestors. A tripartite agreement of November 10-says that all refugees must return to their home land. Our native land is Zangequr. Our native land is Gosycha and Irvans (Yerevan)." These are strong boisterous and incriminating words and loudly spewed by the Azeri dictator. He has no idea of Azeri history because it was not even as an identity before 1918. He can make up what he wants, but it will be pure fiction. Almost every move the tyrant makes is to have Armenia counter strike so that he can say Armenia is starting the war again. Pashinyan has been extremely cautious to avoid this dilemma. Armenia has appealed to the CSTS, but it usually comes up with some excuse such as there were no casualties, but there were casualties.

July 19, the Armenian Minister of Defense (MoD) reported Azeri forces fired on positions on the Nakhichevan border. Vartouhi told her husband that the Azeris have no idea of what a "ceasefire" means.

July 28, after batches by AzerI troops advanced in the area of Yeraskh failed, new attempts were made along the Vardenis-Karvachar line. Armenian forces tried to stop the advances, but due to overwhelming Azeri numbers and the aid of artillery, the enemy succeeded in occupying two Armenian posts. After fierce fighting the following day, the Armenians regained the lost territory and the Russians again initiated a ceasefire agreement. Vartouhi said it was almost like a deadly game. The Azeris attack specific areas of Armenia or Artaskh, the Armenians defend the area, dozens of soldiers die on both sides, then we have a ceasefire again. Sadly, "It's not only stupid and injurious to all parties except, Azerbaijan may believe in her warped thinking that she is demoralizing or weakening Armenia. The notion is absurd in my thinking," she told Simon.

July 28, good news from the other side of the world indicated that the US House of Representatives unanimously passed HR 4373 that blocked US military financing and training aid to Azerbaijan. The bill has to go to the US Senate and be approved then signed by the president in order to become a law.

July 29, the Minsk Group chairmen again issued a statement calling for the parties to resume negotiations of which Azerbaijan basically ignored. The statement this time called for the parties to deescalate the situation and refrain from incendiary rhetoric and actions and fully comply with the November 9 ceasefire. Armenia welcomed the statement, but Vartouhi thought it went in one Azeri ear and out the other. She wrote in her column how Baku has aggravated the situation by refusing to release Armenian POWs, and even worse, killing 60 Armenian soldiers in mock trials and claiming Armenian sovereign territory.

France has gotten more involved in the picture by possibly offering to send troops to Armenia, but is limited in what she can do due to EU and UN restrictions. Russia has gotten strangely silent at Turkish and Azeri aggressions, demonstrating weakness in what is occurring. Rep. Adam Schiff made a statement on how Armenia is dependent on Russia and that he would like to strengthen Armenian-American relations. How this effects the overall situation is a valid question?

July 29, an editorial in the *Washington Post* reported President Aliyev has "blown a gasket" with a "tantrum" that is "threatening to obliterate what remains of independent political forces in Azerbaijan." The editorial continued, "Mr. Aliyev's use of he the iron fist to destroy his critics is the opposite of democracy and why everyone should worry about the intemperate tyrant." This was no surprise to Vartouhi who was well aware of the Azeri dictator's rages, lies, raucous and wild rantings, against Armenians and even his own people. Numerous crackdowns on opposition leaders and critics have turned the country into a quagmire of fear where the political rivals have been silenced or jailed.

Agust 2, President Armen Sarkessian officially signed the order reappointing Nicol Pashinyan as Prime Minister of Armenia.

August 2, the eighth session of the Armenian parliament was opened to elect the speaker and his deputies and leaders of the standing committees. However, all chaos reigned. Instead of working together, the opposition party had come to disrupt the normal functioning of the parliament. Rival members clapped in kindergarten-style, then left the parliament in a dramatic manner. The elections were conducted, but it was not with all members. Pashinyan's Civil Contact Party won 71 seats out of 107 against Kocharyan's Hayastan alliance that gained 29 positions. Seven seats went to Serzh Sargsyan's party. Vartouhi, who was an observer at the session, could not get over the carnival atmosphere of the meeting. Votes were taken for various positions and Pashinyan said he would rule with the iron fist of the law. Fine, except he utilized it against opposition members, not his own. The journalist thought if accusations and court cases were applied to everyone equally, the atmosphere would be much saner. That evening in a discussion with her husband she mentioned how chaotic the session was and the displayed no semblance of professionalism. There was no sign of Armenia being in dire situation. "I thought they acted terribly," she told Simon who is a member of the Civil Contact Party. He responded, "Yes, I agree with you. Sometime they act like they're a bunch of kids. There certainly is no love between a lot of them."

August 3 Armenia reported Russian soldiers set up check points in Tavush Province reversing advances of Azeri troops. However, the Azeris have been causing problems in other areas.

August 4, signs are beginning to show that Russia is taking a more aggressive action to assist Armenia in her struggle against Azerbaijan. The first positive sign came from a private visit from Konstantine Zatulin, head of the Eurasian Integration Committee in the Russian Parliament. When he returned to Moscow he said, "Armenia is experiencing its most difficult times. We will be betraying ourselves if we fail to help Armenia." This was only one phase of potential assistance. Following Zatulin's visit, Stanislav Zas, Secretary General of CSTO, said "We need to remember that Armenia made an appeal to me a few months ago about the incursion of 1000 Azeri soldiers around Sev Lake. I dismissed it as an insignificant border skirmish. Now the current tension falls on Armenian security and the security situation of CSTO zone of responsibility in general." Vartouhi was pleased to hear him say, "One of CSTO's key priorities is to ensure the sovereignty and territorial integrity of its member states."

Vartouihi's statement to her husband was, "It's about time the Russians had a wakeup call, and their actions are well overdue; that is, if they follow-up on what they claim they are going to do."

August 9, at a delegation meeting between CSTO Secretary General Stanislav Zas and the new Armenian Defense Minister Arshak Karapetyan, the defense minister unexpectedly presented a stern commendation at what has been occurring on the Arzeri/Armenian relationship. They also discussed the accomplishments of military cooperation and future possibilities as well as the Azeri occupation of territory of the Republic of Armenia. Karapetyan presented the situation in a dry manner, practically in the form of an ultimatum that was a surprise to most everyone at the meeting. In effect, he claimed CSTO has done nothing to stop the bloodshed, and that Armenia wants peace but will defend her territory. As far as Vartouhi knew the CSTO did not react to the Karapetyan declarations but expected a response. At the end of the meeting, the Armenian defense minister expressed his regret that the mechanism for reaching decisions in the CSTO structure and responding to crisis situations do not correspond to the current need for rapid response.

August 11, Azeri armed forces continued their assaults on Nagorno Karabakh utilizing quadeopters (drones) and ignoring the ceasefire agreement between Armenia and Azerbaijan. Since the end of the war on November 6, 2020, Azerbaijan has initiated all kinds of clashes, but this was the first time Russia has explicitly blamed Baku for violating the agreed upon ceasefire. Vartouhi told her husband the Russians have specifically accused Azerbaijan of carrying out the infringements and invasions. The only problem is that the Azeris continue their transgressions even after the European Parliament, United States, and France have made, and continue to make, official complaints to Baku. Azeri officials have responded to the accusation by declaring Armenia has deployed more troops in the area and falsely committing provocations, yet the Armenians have not shown any aggressive moves. They are more for defense than any other reason.

August 19, Maria Zakharova (b. 1987), official spokesperson of the Russian Foreign Ministry, addressed President Alivey's statement on rearming Armenia and his reiterated demand for the Zangezur Corridor and ridiculous claims on Yerevan and Sevan, "It is Russia's sovereign right and the Russian side always takes into account maintaining a balance of military power in the region." Zakharova then added, "In this regard, I would like to note the absolute counter-productioness of confrontational rhetoric, let alone bellicose rhetoric, which political leaders in the South Caucasus sometimes resort to." Vartouhi told her husband she was happy to hear the aggressive Russian words against Aliyev's warlike statements, but she wondered how much real action would be following? Russia's past actions certainly do not indicate that she is willing to help Armenia. Aliyev is concerned with some of these measures and the fact that President Macron will be visiting the region.

August 23, Azeri soldiers blocked the Goris-Kapan road in Syunik further intimidating travel in the area. Negotiation among Armenian, Russian, and Azerbaijani authorities, to date, have not netted any positive progress on the utilization of the road including some of the rural settlements of Syunik making it more difficult for the villages to obtain food and medical supplies. Four days later, the road was opened. The encroachment of Azeri soldiers has been a problem in many of the Artsak and Armenian border villages due to the vague or nonexistent rules. Vartouhi believes the Russians should take more aggressive action to calm the uneasiness of the Artsakh inhabitants

August 25, a serious brawl occurred in the Armenian parliament as a result of opposition leader Vahe Hakobyan calling PM Pashinyan a "lying populist." Water bottles were thrown at each other and the speaker and fights broke out. One member was hospitalized due to an eye injury. This was not the first time a brawl has broken out in the assembly as there were others in the past, one especially two days ago. Even when there is no fighting or hostility, there is continual finger pointing and accusations at each other as to why we lost the war or how to get Armenia back to a successful state. Unfortunately, the landslide victory Pashinyan received in June has not brought about any peace. In fact, it has gotten worse.

Vartouhi saw an article by Editor Harount Sassounian, *Armenian parliamentaries brawl while the barbarians are at the gate*, where he described the brawl as, "Parliamentarians fiddle while Armenia burns." (Akin to Roman Emperor Nero fiddling while Rome burns). She thought the analogy was very apropos. Sassounian wrote how the brawls were extremely intense where fist fighting fanned out among parliamentary members. He thought European TV stations had a ball showing the violence. Vartouhi thought it was sad.

August 25, the Ronald Reagan Library has digitized and released archive video materials that included Armenian catholicoi visits to the White House in 1983 and 1987. Karekin II stopped-over in 1983 and Vasken I in 1987. President Reagan was the first president to acknowledge the Armenian Genocide and had a good relationship with George Deukmejian, who later became governor of California. The video references to quite a few occasions where he had engagements with Armenian Church leaders and community members.

August 29, Turkish President Erdogan gave a speech on the prospects of beginning negotiations and establishing rapprochement with Armenia. PM Pashinyan has detected some positive signs in Turkey's attitude expressing his readiness to begin negotiations without preconditions. As a good will gesture, Armenia opened up her air space for Turkish planes flying over her territory. Turkey has not reciprocated. Russia has encouraged the potential relationship. An Impromptu analysis of Turkish ambitions is enormous. She has initiated her growth prospect even before any are even started to talk about them. She is well entrenched in Azerbaijan and has made inroads into Libya and Syria. She is planning a future foundation for Turkic federal states of Central Asia and there is even talk about including Armenia and the Kurds. Pashinyan has indicated that he is receptive to the idea of rapprochement, but he should be super cautious what Turkey has in mind. "No preconditions" is a strong stipulation especially where the Armenian Genocide is concerned.

Vartouhi as many other Armenians are concerned with Erdogan's approach. "Turkey has never done any good things to Armenia or Armenians to indicate that she is going to do something now. And why is Russia so receptive to the potential loss of Armenia's relationship. The journalist thought the prescribed conditions were especially tough on Armenia.

August 30, an Armenian pro-government lawmaker hailed President Erdogan's stated readiness to normalize Turkey's relations with Armenia. When Varouhi heard about the statement, she told her husband, "This remark from Erdogan is just another 'blind side' comment by the Turkish president and is only made to dupe Armenia into thinking he is sincere about better relations. It's just another farce. I have no idea who in the parliament encouraged the statement, but I think he should examine the details before he makes another remark."

August 31, Armenian's new Foreign Minister Ararat Mirzoyan (b. 1979) visiting Moscow again accused Azerbaijan of not fully adhering with the Russian brokered peace agreement. One of his remarks to the Russian foreign minister was, "Peace and stability in the region is part of our strategy and we are prepared for active dialogue in this direction. But the situation in the region remains quite tense that is greatly determined by Azerbaijan's destructive policy." He then pointed out that Baku was not complying with the joint agreements as to releasing the POWs and the initiation of hostilities on the Armenian and Artsakh borders. Foreign Minister Lavrov said that he and these and other issues will be discussed. When Vartouhi heard the news, she said, "Good luck."

September 8. PM Pashinyan announced that the government is planning a lavish celebration for the upcoming Independence Day. Instead of an overall rejoicing, there was a condemnation from relatives of slain soldiers from the 44 Day War. Pashinyan tried to explain the 30 year anniversary celebration would be dedicated to the martyrs of the war, but was criticized by not only relatives by opposition leaders and public figures, who demanded that the plan for September 21 be scaled down.

September 8, PM Pashinyan noted at his cabinet meeting that he sees words of normalization from President Erdogan and that we are r ready for such conversation. He told his cabinet, "By in large, this is about transforming our region into a crossroad linking the West with the East and North with the South." Vartouhi again thought how the Turkish dictator can talk about normalization when his troops are performing war exercises with Azerbaijan and Pakistan. She was praying that Armenia does not fall into some kind of Turkish plot. There was also discussion of preserving both Eastern and Western Armenian, but this is another story.

September 11, the international community is finally waking up to the fact that Azerbaijan is torturing and abusing Armenian POWs and captured civilians. The Office of the Human Rights Defender of

Armenians and the Yerevan based International and Comparative Law Center (ICLaw) with the support the Armenian Legal Center for Justice and Human Rights (ALC) in Washington, DC are the organization ding the reporting. Organization interviewed 40 repatriated POWs and 10 captured civilians. Personal reports from POWs stated forcing them to sing the Azerzi National Anthem, to shout "Karabakh is Azerbaijani," to drink tainted water, and to eat food off the floor, and many other abuses. Russia has also demanded that Armenian POWs be treated as Geneva Convention III prisoners but Azerbaijan has continually ignored such requests and while falsely calling prisoners as terrorists.

September 21, Armenia celebrated her 30th year of independence from the Soviet Union in an extremely sober light. There was bitter debates as to how the rite should be performed, yet ended up with a beautiful open air concert by the Armenian State Ballet that performed interpretive dances evoking scenes from Armenian's modern history accompanied by classical and tradition hymns by the Armenian Philharmonic Orchestra. The anniversary celebration was formally dedicated to the memory of the martyrs of the 2020 Azeri War that was noted by PM Pashinyan who also announced the formation of a memorial park on the site of Yerevan's Botanical Garden to immortalize the fallen soldiers.

The conclusion of the report stated that 3,781 Armenian soldiers and civilians were killed during the war; 253 remain missing. This is in contrast to other reports that state 5,000 were slain. Vartouhi did not know which figure was correct. The Azeri death toll ranged from 2,879 to a real number of 6,000, which is even more questionable.

September 21, the London IntellliNews reported the buildup of Iranian infantry and rocket artillery on her border with Azerbaijan as military exercises were performed by the "Three Brothers," Azerbaijan, Turkey, and Pakistan. Iran believes the exercises are to impede the trade between her country and Nagorno Karabakh. One representative of the Iran's supreme leader warned Azerbaijan to not "play with the lion's tail." Vartouhi thought it ironic that Turkey especially, was offering peace, trade enhancements, and economic advances while taking part in war maneuvers in Azerbaijan. Iran has not taken the maneuvers lightly by moving infantry forces, drones, and artillery to the Azeri border. Iran has also been concerned with a "$130 road tax" for her trucks transporting goods to Artsakh.

September 23, talk of a possible invasion from Turkey on Armenia circulated in the area. Greek Ambassador to Armenia Leonidas Chrysantopulos made a statement that Turkey intended to attack Armenia. Major Gen. Eduard Simonyants, Head of Armenian State Department of National Security confirmed the statement and started to establish security defenses realizing that the threat of intrusion was extremely high. Turkey using the pretense of PKK operating out of Armenia had to be contained. Vartouhi thought the reason was more for Azerbaijan having an extremely difficult time on her fight in Nagorno Karabakh. It was not too long ago that Azerbaijan convinced Turkey to stop all relations with Armenia. Fortunately, the threat did not occur due to Armenia convincing Turkey that there were no Kurdish encampments of Kurds operating out of Armenia.

September 25, during the UN General Assembly week, Secretary of State Antony Blinken met with Turkish Foreign Minister Mevlut Cavusoglu and had "a relatively long conversation" about Armenia, Azerbaijan, and Nagorno Karabakh. A senior State Department official noted that the US had "midwifed" a swap of demining maps for the release of POWs and he asked if the US can do more to de-escalate the tension between the two counties. If Vartouhi had been at the meeting, she would have told the Secretary, "You can tell Azerbaijan to do a lot more but the Azers do not abide by rules or agreements. We gave the Azeris those demining maps and they still have not returned all the POWs. Azerbaijan does what she wants to do and never minds being told what to do."

President Erdogan used 76th session of the Turkish assembly to announce that Turkey has become a world player and should be treated as such. Most delegates did not take too kindly to the president's rhetoric as they were well aware of using his troops, jihadists, and mercenaries to interfere and dominate other nations, then often acting as a peacemaker. He also criticized the West for harboring Islamophobia, but this was counter criticized for his weaponizing religion and utilizing it to enhance it to build a world sultanate. He has spread his message of Islamic learning and hate in Europe and to train fanatical Islamic youth. In addition to the above he also covered other issues the West was not happy about. He said nothing about Turkey's financial problems.

September 26, several hundred Armenians and ethnic French people demonstrated in front of the Azerbaijani embassy in Paris protesting the holding of Armenian POWs and civilians. They were supposed to be released as stipulated in the November 9, 2020, ceasefire agreement and Geneva Convention rulings. Several speakers spoke about the Azerbaijani physical abuses, reprisals, intimidation and discrimination, and demanded the recognition of the Republic of Artsakh. One speaker, Armenian ombudsman Arman Tataoyan, revealed that "50 survivors testified to physical torture, abuse and deprivation of food, water, sleep and adequate medical care…Some prisoners testified that the guards forced them to eat food spilled on the ground…." And much, much more was pointed out. Vartouhi heard the same abuses many times and thought, "Is any country or organization doing anything about it?"

September 27, PM Pashinyan and other government officials visited Yerevan's Yerablur pantheon, where most of the martyrs of both the First and Second Artsakh Wars are buried to pay homage to the fallen. Other prominent political figures also did the same. The government pledged to strengthen Armenia politically, economically and militarily to ensure that the children and relatives of those who made the ultimate sacrifice would live in a country worthy of them. Vartouhi prayed "so be it," but wondered how this prayer would come about with Armenia so polarized.

September 28, on the battle front, Azeri troops attacked Armenian positions in the Gerharkunic Provence where three Armenian soldiers were killed. This was part of the continuing effort where Azerbaijan does not understand what a ceasefire means. After heavy fighting, the Armenian troops forced the Azeris back to their starting point.

September 30, the National Security Service (NSS) announced that it had detained former Defense Minister Davit Tonoyan (b. 1967) on embezzlement charges of large sums of money, falsifications, and faulty weapons purchases. The NNS also announced the detainment of David Galstyan, head of the defense contractor supplying weapons to the Armenian Army. Together they were charged with stealing 2.3 billion dram ($4.7 million). Other officials are also being investigated. Vartouhi thought it sad that Armenians could be so traitorous, but Simon added that Armenians are not much different than other people.

October 4, at a joint news conference between Lithuania/Armenian in Vilnius, PM Pashinyan thanked PM Ingrida Simonyte (b. 1974) for the "balance position" on the Nagorno-Karabakh conflict and on its role in the European Union's efforts to ease tensions between Azerbaijan and Armenia. In addition to demining and POW issues Pashinyan publically answered a concern of Tehran that Armenia is colluding with the West in a plot against Iran. Pashinyan stated that Armenia cannot and will not plot against Iran. He also said that he has dispatched Foreign Minister Ararat Mirzoyan to assure the leaders in Tehran that Armenia does not have any such intention.

With regard to the complex issue between Armenia and Iran, inter-mixed with Azerbaijan, Turkey, and Israel, it has been extremely difficult for Armenia to keep on top of concerns. Iran has complained about the Azeri taxing of its supply trucks entering Nakhichevan. In addition, Turkey that is now a surrogate and endorser of Azerbaijan is performing military exercises, even including Pakistan, in Naknichevan. Why? Alarmed and concerned at the movement, Iran stared building up her military in the event the three potential aggressors commit some border incidents. India has also gotten into the picture by seeing Turkey's aggressive moves toward the establishment of the southern corridor through Armenia. India is well aware of Pakistan's support to Azerbaijan and Turkey and her participation the military exercises the two countries. She is also extremely concerned to see any Turkish expansion to the East. We are yet to see what all this movement will affect Armenia, but it certainly does not sound good. The situation does not look promising with all the building up of their arms and having joint military maneuvers. One thing that Armenia has started to ease some of the tensity is to construct additional roads going into Iran. These would allow Iranian trucks tax-free passage into Armenia.

October 9, the Russian Minister of Defense reported the killing of a civilian near the town of Martakert. An Azeri sniper shot and killed a farmer while he was plowing his field. As usual, the Azerbaijani government has denied reports of the shooting. However, the Artsakh authority has repeatedly reported similar attacks in other border towns. The incident caused an uproar of comments and complaints from various Armenian and Artsakh officials to Russian peacekeepers, the Russian peacekeeper's office and Defense Ministry. Spokesman for the Russian Defense Ministry stated it is analyzing the episode and will take further action to exclude ceasefire violations and to insure greater security opportunities. Vartouhi stated the rebuttals are great, but she has seen these before while the Azeris continue to violate the trilateral agreements that they signed. She wrote in her column that it is an ongoing thing that Azerbaijan continually violates the agreements she signed up to and no penalties are assessed against her. The reporter thinks that Arman Tatoyan (b. 1981) said it correctly when he said, "This tragic incident proves yet again that the guaranteeing of the right to life, the right to a secure and peaceful life and vital right of the Armenian population is impossible in the conditions of Azerbaijani policy of hatred and enmity and due to the fact that those who committed these criminal acts, and the Azerbaijani authorities who promote Armenophobia remain unpunished."

October 12, former residents of Karabakh protested in Yerevan accusing the government of not helping them. Some financial assistance was provided in August but was discontinued. PM Pashinyan assured the protestors that the government is establishing new aid programs that should help them. Vartouhi said she would followup on the statement to confirm that it is accomplished.

October 19, Armenian Ombudsman and Human Rights Defender Arman Tatoyan reported the Azerbaijani forces that invaded the Gegharkunik region last May have illegally built large shelters and paved the roads leading to positions. He further reported, "These are the Azerbaijani positions from where the Azerbaijani servicemen commit terrorist crimes against the civilian population of Armenia. They regularly fire on the villages of Verin Shorzha, Sotk, Kut and other settlements in the area. The officers of these positions have committed a large number of thefts of animals of the residents of the Republic of Armenia." Many more abuses have been reported in other areas.

Tatoyan further reported other infringements, and that a proposal has been made to the Parliamentary Assembly of the Council Europe (PACE) to create a demilitarized security zone around the borders of Armenia and the immediate removal of servicemen of the occupied villages should begin immediately. Vartouhi said the proposals are great, except there has been no teeth in them. The Azeris do what they want and they have been getting away with their violations of international law. She agrees wit Tatoyan when he said "...the violations will not end, and the security of the people will not be guaranteed unless the perpetrators are punished."

October 26, President Erdogan visit to Azerbaijan discussed the idea of opening the controversial Zangezur Corridor in southern Armenia. Erdogan claimed that he is still interested in opening the corridor where Aliyev has not been as vociferous lately. The Azeri dictator even surprised Armenia by releasing four POWs. Previous clamors from the dictator had made threats of military action if necessary, but so far they have been spotty inroads into Armenian territory. Armenia has procrastinated on the issue and the international community has toughened up on the loudmouth Aliyev. Iran and India have expressed their concerns as to potential Turian expansion Turkey has been dreaming about for almost a century.

While all this mishmash was occurring, Russia has set up a symbolic meeting for November 9 (the first anniversary of the ceasefire agreement) to sign two treaties. The first one is on the border demarcation and delimitation between Armenia and Azerbaijan based on the old USSR maps. The second one is on the opening of roads and communications. These two treaties will not be easily agreed to. Vartouhi said, "We'll have to wait to see what happens. So far, treaties mean nothing to the Azeris."

President Putin has made an intricate statement asking both sides to make concessions saying, "There are things which require mutual concessions from both parties. There are places where exchanges are required." The only problem with Putin's statement is that Armenia has already given up numerous concessions to date. What more can she give up?

October 26, turmoil continues in the Armenian Parliament as security officers removed deputy lawmaker Gegham Manukyan (b. 1970) from the podium where he was accused of trying to discredit the Hyastan All-Armenian Fund and the Armenian government with various "abominations." Vartouhi explained it was a sad commentary that parliament members could not get along with each other.

October 29 -31, the Armenian capital hosted the Digitec information technology expo over the weekend that included some of the biggest names in the local tech scene and thousands of tech enthusiasts from the world. The expo has been held every October since 2005 with the exception of the war in 2020 and COVID – 19 pandemic. The Armenian tech scene has the distinction of being one of the few sectors that continues to see robust growth.

November 8, former President Robert Kocharyan held a rally in Yerevan against possible territorial concessions. His Alliance Party in coalition with the ARF called the launch of a "national resistance" to oust PM Pashinyan and the "Turkification of Armenia."

November 9, on the first anniversary of the trilateral agreement Armenia took a look at its present day status. The situation for the country does not look too promising but surprisingly the people have pretty well taken the defeat in stride. There are still periodic Azeri aggressions at the borders, but Aliyev has toned down some of abrasive rhetoric and recently released five POWs. Negotiations and talks are continuing, but as far a Vartouhi can see, not a lot meaningful progress. Life in Artsakh has become very difficult due more to the unpredictability and the Azeri continuous belligerence. However, most Karabakhis have been taking the instability in stride.

November 11, two days later additional reflection was given by the concerned parties as to what has happened and what is currently going on. Azerbaijan continues her provoking aggression whenever she has an opportunity. President Biden called for a conference with Armenia and Georgia to discuss democracy on December 9-10 in Washington.

Turkey and Azerbaijan were not invited. Vartouhi was not sure what other subjects were to be discussed, but hopefully Biden would include the violations the Azeris and its allies have been committing and if the US is going to do anything about it. Another element in the picture is the 3+3 formula that no one seems to be crazy about, but Russia endorsed the idea because it leaves the West out.

The 3+3 is the President Erdogan's proposed formula to unlock the economic and transport communications in the Caucasus. Two teams are to be made up by Armenia, Azerbaijan, and Georgia, and the other by Russia, Turkey, and Iran. The idea is to resolve some of the existing problems in the region). Vartouhi did not think the participating countries were particularly too excited about the formula but felt they had to join to make sure their interests were not trampled on. Vartouhi wished them luck. She believes the 3+3 format is a ploy by the three large members to keep control of the regions they are more directly involved. They would rather call the shots rather than the OSCE Minsk Group.

Even though the 3+3 is trying to hinder the efforts of the Minisk Group, the Co-chairs have gone ahead and called on Armenia and Azerbaijan to continue their talks on the progress of humanitarian issues by including such as detainees, demining, missing persons retuning displaced persons, border demarcation, and the protection of historic and cultural sites. When Vartouhi saw the list she again thought to herself that Armenia and Azerbaijan would agree to all those issues, but Azerbaijan would never adhere to them.

Other occurrences included the Parliamentary Assembly Council of Europe (PACE) that has blamed Azerbaijan for violating one of its fundamental principles of membership, resorting to war to resolve conflicts, which warrants sanctions. Azerbaijan has also violated stated principles of the OSCE by resorting to war. To date, no party has reprimanded Baku for that violation. Vartouhi stated that many other violations have been performed and the Azeris continually bypass any punishment that they have been called on. . In most of the set-up meetings there was no talk about the status of Karabakh. Russia thinks they can settle that later. In the meantime Azerbaijan continues her dirty work unmolested. Armenia pins her hopes on the Minsk Group, but our journalist wonders about that group.

November 14, Azeri forces attacked the town of Sisian in the Provence of Syunik inside the Republic of Armenia. PM Pashinyan dismissed Defense Minister Arshak Karapetyan (b. 1967) from office and replaced him with Suren Papikyan (b. 1986).

November 15-16, Azerbaijan aggression continued toward the Provence of Syunik until Russia again brokered another ceasefire. Armenian lost one soldier with 12 being captured. There was no confirmation on the deaths. There were also clashes in the Lachin Corridor where the highway was closed for a few hours, but opened soon after. No deaths were reported in corridor area.

November 16, Armenia asked Russia for help after Azerbaijan again started new border clashes. *Reuters* reported 15 soldiers had been killed, 12 were captured, and two combat positions had been lost. Armenian sources believe 14 Azeri soldiers were killed, 37 were wounded, and five were missing. The fighting was the worst since last year's 44-Day War. As of this date there has been no r response from Russia to the Armenian appeal except for the brokered ceasefire. Vartouhi wrote in her column that Azerbaijan has absolutely no respect for the November 9, 2020, ceasefire she agreed to last year. "We are yet to see what Russia does about these most recent clashes?"

November 18, on later reports on the clashes, Azerbaijani Defense Minister stated seven Azeri soldiers were killed, none were wounded. Armenian officials reported one serviceman died, 13 were captured. Both sides accused each other of starting the clashes although Azerbaijan has been a chronic liar in most of like reports. Vartouhi again explained in her column we should not expect any changes from Azerbaijan. She has never has been an advocate for peace and has violated all kinds of agreements. She has been getting away with this malfeasance for years: Because there has been no significant punishment, ceasefires just come and go with no retribution. Later reports indicated one Armenian soldier was killed and 13 were captives, and traces of 24 soldiers are unknown. Azeri losses were believed to be 70 soldiers were either wounded or dead and several of its military equipment were lost. The

Azeri forces continued their firings inspite of the ceasefire agreement. Russia manages to initiate the ceasefires but Azerbaijan takes them rather lightly.

November 23, chess grandmaster Levon Aronian (b. 1982) won the prestigious Tata Steel Blitz Chess tournament in India after defeating India's highest ranking chess player. Aronian dedicated his victory to Armenia, to all the compatriots who fell in the battlefield, and to all who live and struggle for the Armenian nation.

Aronian missed the European tournament that was held near the same week as the Blitz matches. The Armenian teams did very well up until the final meets, ending up seventh in the final chart. The Armenian women's team ended 11th.

November 26, President Putin called for a trilateral meeting in Sochi among PM Pashinyan, President Aliyev, and himself to iron-out some of the problems between the two countries. When Vartouhi saw the results of the three hour meeting, she analyzed that it did not go too well. It was difficult for Pashinyan to agree to any settlements when Azerbaijan was continually attacking Armenian borders and utilizing aggressive rhetoric in his speeches. Putin was aiming to discuss the demarcation and delimitation and the restoration of communication in the region. There was some agreement on communication, but not on the other two aims. When Pashinyan asked Putin to stop the Azeri belligerence, the Russian president said it would trigger an acute political crisis with Turkey. "Is Russia afraid of Turkey?" Vartouihi commented to her husband. Simon just nodded with a shrug. The two leaders agreed to work bilateraly but Vartouhi questioned the sincerity of the Azeri dictator in her mind due to the fact that agreements do not mean much to him.

November 29, at the Ministry of Health press conference it was announced that high rates of acute respiratory infections are starting to plague Armenia and that there is another increase in COVID-19 infections. People are reminded it is essential to wear masks and to keep at six feet from other people. Hospitals are being overcrowded much as in other countries. Armenia has also put a ban on travelers from African.

Decembeer 4, Azerbaijan returned 10 Armenian soldiers in exchange of the Karabakh landmine maps. Hundreds of POWs still are held there.

December 5, former US Senator Robert (Bob) Dole (1923-2021) and World War II hero, died in Washington, DC. He was an outstanding statesman and candidate for vice presidency and president of the US and an honored friend and supporter of many Armenian causes. Dr. Hampar Kelekian (1899-1983) was his master surgeon who helped Dole in the limited use of his right arm due to a war injury and taught Dole about the Armenians. President Armen Sarkessian sent a letter of condolence to Elizabeth Dole and Ambassador Varuzhan Neressyan exalted Dole with the "Republic of Armenia Order of Honor." Congress bestowed the Congressional Gold Metal to Dole in 2018.

December 7, Reuters reported the World Court of Justice ordered Azerbaijan to prevent incitement of hatred against Armenians and to protect Armenian prisoners of war. The court specified that under the UN anti-discrimination Treaty, Azerbaijan must take all necessary measures to prevent incitement of hatred and discrimination. Vartouhi laughed to herself when she read the report thinking what the World Court was going to do if Azerbaijan ignores the order as the Azeris usually do. She was anxious to see what Azeris were going to report on their side of the story,

December 7, Armenian parliamentary members discussed the role of some Armenian soldiers who surrendered during the war. They did not have a happy debate as members argued with each other and accused soldiers throwing down their weapons and yielding to the enemy. Vartouhi thought this was a real "slap-in-the-face" as it disputes all theories on how brave and courageous Armenian soldiers are.

December 9, Azerbaijan again broke the agreed ceasefire by firings at the border. The Armenian Defense Minister said in the evening that Azerbaijani troops "opened intensive fire from firearms of different caliber" at Armenian military positions in the Gegharkunik province bordering the Kelbaja district. The firing continued overnight and resumed the following day. Two soldiers were slightly wounded in the assault. Both side accused each other of violating the ceasefire. Vartouhi told her husband, "I can't believe the Azeris, they lie so much. They agree to ceasefires then forget they made them"

December 14, a trilateral meeting was held in Brussels among Pashinyan, Aliyev, and the President of the European Council. The two leaders pledged to de-escalate tension and restore railway lines. If Vartouhi heard what happened she probably would say to herself, "It's just another lie from the dictator." See addition details on December 15.

December 15, a railway construction reenforcement plan was reached the day after the Brussels meeting among PM Pashinyan, President Aliyev, and President Charles Michel of the European Council. The next day Pashinyan presented a speech to his cabinet that the railway was to be connected between Yeraskh, Julfa, Ordubad, Meghri, and Horadiz. The PM told his cabinet that the construction was approved originally at the November 26 trilateral Sochi meeting. He emphasized the railway will operate in accordance with accepted internationally border and custom rules, under the principle of reciprocity and sovereignity and jurisdiction of the respected countries.

December 24, during an online press conference, PM Pashinyan said he "washed his hands of the Karabakh problem." The simple statement caused rumpus between him and the authorities in Artsakh. The PM felt there were organizations set up to manage the problems between Azerbaijan and Artsakh. A few people thought it was good that Karabakh could take care of her own problems and Armenia could relish a calm life by herself. Other people thought the PM was abandoning the Armenians of Artsakh.

December 31, the finger pointing for losing the war continued into the new year with PM Pashinyan on public TV again openly blaming Armenia's past leadership opposition on the disaster. Opposition politicians in Armenia and Karabakh quickly denounced the remark stirring controversy between Armenia and Artsakh. Karabakh President Ara Harutyunyan said in a statement, "There can be no return to the past in terms of not only status but also of demography." He stressed only the authorities in Stepanakert can speak for the territory's predominately Armenian population.

2022

January 14, the first round of talks to normalize the relationship between Armenia and Turkey was held in Moscow. The two representatives of their respective governments agreed they should work to regulate ties "through dialogue" and without preconditions. The representatives stated that the date and place of the second meeting will be determined via diplomatic channels. Armenia expects that the talks will lead to the establishment of diplomatic relations and the reopening borders after decades of animosity. Vartouihi was not too encouraged by the report, but hoped something positive materialized in the future.

January 17, Philippe Raffi Kalfayan again got into the conglomeration of report writing by commenting on the frenetic diplomatic pace challenges for Armenia and Artaskh in a report to the *Mirror Spectator* in which he discusses clashes in relationships. He talks about the need for Armenia to elaborate and implement a new legal–diplomatic paradigm where he proposes several ideas on how this could be accomplished. The self-determination process of Nagorno Karabakh has remained unachieved to date, yet even worse; its very existence is threatened. He points out there were opportunities in the past, but Armenia failed to initiate any progress in that area. It is easy to point fingers, as many others have done, but he strongly believes in improving the diplomatic corps of nation. He does not provide on how to find or create these super-political indivduals, yet it is a requirement that has to be accomplished. Kalfayan does say that it was a good measure that Armenia brought Azerbaijan to the International Court of Justice. The court hearings have not started yet, but the Azeris cannot take the risk of continuing their crimes of torture, summary executions, beheadings, and other international violations that they have demonstrated in the past.

Kalfayan is concerned about the opening of borders and the development of land and air communications with Azerbaijan and Turkey. He feels this would be more beneficial to the economic and financial strengths of the two Moslem countries where Armenia could be colonized economically and demographically. The opening of borders could also accelerate the alarming rate of emigration of Armenian citizens.

Other issues that should be reviewed are introducing preconditions in the talks. The French Armenian thinks there should be no prerequisites. Another is to take advantage of Turkey's current financial crisis and all-out military adventures. Armenia should refuse to sign any agreement with Azerbaijan until all POWs are released. The negotiations with Azerbaijan should not exonerate her with the crimes she has already committed. The main concern at the present is the safety of the population of Artsakh. When Vartouhi saw the report she thought Kalfayan did a good job in putting it together, but she was concerned with people working together to make it work. If the policy of institutionalized hatred and discrimination still prevails, she has her doubts.

January 23, President Armen Sarkessian announced his resignation on his presidential website along with several statements. He spoke on the history of Armenia since independence and how he attempted to keep the nation on a well-managed course. He talked about the importance of building a country that would insure the security, progress, and prosperity of Armenians. He emphasized the importance of having the tools and opportunities to influence foreign political, economic, and investment policy and relations with the Diaspora, as well as to promote national interest in the international arena, and shape a new scientific-educational and high tech environment. He said he wanted to create a state system based on checks and balances. He said he was glad that a commission has been set up where he hopes an eventual constitutional change will take place, and the next president will be able to work in a more balanced, coordinated environment.

Days after the announcement, comments generated from several sources. His request to have a constitution review was originally rejected, but later was told it would be done. Some politicians said he resigned due to his lack of power and that Armenia did not have a "balance of power" government. He had a secret illegal citizenship with St. Kitts and Nevis (a nation of two small islands in the Caribbean Sea with its east shore on Atlantic Ocean and its west shore on the Caribbean). Sakessian claimed he was offered the dual citizenship years ago, but never accepted it, although the record indicated he has the dual citizenship from the two island nation. He claims he told the investigating company that he was not interested in any passport. According to *Hertq.am*, an online Armenian newspaper in Yerevan, Sarkessian has held a passport from the Caribbean nation as late as 2017, shortly before his election as president. There are many more questions about president's past that *Herq.am* has brought out. The National Security Service (NSS) is currently investigating his background.

Sarkessian has had a history for working for the government shortly after Armenian independence. He was the first Ambassador to London. He served as Armenia's Prime Minister from November 1996 to March 1997, and then was appointed as special advisor to the president of the European for Reconstruction and Development (ERBD) and later as governor of EBRD from 1998 to 2000. After he served on the Dean's Board and Advisory Board of Harvard University and University of Chicago and several prestigious international organization until he was elected as president under the new constitution in 2018. He was often disappointed due to the constant criticisms and continued attempts to underdermine his activities.

February 2, Artsakh Foreign Minister David Babayan (b. 1973) spoke at a Zoom press conference organized by the Armenian Democratic Liberal Party (ADL) in Watertown, MA. The talk enlightened a lot of people who had no idea as to what was going on in Artaskh. Babayan stated that Artsakh has lost all but 20 percent of its territory and is completely surrounded by Azerbaijan, which is supported by Turkey. He compared Artsakh to a heavily wounded but alive and in the course of recovery. Azerbaijan cannot destroy her due to the Russian peacekeepers but instead attempts to psychologically destroy her. He talked of the unity of Armenia, Artsakh, and Diaspora as being essential. He told of Azeri forces infringing on Armenian and Artsakh territories, but are often forced back. The destruction of Armenian monuments has been rampant. When the Azeris cannot get to the sites they falsely claim they are Caucasian Albanian. If that does not work, they claim them Russian Orthodox. Another ploy the Azeris use is not to permit foreign researchers or UN personnel to investigate the sites. Babayan claims the Russian peacekeepers are doing a good job and that he would like to keep them on to continue their mission well pass 2025. He answered audience questions after his talk.

February 15, a report was issued by the government stating what the 2021 inflation rate was in Armenia. Inflation started in 2020 but increased almost eight percent during the year. Food prices rose 11.2 percent, household goods 8.7 percent, leisure by 3.8 percent, alcoholic beverages by 9.3 percent, clothing by 8.1 percent, transport by 9.1 percent, and healthcare by 5.4 percent. Other areas were not quite as bad, however the figures for first months of 2022 got worse. The Armenian government has attempted to find the cause of the rising prices but it has been a universal problem in most countries due largely to rising energy, mineral, and food prices. To date the government has not much to stem the rise.

February 13, a 5.2 magnitude earthquake hit Armenia in the Armenian-Georgian border about 40 kilometers north of Gyumri. Fortunately, there were no deaths and there was minor damage.

February 23, Dr. Arman Tatoyan terminated his six year term as Human Rights Defender Ombudsman of Armenia. Former Deputy Minister of Justice Kristine Grigoryan (b. 1981) was elected to replace him. Tatoyan was especially critical of Azeri human rights violations where POWs were tortured, the burning of tattooed crosses on hands of captives, and the killing of anyone who was wearing a cross.

February 25, a new problem has been created in Europe that significantly affects other countries. Russia started an invasion of Ukraine that she threatened for months. The US and other nations have imposed huge sanctions on Russia while condemning the attack. Implication for other nations has been dramatic as trading barriers and financial relations are not as clear as before the attack. At the present, it is not clear how the UN and USA sanctions on Russia will affect the Armenian economy, but if the 2014 sanctions on Russia were any indication, the Armenian economy will falter. The delimitation and demarcation process has made no headway, and will probably will stay at a standstill. Armenia is sure to encounter a loss of the modest flexibility it had with the West. Armenia is in a real dilemma as how to react to any siding in the conflict. Armenia should do everything possible to maintain her relationship the Euro-Atlantic community, but still stay within the Russian economy. Yerevan should be careful not to disrupt her relations with either the West or Russia.

PM Pashinyan has expressed concerns over the impact of Western sanctions on not only Russia but on how they will affect other members of the Eurasian Economic Union (EEU). This includes Armenia, which has not officially reacted to Russia's aggression, but essentially has taken a neutral stand. Armenia considers both Russia and Ukraine as "friendly countries" and hopes they will resolve their conflict through "diplomatic dialogue." Still even if he does nothing the PM feels the tourist trade will reduce and the transfer of Armenian worker funds to Armenia will greatly diminish. One thing that bothers Pashinyan is that he remembers how Ukraine supplied Azerbaijan with a lot of military equipment during the 44-Day War and that President Volodymr Zelenskyy personally congratulated President Aliyev in winning the war. In addition, the Ukrainian president has no particular love for Armenia. The situation puts a hard decision on Pashinyan.

February 26, Azerbaijan continues her aggressive tactics even while Russia and Ukraine are in turmoil. The Arzeris conducted psychological and physical attacks on the village of Khramort in Artsakh and nothing is being done about it. The Azeri troops in the past have occasionally fired upon the villagers, but this time they entered the village threatening the inhabitants carrying out farm work by demanding that they leave the village or submit to them. The soldiers claimed the village was located in Azerbaijan territory, which it is not. Artaskh Human Rights Defender Gegham Stepanyan (b. 1991) referred to the incident that a stunned atmosphere prevailed in the village. The Azeris located just outside the village intiminiated the villagers using loudspeakers threatening and telling them to abandon their homes. The provocation is an outright violation of human rights and nothing is being done about it. The worse part of this scenario is that the Azerbaijani troops are doing this openly in a lot of localized incidents and they are getting away with it.

March 10, the European Parliament adopted a resolution chiding Azerbaijan for destroying Armenian heritage in Artsakh. The long overdue resolution vote tally was 635 in favor, 2 opposed and 42 abstentions. The text drew on the series of previous resolutions and conventions, but this one put all the charges skillfully together so there was no question about each one. Recap of the charges are summarized below;

- Physical destruction was sustained to 1456 structures, mainly Armenian churches and monuments.
- The falsification of history that includes the denial of the existence of Armenian physical monuments and the actual changing of historical records.
- Azeri policy of Armenophobia, erasure of Armenian cultural heritage, historical revisionism and hatred toward Armenians, including dehumanization, the glorification of violence and territorial claims, and other damaging issues.

The welcoming of the UNESCO proposal to send an independent expert mission without delay and that demands Azerbaijan to grant unhindered access to all heritage sites in order for the mission to determine what has occurred at the sites.

Vartouhi understands how some Europeans are reluctant to condemn Azerbaijan due to Russian's measure to stop oil shipments due to UN and other national support for Ukraine. By the same token, she thinks they should understand what Nagorno Karabakh (and especcially Nakhichevan) has gone through the last few decades. However, she is thankful for the European action because it opens the doors for other organizations and nations to condemn Azerbaijan for what she has done and is continuing to do.

The document will be delivered to officials and organs of the European Union, the governments and presidents of Armenia and Azerbaijan, the Director-General of UNESCO, the secretary generals of OSCE, the Council of European and the UN, and Europa Nostra. Vartouhi prays that something positive results from all this action.

March 12,

March 25, Azerbaijan armed forces broke another peace agreement by infiltrating into the village of Parukh in Artsakh. Baku again demonstrated its intention of violating the measures set up for the peace process.

March 26, Azerbaijan continued to attack Karabakh in the eastern section of Askeran district. Ilham Aliyev talks peace with one side of his mouth while the other side commands his military to continue to assault Artsakh and Armenian border towns.

March 26, *The Armenian Miirror Spectator* included "The Artsakh and Ukraine Conflicts Need to Be Recongnized as Two Separate Battles of the Same War" by Dr. Arsgavir Gundjian. The article points out quite adequately the similarities and differences between the two conflicts. He tells about how the West and other nations in the world have come to Ukraine's aid with food, military supplies, financial resources, and residency of refugees in their countries. Gundjian is not criticizing this action, in fact supporting it, but he questions, where was, and still is not, that kind of support for Artsakh? Azerbaijan has literally been getting away with murder and the world has been deaf and blind as to what has been occurring in the Caucasus, and still is occurring. Artsakh has received the same brutalities, and possibly the worse atrocities, than what Russia has bestowed on Ukraine. The free world has done nothing much to help Artsakh or inflict guilt on Azerbaijan.

In addition, Gundjian also points out to the world that Artsakh is also a de jure independent state by accepted standards of international law. The country followed all the international steps and held a referendum of self-determination around the time of the Soviet Union fall in 1990. In addition, the genocidal state-sponsored policy of Azerbaijan that s being openly applied in occupied regions, doubly qualifies and reinforces Artsakh's right for independence. He feels the international press has been notariousl unfavorable toward Armenia's plight.

One other point Gundjian addresses is Armenia's diplomatic policy. The country has to develop a strong loud and clear awareness of what the Azeris and Turks are doing to Artsakh dispite their talking of peace.

Gundjian recommends a two-prongedged relentless campaign, one an aggressive and active outreach to the Western world and the other, Armenian information and media services be provided in European language.

April 6-7, European Council President Charles Michel called for a meeting between PM Pashinyan and President Ilham Aliyev in Brussels to settle some of the issues between the two countries, Michel called meeting a success, but Vartouhi wanted to know the "details of the success." The three sides signaled a positive movement toward a peace agreement for the Caucasus, but Vartouhi questions how Aliyev can agree to peace when his troops are constantly raiding Armenian and Artsakh border villages and cities killing both civilians and soldiers. Another thing was that none of the statements touched on the Karabakh core issue. To make matters worse Aliyev thinks he has solved the problem militarily and that OSCE Minsk Group has no longer any function. "How can you talk peace with someone who has a relentless attitude and lies so much," she told her husband one evening.

Russia is concerned about the meeting because she feels the West is taking over issues related to the conflicting counties and may be countering her guiding principles. Her aggressive war against Ukraine does not help. Armenia has to exercise some real diplomacy in her relations when dealing with both the West and Russia. Pashinyan plans to meet with Putin on April 19 to bring him up to date and to assure him that Armenia still relies on Russia for support.

April 13, Artaskh leadership criticized PM Pashinyan warning him against helping Azerbaijan regain control over the Armenian populated territory. Passhinyan claimed the international community was pressuring him to "lower the bar on the question of Nagorno-Karabakh status" and recognize Azerbaijan's territorial integrity, Artsakh believes Pashinyan's remarks signated Yerevan's intention to make concessions to Baku for Azeri control over Karabakh. When Foreign Minister of Artsakhs Davit Babayan (b. 1973) heard about the statement he said, "Even if the whole international community is against us ...we will still fight till the end."

Pashinyan tried to soften his remarks by addressing the Armenian Parliament on the same day, "What I've been saying is all about not surrendering Karabalh…If we follow a different path we will surrender Karabakh." He followed with an additional remark, "I have the impression that there are people who dream about seeing the population leave Karabakh as sooon as possible, No, what we are saying is that the people of Karabakh must not leave Karabakh, the people of Karabakh must live in Karabakh, the people of Karabakh must have rights, freedoms and status." As far as the Artsakh leadership was concerned, Pashinyan's parliamentary statement did not soften the feelings against him.

April 16, *The Armenian Weekly* newspaper carried the headline, "Pashinyan ready to recognize Azerbaijan's territorial integrity." The article pretty much carried the remarks that the prime minister presented in previous speeches. When Vartouhi read the article, she was extremelly disappointed in her former student in that he has learned to speak "double talk." How can Karabakh be a territorial integrity of Azerbaijan, and the same time say, "the people of Karabakd must live in Karabakh, the people in Karabakh must have rights, freedom and status?" Pashinyan as well hundreds of thousands Armenians know what happens to a territory when it is governed by a Muslim country. Look at Nakhichevan.

April 17, opposition leader Arthur Vanetsyan (b. 1979) announced that he and several other party leaders in parliament would hold indefinite sit-in in central Yerevan to protest the Armenian government's apparent openness to ceding control of Karabakh to Azerbaijan. He and his allies demanded that Pashinyan resign in a prepared statement. Vartouhi could understand the frustration of other parliamentarians due to Pashinyan's lackluster performance. She also noticed that there was not much support from the international community. Azerbaijan can offer oil, Armenia has nothing to offer.

April 24, President Joe Biden again acknowledged the Armenian Genocide of 1915 by the Ottoman Turks as many other nations in the world. Turkey still denies that was a "Genocide" where her ancestors murdered one and half million Armenians.

Chapter 10 more or less ends the time sequencing in the book and continues on with what is going on in a broader sense. Ceasefires are still going on ending most of the time in Azerbaijan violations. The war in Ukraine is continuing with Russia bombing and killing thousands of civilians. Conciliatorily talks are ongoing between Armenia and Turkey and the Brussels EU peace talks are long-lasting between Armenia and Azerbaijan while the Azeris remain steady in their aggressive attacks on the border towns of Artsakh and Armenia. The OSCS Minsk Group is still operating, but with a possibility of discontinuing. Armenia and Artsakh are at odds with each other regarding Karabakh independence.

Chapter 11

The Reawakening

When I first started to compose *Never to Die II* in 2017, I had the positive feeling that Armenia had a bright future, but after the Armenian/Azeri 44-DayWar, I now have my doubts. However, I still believe Armenia can overcome her problems, except I think maybe it's going to take much longer than I expected. Armenia has had disasters in the past and eventually recovered, when she earned her independence in 1918 and in 1991; she was really unprepared with professional diplomatic and technical leadership. Management in the various governmental disciplines had to be learned and experienced. She did it before and she can do it again.

When the "Velvet Revolution" occurred in the spring of 2018 my hopes were initially high spirited, but three years later, I'm beginning to wonder? Azerbaijan got herself back to control surroundings of Nagorno Karabakh, and Turkey who has had a continuous scourge on the Armenians for centuries, is intimidating pressure as much as possible by conducting war maneuvers together with the Azeris who by themselves have been extremely inept in their offense of war. At the same time, Turkey is coming out with peace initiatives and rapprochement. This does not make sense to me nor to our fictitious Vartouhi.

At the start of hostilities in early 1990, Azerbaijan was not capable of penetrating into Karabakh territory. Even though the Armenians were outnumbered they were able to soundly defeat the Azeri forces at almost every engagement. After every Azerbaijani offense, she has had to retreat home with her drooped tail between her legs. After the sound defeat in the summer Four Day War of 2020, President Aliyev went crawling to President Erdogan crying for help. The Turks gave him more than help; they took over.

Turkey got involved into the picture. She sent troops and war equipment into Azerbaijan, set up a military base in Nakhichevan, and has played war games together with the Azeris. Turkey together with Azerbaijan has hired thousands of former Islamic State terrorists to help perform their inhuman tactics and do much of their dirty work. This is while Azerbaijan holds Armenian POWs mislabeling them terrorist where in reality the Azeris are the ones who hire terrorists. A few Armenian captured soldiers have undergone mock trials in Azerbaijan and are currently serving prison terms. Azerbaijan also uses every reason possible to engage in skirmishes into Armenia and Artsakh in spite of the November 2020 ceasefire she agreed to. Pakistan has also gotten into the picture where she supplies fighter planes from her air force in the 44- Day War. She continues her support by participating military exercises with Turkey and Azerbaijan.

At the time of this printing of *Never to Die II*, the future of Armenia-Azerbaijan relationship remains elusive. Meetings have occurred between the two countries often with the support of large nations, agreements have been made and signed, and ceasefires have come and gone. Yet, at the time of this writing, no positive settlement has been reached nor has the exchange of POWs been fully implemented. Azerbaijan continues to put pressure on civilians in Karabakh, and attacks on the border almost weekly. Azerbaijan believes she has solved the dilemma by winning the war, but Armenia believes Artsakh still has a possibility of self-existence. Vartouhi thinks it may take years for a real settlement to take place.

Turkish President Recep Erdogan today is playing the role of "piece by peace" much as Adolf Hitler did in the late 1930s. He is attempting to emulate the role of Sultan Selim I (1470-1520) who ruled the Ottoman Turkey for eight years (1512-1520). Armenia is one of the countries that are in Erdogan's agenda. From the Turkish president's actions, this looks like what he is attempting to do in Syria, Libya, Greece, and Lebanon. From his buildup of Turkish forces in Azerbaijan and Nakhichevan it appears to be the same aim going eastward. Turkey has literally made Azerbaijan a puppet state. It appears that Erdogan is slowly accomplishing his intended schedule. To date, Russia has not made any attempt to stop the Turkish dictator's dream, but maybe she will wake up to what is going on in the near future. Iran is also concerned with what is occurring. She is not amenable to the Zangezur Corridor as its construction will impede her trade relations with Central Asia.

One other concern about Erdogan is his rhetoric about relations with Armenia. It depends on what one wants to believe. Good relations help in restoring the Turkish economy that used to be more than satisfactory but is currently in shambles. Inflation has gotten out of control. He talks about peace and opening trade routes and commerce on one hand then about finishing the job of his ancestors on then other hand. At another time he says, "Maybe we have to teach them (the Armenians) another lesson." The launching of peace initiatives may be side issues but have more to do more for completing his dream of a Turian Empire.

Some things will never change in Armenia like half the country caters to Russia ideals and policies while the other half wants to have nothing to do with her giant neighbor. This seems to be true even among her families and people, and also in her parliament that demonstrates its feelings in fist fights and brawls. This is a sad commentary for small nations like Armenia, because it is so crucial that she have a united front. People and organizations can have differences and still get along respectfully.Vartouhi thinks this a tough one for Armenians, but she has her doubts.

Armenia in the beginning of the 44-Day War thought she could defeat Azerbaijan as in the past and did not request any assistance. Later when the situation was more severe where Turkey got involved and the nation needed military assistance, support was not forthcoming when requested. She had a treaty called the CSTO (Collective Security Treaty Organization) and originally did not request assistance but later when asked, none was forthcoming from the treaty members. One excuse after another was utilized resulting in no help. However, when it came to humanitarian aid or the progression of democracy, other countries were willing to help. Armenia had a rude awakening where she was not the strong military power she thought she was. Her soldiers are no doubt probably the best and bravest in the Caucasus, but if a military force does not have proper fighting equipment the bravery does not mean much. Armenia did not have that equipment. There was a lot of finger pointing after the war, yet the fact remains that she did not have the proper battle gear.

After the defeat of the war, families, politicians, and almost everyone attempted to put the finger on who was responsible for losing the war. Unfortunately, PM Pashinyan got most of the blame. The accusations were so bad they were again calls for his resignation. He was called a traitor by some people, but the charge should be more like incompetence. He was, and is known for his patriotism. Pashinyan countered accusers by asserting that the former presidents should be accountable also for not keeping the strength of Armenia up while they were in office. As far as keeping him as prime minister, the June snap election votes were 53percent for Pashinyan where only 23 percent were for Kocharyan. This had to be some indication that the voters were satisfied with him or they were willing to give him another chance. Another reason for the lopsided count is that there were a lot of voters who remembered the corrupt government Kocharyan ran. One thing that would help Pashinyan's administration is to hire a super foreign minister; there has to be someone in Armenia who can accomplish this role. We are yet to see what the future is going to unfold.

Some critics say Pashinyan does not have the competence to run the government, while others say it is not him, but it is the people he has supporting him. In contrast, Kocharyan has more college educated personnel who have had more experience. About a majority of Pashinyan's advocates are high school graduates and do not have much government experience. Vartouhi has been telling him for a long time he should be looking for more experienced people to help him run the government. There is no question that it has to have a secure and diplomatic strategy in both the short and long terms. Everyone also says there should be no interpersonal conflicts. Most people probably agree with this but do not know know to practice it.

Armenia has another quandry that has been around since independence and that is the emigrate dilemma. The population has been steadily decreasing since 1991 and nothing has really been done to stifle the reduction. One of the main reasons for the depopulation has been the unemployment rate in the country. It was as low as one percent at lthe beginning of independence, grew to to arouind 10 percent by 2000, ran steady at that percent until 2008 then rapidly increased to 17 percent in two years and has been there ever since. Why? One main reason is Armenian losing her dominance in the technical field. Armenia's title as the "Silicon Valley of the Soviet Union" faded away after independence to what it is today. Several aspiring young men have tried to restart the Armenian leadershisp of the technical industry (TI), but have been hampered by government laxity and taxation. This has to change for Armenia's unemployment rate to come down.

Maybe we were a little too harsh on the TI as there have been some headway in innovation and growth in Armenia. Yet, the progress has not been enough. The Foundation for Armenian Science, Technology (FAST) was established five years ago and has made improvements. Perhaps not enough to state the current TI is on par with what it was during Soviet times. However, most reports indicate that there are several technology experts working on improving and expanding the industry. One of the major contributors to this growth is Armen Orujyan (b. 1974) who was born in Armenia, migrated to California with his family as a teenager, earned his PhD here, founded and served as chairman of Athgo, then as consultant with the UN. In 2017, he founded FAST with Ruben Vardanyan (b. 1968) and Noubar Afeyan (b. 1962). Both men have made other significant contributions to the Armenian culture. Hopefully, Armenia can invent drones that out maneuver and destroy the Turkish and Israeli weapons that were so destructive during the 44- Day War.

If young people cannot find jobs in the nation they have to look someplace else to find employment. Thanksfully, we have seen some improvement in this area. Armenia has to reduce her taxes on new enterprises and encourage new businesses to open. Technical conferences have been held in the country, and corruption has been reduced significantly. Yet again, have these programs been enough? On the other hand, have the people been able to utilize these encouragements to take advantage of any incentives and corrections. The sad part generally as to what has been going on is that a person learns and experiences his skills in Armenia, becomes a respected specialist, then leaves the country for a much higher paying position. Armenia has a wealth of brainpower, but she has to harness that power and keep it in the country. Pay scales, somehow or another, have to be increased together with an improvement in the educational system. Armenia has a responsibility to stop her "brain drain."

One other problem that one does not hear much about is Armenia's agricultural set back since the 44-Day War. Before war Armenian farmers produced an ample ammount of wheat, but since the war, production has significantly cut back. This is mainly due to the lack fertile land that was available before the war and the utilization of irrigation water they require for their crops. Drought and water shortages are natural that crop up now and then, but poor management also contributes to the problem. Politicians have cut back the water supply for some reason. This is true even though the water level Lake Sevan is about one inch higher that last year. Why is the government management holding back? The Armenian Techical Group (ATC) also report that it has developed a drougt resistant seed that produces a higher yield. The government should make the seed available to farmers.

Never To Die II now returns to Vartouhi and her family. The narration wants the reader to grasp an idea of what family life is in Armenia.

In a discussion one evening, Azad told his mother the 44-Day War was the real factor that put Armenia into such bad shape. "And you know we can't blame it all on Pashinyan, even though I don't care for him," Azad told his mother.

"Why do you say that?" responded the journalist.

"Armenia was so outnumbered and overly weaponized we never had a chance. The 44- Day War was so radically different than what happened in the early 90s."

Vartouhi eyed her son with a questioning look, so Azad continued, "You know I don't care how brave and courageous your soldiers are if you see your weapons being demolished right and left before your eyes. When you can't do anything to stop the destruction you feel rather helpless. I spoke to a lot of the wounded soldiers who required care and many of them talked about the drones that were demolishing our tanks, artillery, rocket launchers, and any other offensive weapon system. The Bayraktar TB2 and Israeli drones were overwhelming systems against the Armenians."

"You know none of the experts and analysts said anything about these drones when they were complaining about Pashinyan. Didn't they know the weapons balance was so lopsided?"

"You're right mom. But like I said, I don't care for Pashinyan that much, yet we can't blame him entirely for losing the war. No one except the most advanced war strategist would have had that knowledge. None of our generals were aware the drones could be so deadly."

One evening after dinner, Vartouhi asked Simon if he had seen the videos of Pashinyan and Aliyev that they delivered at the UN General Assembly. "Oh yes, I did and I sure got stirred up with all the bullshit the dictator delivered."

"Why are you saying that?" The reporter asked.

"You know Aliyev talked for 38 minutes reading his speech with his head down. It was full of lies and can you imagine how bored the delegates were? I say he is a real asshole and has no idea what is going on and probably would have lost the war again if Turkey had not intervened. But Turkey did interfere, and then all of a sudden, Aliyev was 'king of the castle.' He's a chronic liar and a corruptor of the truth. He has become a puppet for Erdogan, yet now has an arrogance that is beyond an egotist."

"I know he's a liar, but what are the things you're upset about?"

"I have a bunch of things he lied about. You want to hear them?"

"Yes, of course."

"Number one, he said Armenia started last year's war. I think the world knows the Azeris started the war, and in fact, I think he started all the skirmishes we had for last 25 years. He then talked about Azerbaijan as being an example of tolerance and peaceful coexistence. I'm sure most nations are aware of the Azeri ethnic cleansing in the late 1980s, early 1990s, and during any opportunity to kill Armenians afterward. He accused Armenia of violating international law, including the Geneva Convention rules. This is the exact opposite of how Azerbaijan has acted and continues to act. He said we hired mercenaries. Where did he get all the thousands of jihad killers from? And what about the November 9 agreements he signed and has been ignoring ever since including the release of POWs? Need I say more?"

"Simon, I'm sure there are a lot more lies and issues Aliyev addressed, but what about Pashinyan? What did he have to say?"

"His video was only 12 minutes long, but it was in Armenian. I personally think it should have been in English because it was an opportunity for him to relate more closely with the delegates and other nations."

"I think you're right Simon, because his English is very good and it could have been an opportunity he could have utilized. But what did he say?"

"Like I said, his video was only 12 minutes, but I think he set the record straight. He said it was Azerbaijan that started the war (in fact, started all the wars and conflicts) and immediately violated international law by targeting civilians and vital infrastructures, killing and torturing prisoners and civilians, and utilizing many other documented crimes). I think he talked about Armenian democracy, maybe hoping for support from UN member states. He mentioned the Azeri illegal policy of not releasing POWs and civilians and the reopening of transportation links. He finished his talk mainly on Armenian's desire for continuing the OSCE Minsk peace process."

Last but not the least importance in Armenia's reawakening is the Armenian Diaspora. President Armen Sarkessian rightly calls it Armenia's second army. Discussion with the ambassador to America called it "Armenia's oil." Much was written in the earlier sections of *Never To Die II* that talked about Diaspora's role and assistance to her mother nation. The roughly seven million Armenians who do not reside in the land of their ancestors have basically been a tremendous asset to the country. There is no question that Diaspora has been a powerful extensive arm of Armenia. It has raised millions of dollars for the government and various projects and has influenced US legislation supporting the nation in numerous ways. The role of Diaspora is to not only raise funds for the mother land and the plentiful projects, but also to support the viability of the nation. Hopefully it can and will continue to do so.

Special ideas that have been proposed include: 1) re-establishing and strengthing the Minister of Diaspora, 2) having a universal offsite Diaspora Organization with a representative from Armenia, and 3) having a diaspora representative serve as a non-voting member of the Armenian parliament. These are three that stand out. As for the Diaspora Armenians, they too can assist many businesspersons by contacting them and working with them in improving their businesses. This can be in not only the IT (Inteligence Technology) field but also in other ventures. This can be accomplished in both Armenia and Artsakh.

Dr. Arshavir Gundjian has also commented on Armenia's relationship with Diaspora. He believes that Diaspora should be better organized in a unified general manner where it can provide many fruitful activities. Armenia should look for any special talent that she is sure Diaspora would offer if requested. Gundjian recognized the abundant financial assistance Diaspora has provided, yet he thinks there are many individuals who have achieved extraordinary successes who would be more than ready to help if called upon.

Gundjian has two other points to offer. He thinks the present regime has restricted itself to loyalty rather adeptness. The government has to have experienced, capable, political acumen, and competent personnel. The second idea he proposes is that powerful people with authority outside the government be utilized in their expertise to make constructive and practical improvements. The intellectual and spiritual elite of the nation through speeches, appeals, and opinion pieces have to encourage these concepts. Vartouhi noted that several of these Canadian Armenian ideas and opinions were similar to other specialists and gurus. She has said before and says it again, "It won' be easy, but these ideas have to be initiated. We all have to work together to make a strong Armenia."

Vartouhi noticed another article that is food for thought with regard to Diaspora. Avo Piroyan (b. 1936) wrote "3 Steps Toward Resetting the Diaspora-Armenian Connection" in the February 14 *Armenian Mirror Spectator*. Piroyan outlined the importance of having a model for Diaspora to have a relationship that has significant and long term financial involvement. This includes special dual citizenship in Armenia with special non-residence status with different rights and responsibilities that regular citizens of the country have. These Diaspora citizens should be encouraged to invest in land and build dynastic or holiday homes. This will support construction jobs and create a space for Diaspora citizens to visit. This will present an opportunity for Diaspora Armenians to get involved and to help reduce the bureaucracy that Piroyan thinks is too convoluted. He lauds the contributions Diaspora makes to Armenia but believes it will develop even further if additional relations are encouraged and promoted.

In closing of the time line of Amenian occurranlces, I would like to quote a saying by William Saroian (1908-1981):

> *"I should like to see any power in the world destroy this race, this small tribe of unimportant people, whose wars have all been fought and lost, whose churches have crumbled, literature is unread, music is unheard and prayers are no more answered. Go ahead, destroy Armenia. See if you can do it. Send them into the desert without bread or water. Burn their homes and churches. See if they will not laugh, sing and pray again. For when two of them meet anywhere in the world, see if they will not create a new Armenia."*

I thought the expression is apropos for what has been occurring in Armenia. We have managed to back every issue eventually in time and have kept going. We can do it again.

Epilog

As I said earlier, in 2017 when I first started writing *Never to Die II*, I had high hopes that the Republic of Armenia was on her way to a renaissance. In 2018 that hope was reinforced after the Velvet Revolution. From 2018 to 2020 the renaissance appeared to progressing until Azerbaijan, assisted by Turkey, initiated the 44-Day War. Armenia and Azerbaijan had problems since 1988, but somehow or another managed to overcome any serious difficulties until the 44-Day War where all hell broke loose.

Major events came and went. First was the massive public demands in1988 where Soviet Armenia's request for the enclave of Nagorno Karabakh be restored to Soviet Armenia. The movement initiated riots and eventual pogroms in Azerbaijan and ensuing conflicts generated between the two Soviet Republics and continued on following their independences in 1991. The conflict generated into a major war from 1992 to 1994 where Azerbaijan lost not only Nagorno Karabakh but much of the Azeri territory surrounding the enclave. Many military analysts claimed Armenia could have marched all the way to Baku at the time, but Armenia was content with the territories she had under her control.

From 1994 to 2020 it was not a peaceful environment. The Azeri's continuously conducted occasional border skirmishes causing unrest and local damages and sometimes sporadic deaths. In April 2016 the Azeris initiated a major attack that continued on for four days (press labeled it the Four Day War). In July 2020, a small scale encounters turned into a major attack. In both four day wars, the Azeris initiated major damages and deaths, but were soundly defeated. Sadly, 16 Armenian deaths occurred.

It is not only these conflicts that the Azeris keep doing. They are continually conducting cultural campaigns on Armenian churches and traditional structures at every opportunity they can gather. Ilham Aliyev promised President Putin that he would not damage or destroy, but protect Christian structures; however, Vartouhi thought the pledges went in one ear and out the other. The Azeri dictator does not know the meaning of a promise. He also has a habit of making up fables such as the churches in the region were original Caucasian Albanian constructions. Azerbaijan has actually boasted such practices, being a Turkic nation. The United Nations Education, Scientific and Cultural Organization (UNESCO) and a few civilized countries are well aware of these destructive violations and have alerted Azerbaijan about them, but have literally done nothing to stop the falsehoods and devastations the Azaris come up with.

In addition, the International Court of Justice (ICJ) has ordered that Azerbaijan "must take all necessary measures to prevent and punish acts of vandalism and desecration affecting Armenian cultural heritage including, but not limited to churches, and other places of worship, monuments, landmarks, cemeteries and artifacts." Aliyev has ignored all commitments and warnings and in challenge to the world community he has assigned a committee to carry on his determination to deface and desecrate Armenian heritage and launched his war against Armenian history. To date, the ICJ has not inflicted any punishment or penalty against Azerbaijan.

Jean-Christophe Buisson (b. 1968) the deputy editor-in-chief of the French newspaper *Le Figaro*, has been the only scholar to date, who has sighted anyone or organization for malicious moral grounds. Edmond Azadian called this fact out where the newspaper has criticized Europeans for diving into close cooperation with Baku amid the Azeri cultural genocide against Armenian heritage and yet there is no reaction to it from the French government or UNESCO.

On September 27, 2020, it was an altogether different war that resulted where Armenian bravery and superior military valor played a secondary role. Turkey entered the battle scenes with her military and modern weapons. The TB2 drones were much too much for Armenian soldiers who were unable to halt their devastating destruction. The 44-Day War resulted in 5000 Armenian deaths and a humiliating defeat. Finger pointing, incompetence, unpreparedness, and other accusations ran wild. There was little or no mention of the overpowering Turkish influence and weapons. Armenia fell into a quagmire. There should be no question that Turkish influence was the cause of the catastrophic defeat. It's clear what Turkey (Erdogan) wants more nations under his control and influence, and if possible, initiate another Armenian Genocide. He speaks with forked tongue when he talks about reconciliation with Armenia, then on another occasion about "finishing the job his ancestors never completed."

This book is not an end to *Never To Die II*. Armenia will continue on in one form or another for many more centuries. She has lasted this long and she will continue on. For a while from 1994 to 2020, I personally thought we were on our way to becoming a mini-super state, but Turkey in her hateful and long persistent goal to eliminate the Armenian race will still be trying to continue the Genocide. I believe this is a true statement even though Turkey talks of peace out the side of her mouth. This scenario continues on no matter what kind of proposal or testimonials she comes up with. There is an inner plague on Turkey's conscious, but she refuses to erase it. No one can predict the future, but who predicted the collapse of the Soviet Union and the forming of a free Armenia.

One of the major lessons Armenia learned during the 44-Day War was that patriotic and courageous soldiers cannot always win battles when they are faced with superior weapons. The Turkish Bayrajtar drones were just a little too much for courageous Armenian troops. Armenian soldiers proved their invincibility in all the previous wars with Azerbaijan, i.e. before Turkey and Pakistan got into the engagements. All Azeri battle scenes during 1994 and prior to 2020 were lock-down loses for Azerbaijan. However, the picture changed after her big brother got involved. I guess it is a different scenario against the Kurds who live in Turkey.

I personally look forward to a reawakened Armenia, but it is going to take some time. The nation will require a strong dedication in leadership and demonstrate a formidable diplomatic corps. This corps has to establish relations with allies that she can depend on in time of need. Treaties have to be faced with reality and not be wishful thinking imaginations. They have to be locked solid and with no question marks. Armenia's army has to have the modern weapons to counter those nations that wish to destroy her. Armenia has to allow her Diasporaians to participate in nation building projects, have farmer and engineering experts manage the agricultural programs, improve her economy and trading policies, encourage people to remain in Armenia and Diasporaians to migrate to Armenia. All of the above will not be easy. Armenians have to learn how to work better with each other and not be enemies in their relationship.

This book has no ending. Armenia has been around for over 5000 years and will probably be around for at least another 5000. She has outlived the ancient powers of the Assyrians, Urartians, Parthians, Romans, and Byzantines. In some sense, she has even outwitted the Ottoman Empire that sought to annihilate the Armenian race. Armenia, like the phoenix bird, has risen from her ashes to thrive into another period. In one of the ancient time periods Armenia was even a powerhouse competing with superpowers Rome, Persia, and Parthia [reign of Tigranes II (Dickran) the Great, 140-55 B.C.]. Today Turkey and Azerbaijan are in the process of still trying to eliminate Armenia from the map, but even if they do, remember the phoenix bird.

List of Acronyms

ADL	Armenian Democratic Liberal Party
ARA	Armenian Revolutionary Army
ARF	Armenian Revolutionary Federation
ASALA	Armenian Secret Army for the Liberation of Armenia
AYF	Armenian Youth Federation
CSTO	Collective Security Treaty Organization
ERC	European Research Council
EP	European Parliament
EBRD	European Bank for Reconstruction and Development
EU	European Union
FAST	Foundation for Armenian Science and Technology
LOC	Line of Contact
NATO	North Atlantic Treaty Organization
NKAO	Nagorno Karabakh Autonomous Oblast
OSCE	Organization for Security and Cooperation in Europe
PACE	Parliamentary Assembly Council of Europe
TI	Technical Industry or Technical Intelligence
UNESCO	United Nations Education, Scientific and Cultural Organization
USSR	Union of Soviet Socialist Republics

www.ingramcontent.com/pod-product-compliance
Lightning Source LLC
Chambersburg PA
CBHW022127050726
47590CB00002B/442